Nine Strangers

Matthew Pippin

Hold on tight
and enjoy the ride,

Love

[signature]

I

For: Mother, Dad, Jon, Ray, & Andrew

CONTENTS

PART I

December 27TH, 2006

A SIMPLE DETOUR

1:01 a.m.

"If only I could sleep. Sleep. Sleep. Sleep."

Jeremy Henderson was simply dead tired. He just wanted to get home, pull the covers over his head and forget that the rest of the world existed. His light was the only one illuminated on the half-empty, 31-seat TransCoach bus.

Jeremy had made this bus trip from Buffalo, New York to Boston, Massachusetts every Christmas. *'There's No Place Like Home for the Holidays'* as the song goes. Fifteen years earlier, just after Jeremy moved to Buffalo, his doting parents, Peter and Megan Henderson, burned to death in a horrific house fire. Since then, for every single Christmas holiday, Jeremy spent three days in Boston. One day always dedicated to the graveyard and the other two getting plastered.

Jeremy left South Station in Boston with a massive hangover some eight hours ago with two sleeping pills and a NyQuil chaser in his system but only felt dried out and groggy, not sleepy.

The bus trip had been tortoise-like, quiet, and uneventful. Two people boarded in Saratoga Springs, with extremely slow-going progress from there. Snow had been falling all day and there was no sign of the gently falling blizzard letting up. Jeremy had noticed only a half-dozen or so vehicles on the road since departing Saratoga. An hour earlier, the bus was forced to take a detour to I-90 due to an overturned snowplow on the 29.

"Watch it!" the large man in the row diagonally in front of Jeremy snapped at an elderly woman.

"Oh, dear. I'm terribly sorry. Excuse me," the woman said and then continued her journey toward the lavatory in the back of the gently swaying bus.

As the woman made her way down the aisle, her clawlike hands gripping the seat backs as hard as she could, Jeremy threw her a tired wink and a grin, and she winked back with the slyest of smiles tickling the corners of her thin lips.

Seeing her wink made Jeremy's grin widen as he thought, "*She's a fighter.*"

Jeremy rested his forehead against the cool window and felt the opposing puffs of heat coming from the vent below his seat and desperately wished he was in his own bed this very instant. Maybe next year will be different. Maybe next year he would have something better to do than going back to Boston. Maybe, if he did have to go, he wouldn't be getting blind drunk and wasting his couple of days off in a stupor. He was getting too old to put up with the recovery time.

The bus pitched to the left slightly in the hushed evening.

"Home and quiet," he muttered to himself.

Jeremy was thrown with a violent blow against the seat in front of him and then pitched the width of the bus, slamming onto the window that had been opposite his row of seats a moment before. A surprise weight thudded on his right arm as Jeremy realized that the little boy who had been sleeping in the row in front of him was sitting there, looking around wildly.

Metal was tearing and grinding as the bus continued its

death roll.

The large man, who had barked at the old woman just a few minutes before, rolled heavily onto the window in front of the one Jeremy and the boy occupied. The man's window spider-webbed out then gave way, his massive bulk gone, instantly replaced by freezing water.

"Holy shit," Jeremy managed as he stood up on his window trying to distribute his weight on the glass with as wide a stance as he could.

"Help!" the kid squeaked out as the dark waters tried to swallow him.

Without thinking, Jeremy laced his fingers through the child's hair and hauled him up into his arms. Water swirled in fast and Jeremy was trying to get a grip on his surroundings as the child trembled in his arms. That's when he realized that the front half of the bus was gone, snow streaming through the massive, torn hole and disintegrating in the swirling water pouring inside as the back half labored to remain afloat.

Behind him, there was some movement from other passengers, but Jeremy couldn't make out how many people were there or what was going on with them.

As he was calling out to the frantically moving shapes, the window Jeremy and the boy were standing on gave way and dropped them into the waters. Having the kid wrapped around his middle didn't help Jeremy's new predicament, but at least the kid wasn't thrashing around.

Making a swim for it, Jeremy rapped his head on the side of the sinking bus twice before he finally broke the surface, sputtering for air along with the kid. It was at that moment that the cold really bit into him, its teeth sinking into his skin anywhere it could.

"Help!"

It was the kid, trembling and choking. Jeremy paddled laboriously to the edge of the river in which they now found themselves. His jeans and boots trying to weigh him down as he fought the cold waters with the child clinging to him. Climbing out of the river onto the rocky shore, Jeremy stood the kid up, and knelt down to his eye level. "Stay here. Don't move. I... I gotta see."

The kid only nodded as he brought his trembling fingers to his mouth, his eyes wild and wide.

Jeremy walked as best he could on the wet rocks a few steps away to have a look around at the scene. A small bridge crossed the river and half of the guard rail was sheared off on the opposite bank. The sky was lit up with the orange wash it gets from a snowstorm. There were no street lights or artificial light coming from anywhere, but there had to be dazzling light coming from somewhere. Between the cold water and the dried out, hangover brain, Jeremy was having a hard time processing everything as it was coming at him.

That's when he saw why the surroundings seemed to be brighter than just the reflecting snow. The front half of the bus sat right side up on the opposite bank of the tattered guardrail, consumed in flames.

"Get out of the water!"

It was one of the men who had been picked up in Saratoga Springs. The man had looked haggard with the weight of the world on his shoulders when he had boarded. He didn't seem as exhausted now.

"Is there anybody else over there?" Jeremy called.

"No. Is it just you and the boy?"

"I think Mama's in there." the boy simply said.

The man slid down the snow-covered rocks to Jeremy. He had a gash above his left eye which seemed to be quickly swelling shut. Amazingly, he didn't seem to be as wet as Jeremy and the boy, only dripping from his cuffs and with wet patches on his knees.

"This is some kinda' fucked up going on," the man said through a wild, lopsided smile. "Where's everyone else? There must be other people."

"I saw a few others back at the... the other end. I don't know how many... it's so cold."

The man picked up the kid from the rock he was trembling on.

"Let's get near the fire. It'll keep us awake and dry you two out."

As the three started for the tempting flames, a voice cried out from the river, "We need help! Please!"

Jeremy turned to see three people paddling towards the bank, fighting the frigid current. The effeminate young man, who had been in a yelling match on his cell phone hours ago in Boston, was assisting the young black man who also boarded in Saratoga Springs. They were both attempting to carry the old woman with whom Jeremy had exchanged a wink, both men doing their best to keep her head and most of her body out of the water.

Jeremy waded back in and took the woman from the two men, "Are you two all right?"

"We're fine," the effeminate one said. "It's her. We can't get her to wake up. There's... oh... there's, uh, there's two others. Two others back... back-"

"*He's going into shock*," Jeremy thought then said, "Let's get up to the fire. It'll keep us from freezing to death."

"You do that. I'm going back for the others."

The black man was instantly back in the water, pumping his arms toward the sinking half of the wreck.

"Oh, God... come back... what do we do?"

"Come on, man. Help me get this lady up and over there. We need to get warm, or we are going to die."

The mention of death seemed to bring the effeminate one back from the edge of panic a touch. He removed his soaked, black scarf from around his neck, tossed it into the river, and said, "Yes, of course. Yes... let's move her."

The two of them slipped up and over the rocks on the frozen bank to where the man with the swelling eye and the boy were. The large man was there, having crawled to this impromptu meeting spot. The expensive-looking sports jacket he had been wearing was laying in the trail he'd made and he was still coughing out river water from his throat.

"Is there anywhere we can put this woman down?"

The man with the swelling eye looked at the three survivors and ran towards some clumps sticking out of the snow. He hefted two large suitcases that had been thrown from the torn innards of the bus and hauled them over next to where the fat man was lying. They made a lumpy but somewhat dry bed to lay the old woman on. Jeremy grabbed her wrist and felt a strong pulse pushing against his frozen fingertips.

"You are a fighter."

"W-what?"

It was Effeminate.

"Nothing," Jeremy said, "See if your friend is out of the river yet."

"Sure, but he's not my friend. I mean, he needed help... with that lady, and I just...he was sitting behind me when... when we... the water... Jesus, what happened?"

The guy was losing it again.

Swollen Eye crossed to Effeminate and shook him gently but firmly by his shoulders. "Listen, what is your name, my guy?"

Effeminate stared at Swollen Eye for a moment as if trying to remember what his name really is and quietly managed, "Mark."

"Mark what?"

"Mark Navarette," he said with a little more confidence.

"Okay, Mark Navarette. I'm Jack Doll. As you can see, we are in serious trouble here, Mark, and we need you to stay totally here with us. Do I make myself clear?"

Certainty was coming back into Mark's wide eyes. He nodded slowly and looked around carefully, "Yeah. Yeah. What should I do?"

"Just do what, uh..." Jack was waving a hand in Jeremy's direction.

"Jeremy."

"Do what Jeremy here just told you to do. Go keep an eye

6

out for your friend and then get back here with him as soon as you can to get yourself warm."

"Of course, sir, um, Jack."

"Excellent. Off you go!"

Jack left Mark facing the dark river and walked over to the large man. He was still lying on his right side in an indent he had made on the ever-filling snow bed, spitting away snowflakes off his lips.

"Can you move?"

"Of course... Of course, I can," he heaved, "I swam outta that and I'm staying here near the fire."

"At least stand up and get most of yourself out of the snow."

The fat man blinked up at Jack and considered this logic and had a look on his face that said he was trying desperately to think of something that would make Jack incorrect. After another moment, the man rolled onto his knees and stood up with Jack holding onto an enormous elbow.

"I'm Jack Doll."

"Name's McQueen. Harold. Thanks," McQueen said stiffly.

Jeremy was rubbing the old woman's hands and doing his best to keep her face free of snow. She had moaned once or twice, and Jeremy wasn't sure, but he thought he saw her eyes try to flutter open once when his hand had lightly brushed by them on another snow sweep.

"How is she?"

The boy was suddenly standing by Jeremy. All things considered, he seemed really calm. Hadn't he said something about his mother?

"Well, kid, I think she's a strong lady. She's going to be just fine once she warms up."

"I think my mama's in there."

The boy said this statement so matter-of-factly, it was as if he was pointing her out window shopping across a town square rather than the disaster that surrounded them all.

"Where at, Kid?"

The boy had been pointing and now Jeremy followed his little finger to the flaming section of the bus. It was the first time that Jeremy really focused and took in this part of the wreck. Flames leaped out the bulk of it, streaming up through the destroyed windows, while blackening and bubbling the bright white, red, and blue paint that used to encircle the vehicle. The huge flames were terrific as Jeremy scanned the wreck. Even through the massive blaze, Jeremy could still see the driver.

The *driver*!

"Hey, Kid, see how I am rubbing her hands? Can you keep doing that while I go have a quick look at something? Be careful keeping the snow out of her face."

After the kid took over the massaging, Jeremy hurried over to the front end of the bus, having to step over a long length of guardrail that was lodged deep into the grill, sticking out like a long, twisting steel tongue. He got as close as he dared to the tremendous heat of the flames. Clearly seeing the driver now, it was obvious that he was dead, the driver's ribcage collapsed over the large steering wheel in an odd way. Jeremy could just make out the name "Leonard" stitched on the jacket. The most horrible part of this sight was the flask that was jammed into the driver's mouth. The curvature of the flask made Leonard look like the most disgusting of clowns, flaring out his cheeks and splitting his lips.

"Bastard."

Jeremy realized he was rapidly blinking to keep his eyes moist in front of the fire. He could just barely see the body of a woman lying in the center aisle. She appeared to be curled up in the fetal position and what was left of her hair had melted to her scalp in a sticky, blonde skull cap.

"That's the boy's mother," he said

He remembered her now, just after the detour had been announced, that she growled at the boy to sit in the row away from her in front of Jeremy. She seemed to be suffering from the same ailment as Jeremy and must have wanted to be left alone. That action had saved the boy's life.

"Les, for Christ's sweet sake, will you just leave me alone and go sleep over there."

"*The boy's name is Les.*"

Jeremy checked his watch.

1:21 a.m.

It might have been a little over 15 minutes since the crash.

Jeremy turned to go back to the boy, Les, and the old woman, when he kicked what turned out to be the driver's clipboard. He picked it up and carried it back with him to the others. It may help in identifying who was still among the living.

Along with Jack, McQueen, the boy, and the old lady; the black man and Effeminate had shown up with two other women. The younger looking woman, who had stringy black hair, clung to the lean body of the black man, her hair spilling around her face, her entire body quaking. The other woman, shorter and with a perfect caramel complexion seemed to be checking the old woman's vital signs with expert movements.

Jack walked up to Jeremy, his eye now completely swollen shut. He was holding a small chunk of ice up to his wound.

"The lady with the old woman is Maria. She's a nurse. Told me to keep some ice up here on my new shiner. A lot of that around, isn't there?"

Jack laughed at his own words and looked at what Jeremy was carrying, "What's that? Find something interesting?"

"I found out that the bastard driver was drinking. His flask is shoved half way down his throat. This clipboard has a passenger list. I thought it would make roll call a little easier."

"It's... so... cold..."

This was Stringy Hair. She was shaking beyond control now, no matter how tightly the young man held onto her, "Shh," he quietly soothed, "try to focus on breathing. We're going to get us all warmed up soon."

Hearing his voice clearly, Jeremy thought the young man wasn't quite an adult yet. 16? 17?

"You have been through a lot. It's okay to be scared. Just try to keep breathing deep and exhaling slow with me."

This boy must have seen his share of emergencies. Son of a fireman? A doctor? A policeman?

"She's coming around!"

The nurse was holding the old woman's hand, the elderly lady's blue eyes were open and glancing around carefully at the faces above her.

"Ma'am. I'm Maria Crosser. We were on a bus together and had an accident."

The woman looked at Maria a little bewildered and said, "I can see that. My name is Hester. My husband is Nate. Where is he?" Hester began a wild-eyed search for her husband, "I dreamed he was dead and trying to put me into a lifeboat. 'A lifeboat without you?' I said, but he kept helping me in. Oh, my goodness is it cold!"

Jeremy felt a pang of grief for the woman. He remembered better now through the hangover, the elderly couple sitting in the seats behind the driver. Nate was probably still there.

"Where are we?" Hester sputtered as she wiped more snowflakes from her face, "It sure is coming down. Could we maybe move under that bridge over there?"

They all turned their gazes to the little space hiding in the shadows under the bridge.

Maria took one of Hester's hands again, "Can you move?"

Hester squirmed a bit and let out a little, surprised shriek, "Oh, me. Ouch. I'm... not so sure. Oh, my leg."

Maria ran her hands expertly down Hester's right leg and then the left, pausing at the knee, "This is really swollen. How does this feel?" Maria tenderly squeezed the knee.

"That really smarts," Hester whimpered.

"The good news is, it doesn't feel broken or out of joint. You must have really wrenched it during the accident."

"Well... oh, me... I am sorry, but I can't seem to move my leg very well."

McQueen suddenly snorted, flapping a hand at the flaming end of the bus, "What we have to do is get out of this cold. That barbeque there isn't going to last all night long."

The group stared at him, everyone too stunned to say anything after this callous remark about the dead, except Hester, who said in a shaky but dignified voice, "I don't like my husband being referred to as a 'barbeque.'"

"I just mean that we gotta get out of here before we freeze to death, lady!"

Jack turned to McQueen, casually discarding the piece of ice from around his eye, "Well then, Colonel, what do you suggest we do?"

SHELTER

Stringy Hair had stopped shivering for the moment, "I saw... a house just before we cr... crashed."

Jeremy bent slightly to meet her frightened eyes, "Where did you see it? How far away do you think?"

Stringy Hair sniffed, "I had been looking at it not long... not long before it all happened. My friend was sleeping across from me. She must still be sleeping, I think." Her eyes drifting towards the river.

Jeremy took her frozen hands in his, "What's your name?"

"A- Alicia."

"Alicia, I am Jeremy. Where exactly did you see the house?"

She raised her head off the young man's shoulder and squinted hard across the river, "I think if it wasn't snowing so hard you could probably see it over there through the trees. It... kind of scared me when I saw such a dark shape sitting out there alone when everything else looked so orange, pink, and pretty."

Jeremy straightened up. "What does everyone think? Shall we make a go for it?"

"Beats the hell out of freezing our asses off out here," McQueen said, "We gotta start moving now."

Hester sat up with the help of Maria, "If I can get someone on this other side of me, I might just be able to walk it."

Jack smiled, "I'll see if we can figure out another way of getting you up and out. What's your name, Kid?"

"My name is Leslie. Mama calls me Les, but I never liked that."

"Alrighty then, Leslie. Can you help me scout around for some large suitcases?"

"Sure," Leslie replied brightly, and he was off, looking as if he was in a Siberian Easter Egg Hunt.

Jeremy watched Leslie for a moment and then cleared his throat, "I have the passenger list here and I think we should do a roll call. So, I'll say a name and you say if you need any assistance."

McQueen growled something under his breath that Jeremy didn't quite catch and decided to let the flare of irritation for the man extinguish itself.

"Alicia Brooms?"

"I'll be able to walk okay."

"Kimberly Such... is that your friend?"

Alicia nodded once and shuddered.

"Jack Doll?"

"You know I'm fine, but my eye is starting to make me look like a pirate. Captain Jack to you all. Arrrrgh!" Jack laughed to himself and continued his search through the snow for large suitcases.

"Roger Watson?"

"I'm good," the young man who had been supporting Alicia said. "I'll be alright."

"You did a hell of a job getting both of us over here," the nurse said.

Roger looked at the ground, the dancing flame light concealing his expression, "I'm a lifeguard during the summers in Atlantic City. Just doing my job."

"Thank you," Maria said.

"Maria Crosser."

"I'm ready to go."

"Dylan McPike?"

No answer came.

"Libby McPike?"

"Oh, dear me," it was Hester. "That must have been the young couple behind us. They were in Boston for their first anniversary. Uh... well, they seemed to be having a... a disagreement about... well, something in South Station..."

Jeremy thought, "*Not only is this woman a fighter, she's a lady and probably never told any gossip to anyone, let alone this large a group.*" If the light conditions were better, Jeremy was sure he would have seen the old girl blush.

"Well, sometimes you just can't help hearing..."

"For Christssakes, let's get on with it and get the hell out of here. I'm freezing to death!"

"Harold McQueen?"

"You know how I damn well feel. Let's go and stop so much yakking."

Maria Crosser stood, "I agree. We need to get warm and dry as soon as possible. Hypothermia is already trying to sink into us."

Harold McQueen puffed up, getting to the end of his tether, "Alright then, let's move it, move it, move it!"

His great mass shook uncontrollably. He looked to Jeremy like one of those large men in the old 1980's television commercials, wearing a fabric waist belt that just magically shakes the lard away.

"Mr. McQueen, please try and stay..."

"If you even try to tell me what to do, I'll fuck you up the same way that fairy princess over there wants to do to you."

Mark looked hurt and wrapped an arm around himself. He dropped his stare to his water-logged, useless cell phone as if that was what had just rudely insulted him.

Jeremy took a step closer to McQueen, "Losing our heads isn't going to help anybody. We are in this together whether we like it or not. Now, I suggest for your health that you keep your goddamn mouth shut."

McQueen's jaw dropped in surprise then he closed it with a snap, keeping his grizzly eyes locked on Jeremy.

Leslie clambered over some small boulders from the water's edge, pulling a large, black canvas suitcase with MALTBY stenciled in gold over one of the large pockets behind his little legs. "How's this, Mister?"

Jack smiled down at the boy, "It's perfect and just call me Jack."

"Sure, Jack!"

Jack knelt down to the boy's eye level. "Say, Leslie, my man, did you by chance see an old-looking, green suitcase lying around anywhere in your hunt?"

"No, Jack. I saw a small blue one and a big grey one, but this was the biggest. That's what you wanted, isn't it?" The boy looked instantly disappointed, thinking he had done something wrong.

Jack smiled and ruffled the boy's stiffening, wet hair, "Nope, you did a fine job. This is perfect."

Taking Leslie's hand, Jack hefted the long, wheeled suitcase up and brought it over to the group, "Hester. We're going to lay you on this and pull you along. Think of it as a small sled."

Hester smiled, "It's fine with me. It's my husband's suitcase, anyway. Mine has MALTBY stitched in silver on its side."

Hester's arthritic fingers grasped the two zippers and pulled them apart, opening the top a little and then stuck one of her hands inside. She pulled out her hand and then unzipped the suitcase completely.

"We were at our daughter's house for two weeks. She and I just washed Nate's sweaters last night. They're dry. It'll help us with the cold. Here, hon," Hester stretched out an old, white sweater to Alicia, "it'll keep your shakes down."

"Thank you," Alicia brought the soft fabric up to her face and buried her eyes into it.

Jeremy took a red one, "It's a very nice thing to do."

Once everyone was wearing something relatively dry, Jack carefully lifted Hester's thin body onto the canvas top of the suitcase then helped her slide her arms through the handles on either side as if she were wearing a large backpack.

"Now I am going to pull you along as best I can from the handle on this end. A pre-New Year's sleigh ride," Jack said.

Maria nervously giggled out, "I doubt that we'd be here for five days. Someone is bound to be along in the daytime."

Jeremy looked the survivors over. Nine people in wet pants and a dead man's sweaters, standing next to a half burning bus in a blinding snowstorm. This definitely wasn't his idea of a

Christmas card.

"What we're going to do is get back up on the roadway, cross the bridge, and continue back the way we came until we see the house Alicia saw. Then we'll cut through the woods to it and hope like hell that somebody's home."

They all took a breath and started their walk up the slope to the road and beyond. Jeremy was leading, followed by Mark, Jack with Hester, Maria, Leslie, Alicia, Roger, and McQueen.

The snow was nearly knee deep and making Jeremy's calves burn by the time he reached the top of the buried roadway. There were no ruts over the bridge and the bus tracks on the other side weren't visible from where Jeremy stood looking north. The steam was coming harder out of everyone's mouths as they made their little hike up to the hidden pavement. The snow had turned the 30-foot rolling slope into the final haul on Mount Rainier. The incline would have been bad enough on a wet day, but two feet of snow made it feel like the world's most cruel elliptical.

Jeremy reached out a hand to Mark to help him up the last bit of the hill to the road.

"Hey, thank you... Jeremy, right? I'm so bad with names. I'll remember your face until the day I die, but names just don't seem to stick in my head."

"A little help, please?"

Jack called for assistance to get over the top mound of snow with Hester. Jack pulling from a handle on one end, with Maria pushing from the other end where the wheels were built in while all three of them favoring Hester's left leg.

Jeremy and Mark crouched on either side of the long, duffle suitcase, "Lift on three- THREE!"

Hester rose into the air and the four supporters carried her almost gracefully over the top of the snow mound.

Once she was back on the ground again, Hester said, "That felt like my big entrance in the worst musical Ziegfeld ever produced."

They all giggled at this, Mark especially. He was the only

one who knew who Hester was talking about.

Leslie came rolling down the small mound of snow and landed at Maria's feet. She caught him by his armpits and quickly lifted him upright, "Aren't you bothered by all this cold?"

Leslie flashed a devilish smile of conspiracy, "I never really get to play in it. Mama says it'll make me sick. Daddy doesn't mind, but I live with Mama," Leslie ran up to Hester's side, "You need any help getting pulled, Lady?"

Hester smirked and touched one of the boy's cheeks, "You can keep me company if you like. Call me Hester. It's like Esther Williams, but with an 'H'."

Leslie's face wrinkled, "Who's Esther Williams?"

"Oh, someone who I should know better than to talk to a child about," Hester smiled, "I'll tell you about her if you ask me again."

"What's the goddamn hold up?"

Jeremy looked up to the large man standing on the snow mound, "We were waiting for everyone to get up here, McQueen. We don't want anyone getting left behind, now do we? Let's go."

Jeremy and Maria now led the procession across the short bridge.

"*Just 60 or maybe 75 feet at the most*," Jeremy thought, "*75 feet and we would have been sitting on a warm bus, just stuck in the snow.*"

"Bastard," Jeremy said aloud.

"Are you talking about McQueen?" Maria asked.

"No," Jeremy smiled, "Although not far from it. The driver had been drinking. I saw him dead in his seat with his flask stuck deep in his mouth."

Maria shivered violently for a moment and then it subsided, "I was sleeping, but I thought I smelled alcohol in my dream. I was at some party talking to my ex-husband and I remember thinking it was funny that I smelled alcohol because Dan never drank. I've got a good nose, maybe that's what it was the whole time."

"Aside from Hester and myself, I think everyone was

sleeping... No. McQueen had said something, but he might have just woken up. Hester bumped into him going to the bathroom... Damn. Yeah, she had been back there. Otherwise, she would have..."

A cry came from behind them, causing Jeremy and Maria to spin around. They immediately saw what happened, Jack had dropped the handle of the suitcase. Maria cut back through her tracks to Hester in full nurse mode, "Are you alright?"

Tears twinkled in the corners of the old woman's eyes, "I'm... oh, uh, I'm okay. It more surprised me than hurt anything."

Jack stood straight up, facing away from Hester and the others, holding his face, "Oh, my God, I am so sorry. I just realized where I... where we were... where we *are* and... I am so sorry."

Hester lifted her head, "It's fine. Just, um, surprised me is all."

Jeremy was instantly beside Jack, "You know where we are?"

"Yes."

"Are you from around here?"

"You might say that. I did a lot of growing up around here. That is Chuctanunda Creek and this is Crooked Street. I thought we were on 29..."

McQueen plowed through the survivors. Jeremy expected another outburst, but he simply said, "Ma'am, would you like me to pull you along?"

Hester seemed just as surprised as everyone else, but only replied, "If it gets us moving again, I am fine with that. It'll give you a good rest, Jack."

McQueen grandly grabbed the suitcase handle and lifted half of Hester into the air again, "Then let's go."

Jeremy noticed how dim the light from the flames had gotten. The only real light now was of the muted orange from the reflected snow. Jeremy and Jack now lead the group, followed by McQueen with Hester and Leslie, Maria, Alicia, Roger, and

Mark.

At the other end of the bridge, the tracks from the bus could still be seen, swerving from the south-bound lane in a straight line to where the guardrail had been.

"When the hell did we get off Route 29?" Jack asked.

Jeremy tried looking at his watch but it wasn't bright enough to read the time. It seemed like days ago now when good ol' Leonard made the soft announcement that they would be taking a detour to I-90:

"Should be in Buffalo in six hours, weather permitting."

"Alcohol permitting, you bastard, son of a bitch."

"I don't know. There was an overturned snowplow so we were detoured to I-90. There'd been no one else on the road that I could see, although I'm not surprised with all of this white shit coming down. It might have been a half hour before the crash when the driver made the announcement. Forty-five minutes? An hour?"

Jack spat a heavy snowflake from his lips, "I fell asleep almost after sitting down in Saratoga. I was glad to have seats to myself to stretch out. Damn, man, my row of seats landed on the bank just outside the water. I watched the front half swing across over the top of me and land on the other side. It felt like it all happened in slow motion. When it landed, it sounded like something exploded, I mean, the flames just went up. I rolled off into the snow and bounced my face off of a rock, I don't know how I didn't get totally wet. I don't know why I'm not dead now. Why all of us aren't dead now just beats the ever living shit out of me."

"Did you see the bus break in half?"

"No. Well, I might have. I just remember the front half sparking and swinging above me. I don't even remember seeing anyone else getting tossed around. I guess I couldn't have because the break would have been right behind me. Ah... this is so fucked up. My head is a little foggy, I guess."

Those were the last words spoken for some time as the sad party made their way up the twist of Crooked Street. There was a slight rise to the road leading away from the bridge and everyone was doing their best to follow the quickly filling tracks left by the bus. Each individual consumed with their own thoughts of what they had just lived through:

Why did this happen?

How did I get here?

Will we get through this?

When will a plow and rescue be coming?

Will ANYONE be along soon?

The thought that kept uniting the nine survivors was the penetrating cold. Jack thought to himself that the biggest saving grace was that at least the wind wasn't blowing.

Roger Watson actually felt frightened by the lack of wind because then there would at least be some sort of background noise. All he could hear was the soft crunching of feet into deep snow, sniffles, grunts, and the hushed drag of the suitcase Hester was riding on. The snow's quiet fall deafened and frightened the drums in Roger's ears. A little sob from behind him made the lifeguard jump a little. He turned to see Mark pressing the back of a fist to his mouth. "Yo. You alright?"

Mark looked into Roger's face and seemed hesitant to say anything. He fell into step as best he could next to Roger and said, "It's just... it's been a long 24 hours. I should be in Buffalo now. Right now. Hours ago."

Roger focused on the ground and his steps. "What's up?"

"Nothing I think you could understand. I'm not so sure anyone here could. Forgive me, what's your name again?"

"Roger. You're Mark, right?"

"Yes, Mark Navarette. Roger... to think I almost called you, Rob. My memory for names... Roger, thank you for asking just the same. You know that I'm okay, but are *you* alright? I'm sorry for not asking sooner."

"It's all good, man. Relax. We were only in a bus crash, you know?"

Mark stopped and stared at the lifeguard, then burst out with a laugh that almost shocked Roger and was probably heard all the way to Toronto, "HA! God, I needed that. Thank you."

Mark now seemed to have more of a bounce to his march through the deepening white.

*****

Leslie kept up as best he could next to Hester. His little legs were working overtime and feeling the broil and molten chill of the snow. His lungs were burning a little, too, but he just pretended he was an old steam engine, like the one he saw in a museum Daddy had taken him to last year. Leslie was keeping his eyes on Hester half of the time and the other half on Jeremy and Jack.

"It's like following the leader, isn't it, little one?"

Hester kept her hurt left leg crossed tenderly over her right, "You sure are being a brave boy."

Leslie beamed, "I have to. Mama always said men don't cry. She'd swat me if it looked like I was going to. I almost cried by the water when Jack helped me because his cut eye scared me, but I didn't want strangers to see me do that."

Hester stretched out her left arm, "Hold my hand. I need a brave boy with me. It's okay if you have to cry. I always thought it took a brave man to cry."

"I don't need to now, but I'll hold your hand."

A loud, braying laugh came from behind them, and it made Leslie squeeze Hester's hand tighter.

"Sounds like someone just had a good joke told to them, doesn't it?" Hester squeezed Leslie's hand back while her arthritis told her not to.

McQueen grunted loudly.

"Are you okay, Mister?" Leslie asked.

McQueen didn't answer the boy, he just trudged along in the tire track. Hester turned her head up, "Are you alright, Mr. McQueen?"

"I'm fine."

*****

Harold McQueen was not fine.

This was a damn fine mess he was in, that's all the "*fine*" there was to it. It was bad enough that those damn towelheads had scared him out of flying a few years ago. Now he was stuck in the snow, pulling some unknown old bitch on a suitcase with all of these people in the middle of nowhere. He would never tell his people at the firm he managed that he was scared that some idiot radical was going to get a wild hare up his ass and fly the plane he happened to be on into some random building. So, McQueen just stuck with the excuse of air sickness and would take a bus or a train on business trips to Chicago. It all would have been fine if that spic bus driver hadn't crashed. Now, he was freezing his ass off and his heart had started throbbing like it wanted to remind him of how screwed he was. Harold McQueen was better than this. No, he *deserved* better than this. He had worked too hard and for too long to be stuck in a goddamn situation like this.

Harold McQueen was not fine.

"I'm *just* fine."

*****

Alicia Brooms kept putting one foot in front of the other. Every part of her feet ached, her tennis shoes and thick socks being so weighted with icy water that every step felt so painful and endless. When she tried to think about anything else other than the knifing pain in her frozen arches, all she could think about was Kimberly back on the bus.

Kimberly and Alicia had been friends in high school and now worked at the same library in Provincetown, Massachusetts. They had decided to do a cross country tour to San Francisco to see another high school friend who had moved there two weeks after graduation six years earlier. Stacy had been so excited to have Kimberly and Alicia visit that she had planned an entire New Year's Eve party around their arrival.

Kim and Alicia should have flown, but it seemed like such an adventure going across the country by bus. It was their way to see the country without the worry of driving themselves, as they were both nervous enough drivers in their own town.

"What happened to Kim?"

Something must have kept her underwater. She had latched on to Alicia's wrist as the water began coming in the torn bus but she wouldn't get up. Why? Alicia had kept pulling but only Kim's forearm would ever break the surface of the swirling, dark waters. The two guys had just left with the old lady while that nurse, Maria, stayed behind, pulling on Alicia's other arm.

"Please. Wait. My friend is stuck or something. I can't move her. She's holding onto my arm. She's not moving now. She was pulling before, but now she's just holding on tight. She needs help."

Maria stepped in front of Alicia, around the second to last row of seats. She felt for a pulse on the forearm that stuck out of the water, "I'm sorry... what's your name?"

"Alicia."

"Alicia. I am not getting a pulse. We need to get out of here ourselves or we will be in a lot of trouble, too."

"But she's gripping my arm. She only needs some help."

Tears and panic were trying to make a home in the librarian's heart and the only thing keeping them out at the moment was the nurse with the calm voice, "Please, help us."

The water was waist deep now and churning faster within the interior of the bus, only Kim's hand was above the waterline.

"Hold on," Maria said.

The nurse put one hand around Kim's wrist and the other around Alicia's forearm, "I want you to pull your arm back hard for me. I'm going to help you. Are you ready?"

The pulling hurt so bad. It felt like Alicia's hand would be torn off the end of her arm and only a bloody stump would be waving around in a moment. There was a sort of snapping sound and Alicia was suddenly free. Tiny droplets of blood were forming on her wrist where Kim's nails had just torn by.

"Hey!"

The shout came from the opening of the sinking bus, and Alicia could just make out the handsome black man who had been sleeping in the seats in front of them a moment or two ago. Hadn't he already left?

"Come on. Let's move. You think you can do that for me Alicia?" the nurse had asked.

Alicia Brooms did move, and she was somehow still moving. She rubbed lightly over the tender raised welts on her left wrist and she moved, but she couldn't help but wonder, on this frigid night, why her best friend had not.

*****

Maria Crosser called out wildly, giving everyone a start out of their silent thoughts.

"Look there! Back in the woods. Can you see it, too? A house! There it is. Alicia, is that the one you saw?"

Alicia looked up from the snow and through her black hair, "It is. I thought it was so much closer to the road before."

The party left the roadway and trundled into the woods, making their way toward the large, dark house.

It seemed like every kind of house in the rural New York area; a two story, turn of the century home that should have been torn down well before the beginning of the 21st. Halfway there, they came upon a winding clearing that must have been the driveway. It wrapped its way back up through the trees behind them and they all surmised that it would have been a waste of time walking up the road to find the entrance. Aside from a few whimpers from Hester being jostled by the snow covered underbrush and Mark nearly falling down once, it had been smooth sailing through the woods.

Jeremy turned to everyone as they reached the driveway, "Come on everybody, we're almost home."

"God, I wish," grumped McQueen, but even his heavy plodding had quickened its pace.

From the driveway, snow-covered, black tree branches were covering the top windows as if the house were playing peek-a-boo with the survivors as they approached the large clearing in front of the house.

Jeremy dashed through the front yard, then tripped twice trying to get up the hidden steps onto the porch that ran the full length of the house, "Be careful coming up here. There are steps under the snow."

Jack, Mark, Roger, and Maria hoisted Hester up onto the porch as gracefully as possible while Jeremy knocked on the door. McQueen was leaning up against the front of the house, breathing deep breaths. When there was no answer from the knocks, Jeremy left the group and walked the length of the porch.

Leslie stood beside Jack looking up at him carefully, "How's the eye, Jack?"

Jack touched gingerly above his eye, "It doesn't feel as bad now from being outside in the cold. Probably looks worse than it feels, am I right?"

Leslie nodded vigorously while looking at the dried gash, "Yeah, it looks wicked bad."

Jack chuckled dryly, "I appreciate your honesty."

Jeremy came at everyone from the other end of the porch, "I don't think anyone lives here. There's a window cracked open on the other end of the porch. I'll climb through it and let everyone in."

"Hurry," McQueen gasped.

Maria took a bold step closer to his gasping hulk, "Are you alright, Mr. McQueen?"

"There's that damn question again."

"Yes, I'm fine. I just need… need to get warm, alright? I need to get warm right now."

The rest of the survivors were silent for a moment, listening to Jeremy calling inside the home for any inhabitants.

Hester spoke quickly, "Help me up, please. I'll need help walking inside, but I can't be lying here anymore. Leslie, would you pull the suitcase in, please? There will be more dry clothes in there that we may need."

Roger helped Hester to stand up as gently as possible. She didn't say anything for a moment as her breath hitched and tears threatened the corners of her eyes again, "Thank you, young man. You were the one I landed on when we crashed."

Roger looked down, supporting Hester's slight frame against his, "Yes, ma'am."

Mark spoke up proudly, "He brought you out. Swam with you to the edge of the river and then went back by himself for Maria and... uh... Alicia."

Hester smiled at the young man and then a few tears did drop, "Thank you," she whispered.

Roger only shrugged while McQueen said something under his breath.

The door suddenly opened inward, and Jeremy stood there smiling, "No one's home and no electricity, but it will do. Come on in."

The group made their way in and tried to look around. It was too dark to make out more than a few shapes that were in the large room that they now occupied. There were a few metallic clicks and then sparks and a little flame from a lighter allowed a dull glow to fill in their view. Mark stood sheepishly with his Zippo up in the air, "Sorry. I should have thought of that sooner."

There was an old-looking couch in the center of the room with a leaning coffee table slanted in front of it on the hard wood floors. A winged back chair sat twisted away from the couch and angled table as if the furniture had been having a disagreement. A very worn, carpeted staircase was to the left of the entrance and a swinging door led somewhere off to the right across the room from where everyone had gathered.

"A fireplace!" cried Alicia.

Jeremy and Jack rushed over to it on the wall farthest from the front door across from the couch. There were a few large logs laying haphazardly next to the dark opening along with a stack of newspapers.

Jeremy smiled, "Hey, we're in business. Let's get this puppy lit!"

Jack bent down to grab some newspapers and an inch of snow slid off the top of his head and plopped right down onto the papers he was reaching for, "Shit."

Roger assisted Hester to the couch while McQueen pulled the winged back chair up to the coffee table and poured his girth into it. The chair creaked but held his weight without further protest.

Jack tossed aside the wet newspaper and started crumpling the dry ones that had been laying underneath. Jeremy placed four of the eight logs in the hearth then checked to make sure that the flue was open. Mark had joined them and was standing by to light the newspaper with his Zippo. The paper crackled and Jack immediately shoved the paper between the logs.

"Lucky no snow had piled up in there," Jack said with relief.

Maria called for Mark. He joined her and, after exchanging a few words, followed the nurse quickly upstairs with his lighter glowing above their heads.

"Leslie, hon," Hester said, "Open up that suitcase and give everyone a good pair of dry socks. Then we'll see what else we can give out."

The fire built itself up beautifully, and the warmth was starting to sting Jeremy's numb fingers. "We sure need this. I guess when the logs are finished, we can burn the coffee table."

Alicia leaned against one of the arms of the couch, pulling off her shoes and socks, "Do you think we will be here that long?"

Jack brushed the remaining snow off himself in the corner near the windows, "Let's hope to God no."

Maria came hurriedly down the stairs with Mark not too far behind. Their arms were full of white bundles, "These were upstairs. They are old and musty, but they will help keep us warm. Everybody change into something dry right now. We have been wet and cold for way too long for my peace of mind."

Roger had put on a pair of Nate Maltby's sweatpants and socks. His dark skin shimmered like fresh coffee in the fire's glow and the young lifeguard almost looked beautiful to Jack, making him wish he had taken as good a care of his body as Roger obviously did.

McQueen had put on a red sweat suit, his gut hanging out of the smaller sweater top that would have covered the thinner Nate Maltby. He reminded more than one person in the room of a mall Santa at the end of a particularly long and rough Christmas season.

Mark had pulled on a pair of jeans with no top on, choosing to just wrap himself in one of the dusty blankets he and Maria had found.

Everyone had now changed and were all lying close together on the floor except for McQueen who was already fast asleep in the winged chair and Hester, who was slowly nodding off on the couch with Leslie wrapped in her arms. The boy looked like the Incredible Shrinking Man in one of Nate's hooded sweaters, but he didn't seem to mind at all.

The warmth of the fire in the enclosed space tingled everyone to sleep. Soon, they were all dozing except for Jeremy, who was happily wiggling the toes that he could finally feel. Just before he closed his eyes, he looked at his watch:

2:06 AM

An hour. Only one whole hour since the… since…

Jeremy Henderson slept.

A LONELY HOUSE

7:16 a.m.

Maria felt something hit her right shin.

"The footrest maybe? Are we stopping? No, it's..."

Kick.

Scream!

Maria opened her eyes and tried to take in her surroundings. Everything was grey in the room. Alicia was lying next to Maria, kicking and screaming in her sleep. Fully awake now and ready to help, Maria knelt next to her, shaking the girl's shoulder, trying to wake her from her nightmare.

Maria soothed, "Alicia. You're okay. Alicia, everything is... is alright as it can be. Alicia..."

Alicia's eyes opened wildly and seemed to be fighting off images of unimaginable horror.

"Shh. It's alright. You're with people who understand. You are alright. It's okay."

Alicia sat up and wrapped her shaking arms around Maria tightly, "Why wouldn't she get up? She just laid there under the water holding my arm. Why did Kim just stay there?"

She cried and convulsed into Maria's shoulder, the same shoulder that had taken tears from countless patients and relatives. Happy tears from good news to tears of utter heartbreak and grief. Maria stroked Alicia's tangled jet, black hair.

"We'll probably never know, but you tried. Damn it, you tried. She just couldn't get up and she passed away knowing that her friend didn't leave her, that your love was right there with her to the end. You tried and that's more than a lot of people get."

Maria was sure Alicia's sobs were waking people up. The sun must have been above the horizon, so it was at least after seven in the morning. Maria looked around as best she could. No one was really stirring. She could clearly see McQueen's stomach rhythmically rise and fall. Hester was sleeping but little Leslie's eyes were staring straight into Maria's. Something about his young eyes seemed so much older than they really were and that gaze nearly sent Maria herself over the edge. She bit her lower lip to bring up the toughness she had in her and started rubbing Alicia's back tenderly, "It's okay. It's okay. Shhh."

"Is everything alright?"

It was Mark. He sat up stiffly, pulling the blanket he had over his shoulders. A little patch of brown chest hair was visible through the folds of the blanket as well as his little pot belly. He was rubbing the sleep out of his eyes.

Alicia brought her head off Maria and sighed quietly, "I'm sorry. It's just... I was reliving everything from last night. It was just so bad. I didn't mean to wake you."

Mark smiled sleepily, "I don't mind. My dream wasn't so hot, either."

He stood and shakily walked to the fireplace. He picked up a log and tossed it on top of the weakly glowing coals, "We'll be needing those flames to be bigger."

He padded quietly over to the bank of three windows and put a hand up to the frosted glass, "It's still snowing. It looks as if we never even walked here. Our tracks have simply vanished."

Alicia sniffed and rubbed her nose, "I know we haven't had much this year, but I am already so sick of snow."

McQueen burped and snored.

"Lovely," Mark sighed.

Maria stifled a laugh while Leslie giggled. Mark walked over to where the two women sat and joined them on the wood floor, "Isn't he just dreadful? He just yells and acts like it was our fault this happened. I mean, I don't even know the man!"

This time Maria did laugh quietly, and Alicia smiled.

"There you go. I knew I could at least make you smile, but I was going to draw the line at sticking McQueen's hand in a bowl of hot water."

"Probably the hottest thing that's touched him in a while," Maria said.

That remark made the three of them giggle loudly and only stop when they saw Roger move under his blanket. Mark winked, "Thought we were caught for a second."

Leslie had carefully crawled out of Hester's arms and tiptoed over to the threesome. Maria stretched her arms out warmly to the boy. Leslie smiled and half leaped at her, rocking Maria back, "Woooo. You going into football, Little Man?"

Leslie giggled and snuggled up against Maria, "You sure have been a brave boy."

Leslie looked up at Maria, his greenish brown eyes shining brightly, "Hester said that yesterday. You guys are nice. It makes it all easy."

McQueen snorted loudly again.

"Even he can be nice. He pulled Hester here on that suitcase. I think he just needs more hugs."

Leslie saw them looking at him with humor in their eyes, and he decided to defend his thought on this matter, "My teacher, Mrs. Griffith, says that a hug makes everyone happy."

Mark replied, "Alright then, we'll draw straws to see who gets that job."

They all laughed at this, but Maria was hugging Leslie tighter, so it wasn't a bad laugh like Mama would do. Mama's laugh scared him and he wouldn't ever have to hear it again. Leslie decided it was alright to laugh along, too.

"Is this a party nobody told me about? Is there any cake?"

Jack was shaking himself awake. Mark blushed and looked away, noticing Jack's early morning riser, "Well, I think it will be a nice day."

Mark stood and walked to the window again, "Maybe we should all wake up. Think of a plan of action together. We should all be in on it. Somebody else wake up McQueen, though."

Alicia shook Roger. He blinked once, opened his eyes and then closed them, "I was hoping that had all been a dream yesterday."

Maria kneeled next to the couch and very gently touched Hester, "Hester? Wake up."

Nothing.

"Hester?"

Again, nothing.

"Hester, No!"

Maria quickly clamped down on Hester's right wrist. All eyes were on the two women as Hester shifted, yawned awake, and blinked up at Maria, "What's the matter, hon?"

The fingers pressing on Hester's wrist were feeling a beautifully strong pulse. Maria flushed brightly as she loosened her grip, "I was trying to wake you up. You... I thought..."

Hester smiled, "I've always been a heavy sleeper. I have scared everyone with that from my parents all the way up to you. I'm sorry, dear."

Maria patted Hester's hand in embarrassment now, "I'm normally not so panicky... I just didn't want you to be... how's the knee feeling?"

Hester's legs moved slightly underneath the blanket, she grimaced slightly and then her face cleared, "Well, the right one is a little tired, but the left one still hurts some. It is better than yesterday, but not in tip top shape."

Jeremy stood up and stretched as he walked over to the window with Mark, "Good Morning, New York! I haven't seen this much snow in all my life."

Mark turned to Jeremy, "Aren't you glad this old house was here?"

"Yeah," Jeremy scratched his mussed hair, "We wouldn't have made it under that bridge last night. At least we are a little warmer here. Who put the log on the fire this morning?"

"I did," Mark said, "it was just coals when I woke up a little bit ago."

"For Christssake, I was sleeping so well!" McQueen bellowed at Jack from the winged chair.

"Take it up with management."

Jack strode over to the fireplace, grabbing a bent poker laying next to the wood and jabbed it a little too forcefully into the glowing coals around the burning log. Everyone had a good idea as to who he was thinking about at that moment.

"I'm awake now. What's this all about?" McQueen adjusted himself in the winged chair. He tried tucking his stomach into the sweatpants, but fuzzy rolls still stuck out the sides, Leslie thought he looked like a grumpy muffin.

Maria spoke first, "We need to come up with a plan of action. We all would like to get out of here as soon as possible and we should all be probably looked over at a proper medical facility. Any suggestions?"

Everyone looked at each other but no one said anything. Maria sighed, "That's the same thing I thought of."

Jeremy shifted, "Hey, Jack. You said that you know the area. Is there anyone or any place close enough to help us?"

Jack looked at the floor then brought his gaze up to Jeremy and said gravely, "I'm 100 percent sure there isn't another house within ten miles of here. That road out there isn't used much this time of year. That's why I was surprised about where we were last night. See, uh, this stretch is normally closed when there's too much snow."

The survivors all trembled uneasily at this bit of information. Jeremy swore under his breath and started pacing when something caught his eye. It was the windowsill farthest from the front door, the same one he had crawled through to get inside. There appeared to be faint, pink streaks running down the wall inside the house. Jeremy opened the window and saw that the streaks ran in both directions on the old, white windowsill. He leaned out into the freezing air.

"What the hell are you doing? Close that window!" McQueen commanded.

Ignoring this, Jeremy doubled over and brushed the snow away on the porch, revealing frozen bits and chunks of regurgitated food. Feeling his own stomach twitch at what he had just exposed from underneath the drift, Jeremy lifted himself back inside and closed the window, brushing fresh snowflakes off his arm and from the top of his head. He then twisted the old lock on the window, his fingers shaking as he did it, "I think someone has been here recently."

Jack arched his good eyebrow, "What makes you say that?"

"I just found some, uh, vomit on the porch under the snow. I didn't notice it last night when I was climbing in. Was anyone sick last night?"

"Yeah," Jack quickly said, "I hurled some yesterday. Thought I got it all outside, sorry about that."

Jeremy looked upset, "I just thought...maybe somebody had..."

Jack smiled weakly, "Trust me, my guy. This is one of the loneliest stretches of Upstate New York."

Leslie stood up fidgeting and leaned over into Maria's ear and whispered. Maria's eyebrows raised a little, "Has anyone seen a bathroom here?"

"I'm sure I saw one on our adventure upstairs last night. It's at the end of the hall up there toward the front of the house," Mark volunteered.

Roger stood up, heading for the swinging door at the far right of the room, "I'll look for one on this floor."

Maria took one of Leslie's hands and started leading him up the gently creaking stairs.

"Oh, dear. I hope there's one on this floor," Hester said, "I'm not sure how long it would take me to climb those stairs. I sure don't want to be more of a burden on everyone and be carried everywhere."

"Don't forget, Hester, going to the bathroom saved your life," Jeremy said.

The old woman seemed to shiver on the inside but all she said was, "It must have been the soda I had been drinking."

*****

Hester wanted more than anything to be squeezing Nate's hand, having the chance to rest her head on his shoulder, smelling him.

They had left their daughter's house two days early

because Hester's arthritis had been troubling her more so in the last week than it had all year. Nate wanted Hester to be in her doctor's office the first day that they possibly could. So, December 28th at 10 a.m., Hester and Nate Maltby would be the first people to walk through Dr. Donegan's office door.

"*Tomorrow*," thought Hester, "*I should be waiting in Dr. Donegan's office with Nate tomorrow morning.*"

She knew that wasn't going to happen now. When the bus rolled, she had been on her way back to her seat. She could spot Nate's white hair in the darkness up ahead. One man had a light on above his seat, the one that winked at her when she accidentally bumped into Mr. McQueen.

All Hester remembered from the crash was tumbling onto Roger and banging her head on the young man. She must have cracked her knee on the arm rest. She didn't remember anything until she woke up looking at an orange sky, Maria feeling for a pulse in her neck, and the cold.

The dream she had from the moment of the crash until Maria waking her on the banks of the river was an odd one. Hester had been standing on the cruise ship she and Nate had sailed on last spring. Everything seemed so tropical and warm, but it was so cold. Nate looked fine and was smiling at her, holding her hands.

"It's time to get in the boat."

Hester looked at the empty, lonely lifeboat swaying high above the blue/green sea. It was uncovered and ready to be lowered away.

"Why are we getting in that?"

Nate kissed her cheek and was helping her into the boat, "I have to wait here, but you're going to be my good girl and get in. I'll be right here when you come back."

"I'm supposed to be leaving without you? You're crazy Nathaniel Edwin Maltby if you think I am going in this boat without you."

She didn't want to leave her husband of 49 years on the ship, but she kept stepping down into the lifeboat and taking a seat as if something else was moving her. She turned to face him. He was kneeling on the deck, eye level with her. She was still holding his left hand, his right free to caress her neck, "I'll be right here for you, my love. Just be my good girl."

The lifeboat jerked sideways slightly. The pressure on Hester's neck increased and she could hear someone's voice in the distance.

"Nate, I love you."

Nate Maltby kept smiling at her, holding her gaze with those eyes she has loved for decades. Snow began to fall around and then through him. The picture was fading in her mind's eye.

"I think she's coming around."

Now, Hester was out of the dream and into a real nightmare, but the image of Nate smiling so peacefully at her, with so much love, Hester knew her beloved Nate hadn't suffered.

*****

"Nate, I love you."

The sound of her own voice surprised Hester as it was the only sound in the room aside from the crackling of the fire. She looked around to see if anyone had noticed. McQueen had been looking at her then lowered his gaze to his stocking feet when Hester's eyes met his.

"Hey!"

Roger came into the room smiling broadly, "There's food in the kitchen. Food! Canned food and an opener. Everything!"

Jack started for the kitchen first, "Really?"

McQueen was up and following Jack, every inch of him jiggling with each step, with Alicia following right behind him, and Mark hot on her heels.

Jeremy stopped by Hester, "Tell Maria and Leslie where we are. Will you be alright here?"

Hester patted Jeremy's hands ever so gently, "I'll be alright. I'll tell Maria and Leslie that everyone went outside to make snow angels."

Hester's eyes sparkled and the corners of her mouth were trying to keep her sly smile at bay. Looking at Hester in this moment made Jeremy want to hug her. He just squeezed her cold hands gently and simply said, "I sure like you, Ma."

Hester's eyes widened a little, "Well... I guess I'm always up for having new children."

After the swinging door closed behind Jeremy, Hester threw aside the old blanket and examined her left knee. Getting the forest green sweat bottoms on had been a chore for Maria and Hester the night before. The fabric of the left knee still seemed stretched out more than the right. Hester picked up her left leg and timidly swung it over the side of the couch and pushed herself into a sitting position with her right. This was the moment she hadn't wanted anyone to witness. She slowly lowered her left leg until it bent enough to touch the floor. The knee screamed with pain the entire way down, and it took all of Hester's will not to do the same.

*****

Maria walked with Leslie down the L-shaped hall that led to the bathroom upstairs, "The seat was cold."

Leslie had no idea how relieved Maria was to have a working bathroom, also finding it lucky that it had two rolls of toilet paper in the cabinet under the sink and one sitting on the back of the old commode. The rolls didn't seem very old and that bothered Maria, but, right now, this was a major blessing.

There were three bedrooms on the second floor, two had bedding in them of some sort while one contained an old, dusty looking bureau, its drawer half pulled out and one broken on the floor. A railing ran along the top of the staircase and one could lean over and look at the length of the staircase.

Maria felt Leslie tentatively take her hand. Something told her that this gentle boy's mother never showed him much physical affection. In a way, his eyes seemed to be telling everyone that he was having the time of his life.

Coming down the stairs, Maria only saw Hester in the living room, lying on the couch, her face suffused with color while sweat beaded all over her forehead.

"Are you alright, Hester?"

"Fine," Hester said a little out of breath, "just bent the bad knee a little on accident. It's not a good idea to do that just yet. Everybody else went into the kitchen. Roger said he found some food."

"REALLY? That's WICKED!"'"

Leslie released Maria's hand and dashed through the swinging door everyone else had gone through.

"There's really food? YAY!" Leslie's joyous voice carried through to Maria and Hester.

Maria excused herself and went to the kitchen a little faster than a trained nurse should have.

*****

In the kitchen area, everyone crowded around large paper bags that were sitting on the yellowed and peeling counter. There were several cans of fish, chicken, chili, corn, beans, pears, peaches, ravioli, and spaghetti, with several gallons and small bottles of spring water.

Everyone was holding a can of something, checking out the expiration dates. Roger was digging in one of the bags and brought out a long piece of paper, "Hey, found the receipt. Everything here is listed, and it's dated four days ago. Even the can opener is on here."

Alicia put the can of spaghetti she had been holding back on the counter, "That's kind of creepy."

McQueen was twisting the can opener on a family size can of chili, "Look, no one's here. No one can *get* here. The place seemed abandoned, so who cares? Are there any spoons over there?"

Leslie had opened a door behind the group across from the

rotten counter, "This is another bathroom!"

"Good," said Jeremy, "That will make it a lot easier on Hester."

McQueen was drinking the chili hungrily out of the can. Dark, orange juice dribbled out of one corner of his mouth. Jack was cracking open some peaches, Maria opened a can of mixed fruit. Jeremy had found large packs of plastic spoons and forks in one bag and was handing them out. Roger opened a can of ravioli and passed it to Alicia and grabbed a can for himself.

Jack walked out of the room and came back a moment later, "Can I have a water bottle and a cup, please? Hester just wants some water right now."

"She needs to eat something, too. Food will help with our energy and healing," Maria grabbed a can of peaches, opened it, and handed it to Jack, "Take this to her and tell her to eat at least a few bites. Leslie, you need to eat something, too."

Jack was swinging back through the door, "Hester, I hope you like peaches!"

"Leslie?"

Maria scanned the kitchen and didn't see the boy, "Has anyone seen Leslie?"

Alicia quickly poked her head into the bathroom, "He's not in here."

Mark wrapped his blanket tighter around himself and opened the swinging door, "Is Leslie in there with you?"

Jack was holding the can of peaches as Hester drank sips of the bottled of water, "Nope. He was in there with you all just a minute ago."

On the other side of the drab kitchen was a large archway. Maria and Jeremy stepped into a poorly wallpapered room. A huge, old wooden table was standing in the center with half a dozen chairs lined up across the wall on the other side of the room. A large glass-paned door opened up to the frozen air on the left.

"Leslie?"

On the opposite end of the dining room to the far right,

another door stood open a crack. Jeremy walked over to it and opened the door completely, "It looks like a basement is over here. Leslie?!"

No answer.

Maria followed and stood next to Jeremy as they both looked down the foreboding staircase. There was some dull light illuminating the gloom below just a touch. Maria stood straight, "I hate basements. I'll go down if you will."

Jeremy squeezed Maria's tense forearm, "Together we go."

The stairs creaked and squeaked all the way to the bottom. The muted blue glow was sunlight through the snow piled up on the storm windows. The large room they were standing in ran the width of the house, a tired looking but solid workbench wrapped all around. The floor was dusty with boxes piled high on the workbench and crammed underneath. Two old chairs were also filled with boxes that looked like they hadn't been touched in decades. Just around the stairs behind Maria and Jeremy were two smaller rooms. The one on the right had an ancient washer and dryer, with a clothesline sagging down in the middle toward a rusty drain in the floor. An angry looking boiler stood between these two doors. Leslie stood in the doorway to the left.

"There you are. Why didn't you answer me when we were calling?" Maria asked as she walked up behind the boy. She hadn't realized how much panic had been squeezing her heart until that moment.

In the room that Leslie was facing, a molded pool table stood in the center with a bar near the back. A few old and empty liquor bottles remained there, remembering parties of times gone by.

"Leslie? Leslie, what's the matter?"

Jeremy followed right behind the nurse, "What's wrong, son?"

Maria had just placed her hands on Leslie's shoulders when her voice was choked off her next sentence. She instantly turned Leslie around and buried his face into her chest to save him from the view of the room.

"What happened..." Jeremy finally looked over Maria's shoulder.

Lying between the rotting pool table and the bar, in a circle of frozen blood, was a very dead man.

THE BODY

Maria pushed Leslie into Jeremy's arms behind her. "Take him upstairs."

Her moment of fright had passed, and she was now in full work mode again.

She knelt down over the top of the gentleman. The temperature of the room hovering near freezing, Maria could see her breath.

The man she was looking at was Latino, at least 35 years of age. His shirt front was caked with blood. Maria pulled it open sending a few buttons flying. She pulled up his crusted undershirt and found a quarter size hole just above his abdomen. A bullet had killed him, but it could have taken up to three minutes for this gentleman to bleed to death. Maria tried moving one of his arms but found a lot of resistance. Rigor Mortis. The man had been dead for less than twenty-four hours. Most likely around twelve.

A dark coat was lying on top of the pool table's moth-eaten green felt just above the body. Maria started digging through the pockets and found a beaten-up leather wallet with "Boss" in raised letters on the front. The ID inside read Hector Ortiz, 37 years old, 150 lbs., 5'9, and he was an organ donor with a New York City address.

Footsteps behind Maria made her jump a little. It was Jeremy.

"Do you know what happened?"

"This man, Hector, was shot just above the stomach. I'm guessing that the bullet nicked his aorta. He's in full rigor, so he's been dead for at least twelve hours, no more than fourteen. The cold could have slowed all of that down, though. It's my best guess, anyway, as it's really not my line of work to worry about the dead. I'm a pediatric nurse at a children's hospital in Boston."

"Should we tell the others?"

Maria stood, "We have to. It might be too dangerous for us to remain in this house."

Jeremy shuddered at the thought of moving, "Jack says there isn't anywhere nearby to go, and none of us are equipped to go on a ten-mile hike in deep snow. I think you're right, though. Let's get up and talk to the others and get some other thoughts on this."

"Let's just leave him here undisturbed with the door closed. The authorities will not want anybody else messing with him by the time they arrive."

Closing the door to the pool room darkened the workroom even more, making the boxes look like jagged boulders in the shadows.

Maria shuddered, "I told you that I hate basements."

"Are you okay?"

"No. That's what seems to be bothering me the most. I'm trained to be okay, but I'm not. Obviously. I'm just falling…"

Jeremy embraced her and she clung to him trembling.

"I'll make you a deal, babe. You keep everyone else okay and I'll do my best to keep you okay."

Maria looked up into Jeremy's face and saw for the first time how plainly attractive he was. There were faded freckles and gaps in his teeth just small enough to avoid braces. Without thinking, she stood up on tiptoe and kissed him. His lips were soft but firm and tasted like pizza from whatever he had been eating upstairs.

He pulled her tighter and she could feel him stiffening.

"*This is crazy,*" she thought, "*I just examined a dead man on the other side of this door behind me, in a lonely house in the middle of nowhere and I'm… I'm…*"

Maria broke the kiss and breathed, "Thank you. I needed that."

Jeremy flushed, "Sorry. I… that doesn't get to happen a lot to me. Let's go upstairs."

*****

Once everyone had assembled in the living room, Maria explained to all about Leslie's find in the basement. She spoke clearly and matter of fact to make the horrifying discovery a little easier to take in.

When she finished her observations, Mark was the first to break the silence, "How dreadful! We must get out of here, and surely someone has noticed that our bus is missing by now, right?"

"Maybe not with the blizzard," Roger spoke up, "Maybe we aren't the only people missing in the state."

"That damn detour," McQueen snorted from his winged chair, "They might not even know where to look for us."

McQueen felt a pang in his heart and started massaging his chest again. At 56, he shouldn't be feeling this bad. Sure, he was a little overweight, but it shouldn't be this bad. He just needed some sleep and something better to eat than just canned food, "Maybe we should just burn down the damn house. That would get someone's attention."

Jack shifted, "You know, that's not a bad idea."

"For Christssake, Doll. That was sarcasm."

Jack was smiling to himself, "Not a house fire, but maybe we could find a way to get a bonfire going. Someone would surely see that from the road. A plow could come by at any time."

"I like it," Leslie said, "I'll help you, Jack!"

Jeremy stood from where he had been sitting on the hardwood floor, "I'm going back to the wreck. I want to see if I could bring back some more clothes, maybe be surprised and find some supplies that we could use here."

Maria looked at Jeremy, "I'm not so sure that's wise. We were lucky that none of us froze out there, but to go out there again? I mean, the snow is a lot deeper. I just think it's too risky."

Mark dropped his blanket to the floor, exposing a tattooed torso, "I'll go with you if you do try for it. Anything we can get... get from the wreck would be good... for us... useful. Also, I don't want to be around a dead body any more than I have to. So, I'll go, too. With you."

Jack tossed another log on the fire, "Roger and Leslie can help me figure out how to get a bonfire going. Mark, we're going to need your lighter, please."

Mark had put on a sweater and an old scarf from Nate's suitcase. He was sliding on his semi-dry jeans from the night before, "Of course. One thing first."

Mark pulled out a small, flat, black box from the back of his jeans. He tore the plastic off of the top, opened it and smiled to himself. He took out a black cigarette and stuck it in between his lips, "Filthy addiction, I know, but do you blame me in times like these? I'm just lucky I hadn't opened them before my surprise swim in the river. They would have been ruined and you all would have had to put up with me going through withdrawals."

He zipped up his leather ankle boots, lit his cigarette, and tossed the lighter to Jack.

McQueen narrowed his eyes at Mark, "What the hell is that you're smoking?"

"A clove cigarette. My, uh, my friend Almir puffs on them. Kinda' got me hooked a few months ago."

"Mmmm. I like that smell," Leslie said, "Mama's didn't smell good like yours do. Yours smell like cim-min-um."

Mark smiled and blew smoke out his nostrils, "My friends call Almir and me the gingerbread men."

Jeremy finished lacing up his shoes, "Are you ready, Mark?"

Mark's smile broadened and swung his deep blue eyes towards the front door, "Exit, stage left, already."

This got a laugh out of everyone except McQueen. Maria heard a slur escape from his lips under his breath and was thankful she was the only one who seemed to have heard him.

Once the door was closed behind them, Jeremy and Mark paused on the porch. The snow now stood higher than the old floorboards. Mark stuck his hands in his pockets, with his clove clamped between his lips, "Well? Shall we?"

Jeremy looked at Mark, smiled and then plowed into the deep, blinding-white snow. Mark exhaled his sweet smoke, looked up as huge flakes peppered from the iron grey sky, then quickly followed behind in Jeremy's trails before he lost his nerve.

*****

Jack and Roger were standing at the glass door in the neglected dining room. Leslie sat on the edge of the dining table, kicking his legs and gently rocking side to side with each little kick.

"See that shed, Roger? That's the first goal to reach. Here's hoping that there's things in there that we can use."

"And if there's not?" Roger raised his eyebrows.

Jack shook his head and flashed his lopsided smile, "Then we take McQueen's advice and burn the whole damn thing down."

Leslie giggled, "Yeah. We can burn the whole damn thing down!"

Jack's smile widened and raised his good eyebrow, "You know, if it had been my nephew that said that, I'd have scolded him. After everything you have been through, you have earned a word or two. Let it, fly, Leslie."

Leslie grinned and kicked a little harder, "Mama always swears. Daddy does, too, but not like Mama. She mostly only swears at night when she would get home late, though. She got a new job, so she was taking me over to Buffalo to live with Daddy."

"You like that idea, living with your daddy?"

"Yeah. Mama doesn't like him, but I always did. Do you have kids, Jack?"

Jack sucked on his teeth, "Nope. I'm just married to my job and my babies are the hours I work."

"What do you do?" Roger asked.

"I work in a bank in New York City. Been at the same branch for over 15 years. Math has the only figures that I was ever really good at in life."

Roger smiled, "I gotcha, man."

"One of my better jokes. Well, here goes nothing."

Jack pushed the glass door open, fanning a pattern in the powdered snow.

"Leslie, my man. I want you to wait here. Watch me and Roger. If we need help, we'll get you to run for Maria and Alicia in the living room. Can you do that for Roger and I?"

"Sure!"

Jack ruffled the boy's sandy-blonde hair, "Back in a flash."

After half stepping, half falling down the hidden back steps, Roger and Jack waded in thigh deep snow to the small wooden shed. Leslie closed the backdoor and had his face pressed against the cold glass watching the two intently as they churned their way down the 100 feet or so to the shed.

Roger made it first. He grabbed the small, metal door handle and pushed, suddenly declaring, "Shit, it opens out. Looks like we'll need a shovel to open this door. Damn it."

Jack pulled violently on the door and got it to open a full centimeter, "Fuck a duck."

Roger was already scooping snow away with his bare hands, the cold stinging his pink palms, "Let's hope our fingers don't freeze off."

Jack sighed heavily and started digging in front of the door with Roger. Powdered flakes were sticking to their hands and burning deep into their skin. Falling snow clung to Jack's neck and the back of his head.

"Blows, doesn't it, Jack?"

"Could be worse. I'm not quite sure how yet, but I'll think of something. So, Roger, how did you get stuck in all of this?"

"I was going to see my aunt in Jamestown. Supposed to meet another bus in Buffalo and then on to the hometown of Lucille Ball and see Aunt Vi. She's a helluva lady, everything my moms ain't. She drinks, she smokes, swears, has had three husbands. I love my moms, don't get me wrong, but I always look forward to spending time with Aunt Vi. I always go the week after Christmas, before school starts. I spend my summers in Atlantic City with her, too. That's where I lifeguard all of July and part of August. Aunt Vi has a condo down there."

"I'll bet you wish it was July now."

"Yeah, bet," Roger smiled then jerked on the door handle again. It only opened half an inch.

"Fuck. Let's go warm up a bit and try again. Hopefully it won't snow in all of our work."

"HEEEEY!"

Jack turned and saw Leslie standing at the open back door and he was holding an old shovel and smiling, "I saw this in the basement earlier!"

Jack lunged back through the trails Roger and himself had made on their way to the shed. The slight incline from the shed to the house made it a little more difficult of a journey.

"Will this work, Jack?"

"You did really good, Kiddo."

Leslie smiled wider and wiggled, "I'm glad. You're welcome."

"Yeah, thanks."

Jack walked back to Roger using the shovel as walking stick, "You go ahead and warm up some. I'll dig a while. I'll trade you before I freeze up like the Tin Man. "

Roger was blowing into his cupped fingers, "You got it. I'll see if I can find an oil can for you before I head out here, but don't you be hogging all the fun."

"I won't. I can promise you that."

Roger started trudging back to the house when Jack tossed his first shovel full. The little damage it did to the powdered snowpack made Jack chuckle and just shake his head. He hoped Mark and Jeremy weren't having as much trouble as he and Roger were.

Jack dug on.

IT'S THE LITTLE THINGS

10:05 a.m.

Jeremy glanced over his shoulders at his companion. He and Mark had been walking for almost twenty minutes when Mark finally threw away his butt. It hissed a brief death rattle in the snow.

"Those things last forever."

"Yeah," Mark breathed, "They last a long time. Taste better, smell better, but I am sure they are worse for me than regular ones."

"Everybody has their vices. I tell you, coming through the woods didn't seem as long last night."

The trees appeared closer together in the muted daylight. Jeremy felt like an unwanted child sneaking his way through a party of giants. He definitely felt like he was invading their space and the trees were looking down on him with the utmost disapproval.

"Thanks for coming with me."

Mark sniffed, "I just had to. Everyone seemed to be doing something useful except me. I have never been great in emergencies, and I didn't care to keep that fact alive. I thought helping you would be at least a little redeeming."

"I can see you've got a good heart, Mark. That's more than a lot of people have these days."

The pair walked in silence for a minute or two before Mark spoke again, "There's also a selfish reason for my coming along, too, if I am being honest."

"Oh, yeah? What's that?"

Mark hesitated, his words catching in his throat, "I thought I should tell you. My Grammie always said, 'the difference between a thief and a liar is, you can lock up a thief, but goddamn a liar.'"

"Smart lady."

"She is," Mark smiled, "The smartest and toughest broad born in 1919!"

"So, what is the big motivation for freezing your balls off with me?"

Mark took a breath and then bit the bullet, "I'm hoping to find my suitcase. I don't so much care about my clothes, I really just want to get a picture from it. It's of me and my... my friend, Almir."

"This is a hell of a lot to go through for just a picture. Are you guys posed on a pile of gold or something?"

"No," Mark exhaled, "it was taken in a park across from his job. He works in Wilson's Coffee Shop on Atlantic Avenue. The movie theater I work for is right next to the park."

Jeremy stopped for a moment and leaned his back against a tree to give his legs a quick rest and to catch his breath. The cold hadn't really started to bother him yet, but he was sure that his cheeks were burning as brightly as Mark's. Jeremy looked directly into Mark's eyes, "So, how long have you and this famous Almir been together?"

Mark looked down at the snow and smiled sheepishly, his cheeks somehow turning a brighter red. He looked up and met Jeremy's eyes with his eyebrows raised, "Is it... is it that obvious?"

"Oh, yeah."

"You see, I need to get better at that. It's Almir's first relationship. Well, his first relationship with... with another guy. He's still afraid to tell anybody. It's been hard not to tell as many people as I'd like. I want to shout it from the rooftops. He's getting better at it... I think so, anyway."

Jeremy started moving again, Crooked Street being only 50 yards off. The roadway looked like a solid white river between the trees.

Mark followed, "Is talking about this bothering you?

Jeremy chuckled, "No, Mark. Not all of us straight guys are dumb. Is he handsome?"

"Oh, yeah," Mark answered quickly, "he's sexy as hell. He's

from Cuba. He's just built so perfectly. He's really nice to me, and he's an artist! Well, him and his brother are both artists. Anyway, he'd really like to get into graphic design. My family really likes him, and... and..."

Mark sniffed and his words came out thickly, "It's just so horrible. I should be in Buffalo right now. He was visiting some cousins over there and was in a car accident. He's in the hospital. He's, um... he'll be fine. I just want to be with my baby. My boss didn't understand, and I was yelling at her yesterday in the bus station. I hate yelling in public places. I actually just hate yelling. It frightens me. I just found out yesterday morning about Almir from his twin brother, Aram. He's the only family member of his that knows about us.

"Anyway, I told my boss I was going away for four days whether she liked it or not. Then, just before the bus took off, I got to talk to Almir. He told me that I didn't have to come, but that's just crazy. Of course, I'm coming! I told him that I was bringing that picture for his room. So, I just have to find it. *Need* to find it. I promised."

Tears were streaming down Mark's face, and he didn't care one bit. He had been keeping everything bottled up around the rest of the survivors, and it felt so nice just to release everything, "I'm sorry. I just needed to get that all out of my system. Thank you for that. Thank you for listening to me."

Jeremy gave Mark a side hug as the trudged along, "Get it out. You know, I almost had a little brother, but he was a stillborn. He'd be about 26 now. How old are you?"

"24."

"So, you're a little younger than he would have been. Anyway, I read a scientific report somewhere a while ago that a lot of gay people have an older sibling. Something about the chemistry in the mother's womb after a first child. I'd like to think that I would have had a gay brother just to even out the family. Do you want to be my gay little brother?"

Mark sniffed, "Sure. I've got an older brother, a younger sister, and a younger brother, but there's always room for more.

Are you 36?"

Jeremy smiled, "Next November."

"My older brother is 36. He's from our mom's first marriage. That's why there is such a large age gap. So, I guess you actually could be my brother."

The two men had reached the roadway by now and began the trek down the sloping street to the bridge.

"Are you an only child then?"

"Yep," Jeremy nodded, "my parents always wanted another, though. I think they wanted me to have the role of a 'big brother.' When I was 20, I moved to Buffalo to live in a different setting. I was born in Leominster and grew up in Boston, so I wanted a change of pace. I had been living there about four weeks when my parents died in a house fire."

"I'm so sorry."

"Me, too. Every Christmas, I go to Boston, leave some flowers at the cemetery, spend the rest of the time getting shitfaced, then I hop on back to Buffalo to manage a pizza shop. Oh, the exciting lives we lead."

They continued their walk in silence, stopping once in a while to rest their legs and bat snow off their heads and shoulders. As they reached the bridge, they could just make out a single trail of whispy smoke coming from the wreckage.

"Jesus. Is it still burning?"

"It was a hell of a fire, Mark. It's probably out, but not quite cooled down yet."

The two crossed the bridge and made their way carefully down the slope. Two mounds were visible near the bus. This had been Hester's makeshift bed. Jeremy pulled the two out from under the fresh snow and handed one to Mark. He unzipped the one he was holding. It was filled with expensive looking but cheap women's clothes; the name *Sylvia* was stitched in a label. Jeremy frowned, "I don't remember a "Sylvia"."

"That could be Leslie's mom."

Sure enough, just down below the blouses was a handful of child's clothes.

Mark had opened up his and guessed that it must belong to Alicia or her friend. He zipped it closed and placed it next to Leslie's mother's suitcase. Some of the clothes were wet, but the ones folded closer to the center felt dry.

Jeremy checked his watch, "Fifteen minutes to eleven. Kick around and see if you can find anything we might need. Let's give it half an hour and then head back home."

"Yes, sir."

Mark sauntered toward the river, while Jeremy walked toward the back end of the bus. What was left of it, anyway. It was a blackened crust of its former existence, however *TransCoach* could still be made out on the side. Part of the roof had collapsed and all but one window had been melted completely in the inferno.

Jeremy placed his hands on the floor. It felt warm but not hot enough to keep Jeremy from climbing in. He made his way up the aisle between what was left of the once cushy seating. The stink was powerful and bringing tears to Jeremy's eyes, but he kept walking up the angled aisle. The matting that had been under the carpet was sticking to Jeremy's shoes. Jeremy stepped over what was left of Leslie's mother, careful not to touch the body in any way. He passed two bodies in the seats two rows behind the driver.

"Must be the McPikes," Jeremy said, getting a taste of the bus in his mouth and gagged.

While the bodies were badly burned, he could tell that they had been clinging to one another. An arm from one of the bodies stuck up next to a melted window. Mr. or Mrs. McPike must have been reaching for the emergency exit lever.

In the row in front of the McPikes, Jeremy found the remains of Hester's husband. Nate Maltby's body was sitting on the floor in front of the seats, leaning up against the wall, his hands clasped together between what had once been his thighs. Taking every ounce of strength Jeremy could muster, he reached down and moved the hands apart as gently as he could. The hands were cooler than he had expected, and they had the spongy crustiness of a marshmallow that had been too close to a campfire.

Going by feel rather than sight, Jeremy put pressure on the old man's fingers and found what he was looking for. Jeremy took a breath and pulled. Crispy skin pulled away with a sound like dirty Velcro, leaving a red and white, stubby pulp between black, crackled fingers.

Without looking down, Jeremy pounded the wedding ring he had taken from Nate Maltby on the back of the driver's seat frame.

Finally lowering his eyes for a moment to look at what he had come away with, he was relieved to only see a blackened ring in his hand and nothing more.

A sudden shuffle and clanging noise to his right nearly made Jeremy jump out of his skin. The flask that had been in the driver's mouth was now lying on the steps up into the bus, three of the driver's teeth sticking out of it like charred barnacles.

That sight was enough for Jeremy. He left the wreckage the same way he had come, jumped down into the snow and started dry heaving.

After his stomach had finally calmed down, Jeremy put Nate's ring in his pocket and tried to wash the soot from his hands in the snow when he suddenly heard a shout.

"Mark?!"

If he had heard a cry, he wasn't sure what emotion was behind it. Jeremy stood up and plowed his way around the bus. Mark was doing the same up from the riverbank, carrying what looked like button-down dress shirts over his shoulder and he was beaming from ear to ear.

"I found it! Everything in my suitcase has been ruined. It was all underwater on the river's edge except the top pocket where I kept the picture. It's okay! I found McQueen's bag. I thought he might like some shirts that fit him."

"That's mighty nice of you."

"'Do unto others', right?"

"Let's throw those in Alicia's bag along with a few things

for Leslie and get going. I think we've found all we can get from here."

After throwing out some of the wet clothes from Alicia's suitcase and piling in McQueen's and Leslie's garments, Mark and Jeremy wrestled it up to the roadway. The deeper snow made this journey up so much more difficult than the first time they had done it.

Mark stopped and looked back at the scene for a moment. He wiped a small tear away and said, "I hope this is the last time I ever see this scene."

"You and me both, bro," Jeremy said, "I couldn't see the back half. It must be down deep in the river. I guess I still can't believe we lived through that."

Jeremy lifted the suitcase out of the drift as best he could and started back in the tracks he and Mark had powered through earlier, "Come on. Let's get back home before we freeze like statues."

Mark picked up one side of the suitcase to help Jeremy keep it out of the ever-increasing snow and they began their quiet journey back up the lonely and silent road.

LESLIE

"My turn, Roger."

Jack was making his way out to the shed for his second wave of digging.

"No way, man. It's almost clear enough and I don't want you stealing all the glory."

Roger tossed a few more pathetic shovel loads of powder away from the shed's dilapidated door, "Alright now. You give that a good tug and see what happens," Roger snorted in triumph.

Jack yanked on the handle and the door squeaked open which sounded like music to the ears.

"Yay!" Leslie yelled from the dining room doorway.

Jack and Roger stepped inside, the former rolling the spark wheel of Mark's lighter. Logs were stacked high in the back of the shed and half covered with a blue tarp that appeared to have seen better days. Quite a few cans of oil, paint, and lighter fluid lined up on the wall nearest to the door on some ancient, metal shelving.

"Save that fire, man. It's not that dark in here," Roger said over Jack's shoulder. "What all do we want outta here?"

Jack faced Roger, "We're going to dig a firepit out in front of the house. It should be visible to anyone from Crooked Street and to anyone from the living room windows. If we just keep it burning, we will be fine. Someone's bound to see it, right? Are you ready for more fun in the sun?"

Jack laughed at his own sarcasm and tore away the crinkled tarp from the woodpile.

Roger grabbed a few logs and said, "I'm taking some of these to the living room. We'll be needin' them soon."

"I have an idea," Jack said, grabbing one large log and hot-footing-it back up the path to the dining room door. "Think you can carry this to the fireplace for me?"

Leslie wrapped his arms around the log, excited to be helping, "Sure. It's... ugh, it's heavy."

Jack watched as Leslie waddled with his load into the kitchen.

"You want my ass to freeze off, Jack?"

"Hell, no. Come on in!"

Jack stepped aside for Roger and then made his way back out to the open door of the shed.

*****

McQueen sat on the edge of the footed bathtub upstairs. He'd gone there to get away from everyone. All of this mess was just so unfair.

Pound... Pound... Pound...

His heart ached and he was freezing to death with these people, and now a damn dead body in the basement. What kind of sadistic bastard lived in this dilapidated house? The idea of being stuck out here for any length of time almost frighten McQueen.

Almost.

He was not an easy man to scare. He had not been scared when he had watched a neighbor's dog maul his best friend nearly to death in the first grade. He had not been scared when his father had dropped dead of a heart attack at a family reunion when Harold was 15. He had not been scared when he moved from Bangor, Maine to Boston to further himself in the stock market trade. He had not been scared when Mr. Anderson took the rap for embezzlement and Harold took Anderson's spot on the board of directors, while Anderson spent ten years in jail. He sure as hell wasn't scared when his wife, Katherine, divorced him and threatened to take everything away from him.

Pound... Pound... Pound...

These had simply been tools of inspiration to get to the next level. So, there was no way in fucking hell he was going to be scared of being stuck in a rundown house with a bunch of good for nothing nobodys that he couldn't give a shit about. Not to mention the two colored people and a faggot among them. Jesus!

"Good for nothing bastards."

Pound... Pound... Pound...

McQueen sat on the edge of the footed bathtub upstairs, massaging his chest.

*****

Leslie almost made it to the fireplace when he stumbled and fell with his burden, the log smashing down heavily on his right hand. He stood up and gasped, biting into his lower lip. Shaking his injured hand vigorously, he was trying desperately to keep the tears he felt stinging his eyes away.

"*Les, real men don't cry,*" Sylvia Pink would slur out as she lit another cigarette having just slapped Leslie, "*You ever seen a cowboy cry? No. No, you don't ever see that. Now, stop it.*"

"Stop" being punctuated by another slap. Half the time, Leslie had no idea why his mother would slap him.

The moment Leslie stood up, Alicia and Maria were up and over to Leslie's side.

"Are you okay, Little Man? Did you hurt your hand?"

Leslie gasped and fought his brimming eyes, "Yeah."

Maria soothed, "Here. Let me take a look at it. I'll try not to hurt you, but you tell me if it does."

Maria gently examined his hand. It looked red and puffy, the back of the hand slightly scraped from the wood. Leslie's nails felt like they wanted to pop off backwards. He stood very still trying his best to hold in his breath while Maria examined him.

"It doesn't feel like you broke anything. I'm going to go get you some ice for it," Maria said going for the front door.

"Come over here, hon," Hester beckoned from the couch.

Leslie walked slowly over to Hester, fanning his injury at his side the whole way.

"Here," Hester stretched out her old, gnarled fingers to the injured boy, "let me see."

Leslie presented his throbbing hand to Hester. She carefully held it, her cool and smooth hands bringing a little relief.

"This cure always worked on my daughter."

Hester carefully kissed Leslie's knuckles and smiled at him. She looked so beautiful to Leslie, so caring and loving. Leslie felt a single tear fall from his left eye. He held his breath tighter and bit the inside of his cheeks. Leslie Gabriel Pink wasn't going to cry! He didn't want to get a slap from someone so beautiful and caring.

Yet, Hester kept smiling at him, her eyes shining, "Remember what I said about brave men? It's okay to be brave now... oh, hon, just let it out."

Leslie flung his arms around Hester's neck and cried. And cried, and cried, and cried.

Hester felt a lump in her throat and hugged Leslie's little body as tight as her old, arthritic arms could let her, "Yes, hon. It's okay. You've been such a... such a strong, brave boy. You just let it all out."

Hester held and rocked him. The old woman hadn't noticed when Maria had come in off the porch, holding an icicle while standing in awkward silence behind the couch. She hadn't noticed Roger and Jack carrying in wood and then leaving the room as quietly as possible. She hadn't noticed Alicia cover herself in a blanket on the floor with her eyes shut tightly. Hester hadn't even noticed that she, too, had started crying. For the boy, for Nate, for the whole damn show.

"I've got you. You keep letting it out. You're doing just fine."

Hester rubbed his back and stroked his hair. Leslie's all too thin body jerked and heaved with each sob, and each one was a powerful release of pain, anger, hatred, and sorrow. Each slap, pinch, poke, curse, and even the occasional cigarette burn from his dead mother was washing away into Hester's safe arms.

Leslie Pink, for the first time he could remember, let it all fall out. The sound of Hester's warm and calm voice was bringing Leslie back, and his sobbing diminished to a few snuffles and silent tears.

"Here, Hester," offered Maria, "rub the back of his hand with this."

The melting icicle was exchanged between them, and Maria walked off into the kitchen.

"Okay, now, you sit up here right next to me. Let's see that hand again."

Leslie held his hand up for Hester to rub the ice over in little circles. His eyes and cheeks as red as his hand. She glided the ice over his puffy digits, her touch as skilled as her teaching days when she nursed many a banged knee or elbow on the playground.

"Who's Esther Williams?"

Hester stopped for a moment and looked up at the boy, "You remember me saying that? What a good memory you have."

Leslie smiled a little, "You said you'd tell me if I asked again."

Hester smiled as her mind put a spotlight on one of her favorite memories. "Yes. I sure did. She was known as 'America's Mermaid' back then, although she is retired from all of that now. She did a lot of swimming in MGM movie musicals a very long time ago. The first movie Nate ever took me to see was *The Million Dollar Mermaid* with Esther Williams and Victor Mature. After seeing that picture, whenever I was in a pool or at the beach, Nate called me 'Hester Williams.'"

"Do you still swim?"

Hester wrinkled her nose and giggled at the wonderful idea of being able to swim again, "Oh, me. Not in many years, but I still go wading in lakes and the Atlantic once in a while."

Leslie pulled his hand away and bent his fingers. The hand didn't hurt so bad now. He took the ice from Hester and tossed it into the back of the fireplace beyond the flamming pile, "Thanks,

Hester. Can I bring you anything?"

"If you'd get Maria to help me get into the bathroom, I'd be most grateful."

"Do you need anything, Alicia?" Leslie asked, bending over to look into the librarian's face.

He stood up quickly and looked like a kid with his hand caught in the cookie jar. He whispered to Hester, "Oops. She's sleeping. I didn't know."

Leslie started for the kitchen, stopped, and ran back to Hester with a huge smile on his face.

"I'm moving to live with my daddy in Buffalo. There's a pool in the park across the street from his house. If you want to come over sometime, I'll take you there with me."

Hester flashed her sly smile at the boy and ran her fingers through his hair, "There is nothing in this world that I would like more."

"Great!" Leslie exclaimed and then put both hands over his mouth to quiet himself again for Alicia's sake.

Hester lovingly watched as the boy turned and ran on quiet tiptoe through the swinging kitchen door.

THE FIGHT

Jack and Roger were once again taking turns digging in the snow out in front of the house.

"I hope to hell I hit roadway instead of grass!" Jack yelled out to himself on his second turn at digging.

The pit had to be large enough to keep the snow from falling in and extinguishing the future bonfire. With the snow being just over three feet deep and becoming denser towards the ground, it made the work long and laborious. Jack wanted at least ten feet around the center. With the snow continuing to fall, switching in and out had to be done as quickly as possible. Jack's toes felt like frozen sticks and his arms burned and strained. It wasn't so much the weight of the snow that made the work so tiring, as most of it was powder, but the feeling like every shovel toss was being filled in as soon as it had been thrown aside.

"My kingdom for an actual snow shovel... or a damn flame thrower!" Jack cried.

Once it finally became time to get the bonfire going, Jack hoped it would be mostly on the hidden driveway instead of on grass. Getting a blaze going in this mess was going to be difficult enough, the idea of freezing grass that then melted into wet grass didn't help Jack's hope.

Jack speared the snow with the shovel and leaned backward as far as his back would allow, feeling a delightful crunch between his shoulder blades. He remained a moment, looking straight up, watching the massive snowflakes fall to the earth, looking like cotton balls being scattered from the sky.

A huge flake floated into view with Jack's name written all over it, falling straight towards his bruised, upturned face. Instinctually, Jack stuck out his tongue and caught it. He grinned, "We're gonna beat you sons a bitches!" Jack yelled and turned back to his digging.

*****

Mark and Jeremy tripped and stumbled over the same hidden log, dropping the suitcase and both falling face first into the snow.

"This is no time for games," Mark said, spitting out fat flakes from his red lips.

"You alright, bro?"

"Yes. Just hurt my pride a little. I'm really too cold to feel much of anything else."

After dusting themselves off, they continued their way back to the house.

11:36 a.m.

"You know, we have been at this for an hour and a half. I think we are doing pretty good. Even though I think all of my good features froze and fell off a good thirty minutes ago."

Mark smiled, "That's okay. You aren't my type, anyway."

Jeremy exclaimed in mock pain, "And just what is *that* supposed to mean?!"

"I'll put it this way to your ice covered self. I'm not into snowmen."

They both had a good, little laugh at this. Trudging through snow was only slightly easier on the way back, following the filled in trails from before.

"Jeremy, I am sorry. I have to switch one more time."

Mark and Jeremy traded places on either side of the large suitcase to give their tired arms a rest that had been half dragging and half carrying their finds from around the crash site.

"You know, this is like a weird reality show."

"How so, Mark?"

"Well, think about it. Here we are all these different types of people, thrown together in a lonely, isolated house for who knows how long. Fox would probably love it! Although, with a dead body in the basement, it could be an Agatha Christie novel and we're just waiting for the man with the "little grey cells" to show up."

Jeremy tilted his head to one side in thought a moment before he said, "It's a little like a stranded family during a reunion."

"I am intrigued, go on."

"Alright, Hester is the widowed matriarch. You, Jack, and I are brothers. McQueen is the uncle that nobody cares for, but he still shows up at all of the family functions, even without receiving an invitation. Maria is my wife and Leslie is our boy. Alicia is Jack's scandalously younger fiancé and Roger is your boyfriend."

"Oh, husband, please! I want to be married in this version of the story."

"Alright, husband. We got stuck in Mom's house after Christmas day, so the party must keep going."

"Until the thaw, of course."

"Of course, but suddenly no one wants the thaw to come because the family is learning to bond together in a different way and love is growing with everyone's company. Even with the grump uncle."

Mark couldn't help but smile, "Your idea is so much more light hearted than mine. It also leaves out the mystery of the dreadful body downstairs."

They walked for a while in silence, the only sound of crunching snow and heavy breaths falling on their ears. After a few minutes, another repetitive sound joined in their trooping.

Crunch... Shook... Crunch... Shook...

"What the hell is Jack doing?"

Mark could just make out Jack shoveling snow with a regular shovel in front of the house, "Maybe he's looking for a car?"

They watched him stop for a moment, stretching his back, and looking up at the sky. Then Jack opened his mouth and started catching snowflakes on his tongue.

"I'll be damned," Jeremy laughed, "there is a little kid in all of us."

Jack yelled something that the two couldn't quite make out and then he began his digging again.

Crunch... Shook... Crunch... Shook...

Mark giggled, "Maybe he's angry that Mom made him shovel the driveway again."

Jeremy flashed all his teeth but said nothing.

When they were close enough, Mark yelled out, "Hey, is there a room available here for two weary travelers?"

Jack swung the old shovel above his head and cried, "This here is private property! Find yourselves a motel!"

Meeting up with Jack, the three of them walked to the porch, assisted in dusting each other off, and entered the house.

*****

"Jeremy, Mark! Welcome back!" Maria beamed with relief.

Maria was assisting Hester to the couch from the kitchen while McQueen was coming down the stairs. Jeremy stomped his feet for a moment before heading to the fireplace. Mark had already pulled off his boots, socks, and jeans and was hastily sliding on a pair of Nate's dry sweats again over his brightly colored briefs.

Jeremy rubbed his hands near the lovely flames, "We found a few suitcases. We brought back Alicia's with more women's clothes to go around and some of Leslie's from his mother's suitcase."

"Thank goodness for the women's clothes," Jack said, "my bra was beginning to feel so sour after all of that digging."

Maria playfully smacked Jack's arm, "Ha. Ha. Thank you, Jeremy. I am so happy you both came back safe."

"You are most welcome. How are things going here?"

Jack handed off the shovel to Roger. "We have been out there digging a pit for the bonfire we are going to make. We found a decent size woodpile in the shed out back. Since then, we have been taking turns digging a pit that will be big enough. I sure wish we had a snow shovel instead of a regular one, though. It's about as useful as a glass of orange juice after brushing your teeth, but it's better than nothing, I guess."

"Don't worry," Roger said, opening the door and facing the freeze again, "we'll have that fire going in no time."

"Wait!"

Everyone froze and stared at Jeremy.

"We should hold off on that."

Harold McQueen planted himself back in the winged chair, "What on earth for?"

"Two reasons. Mark and I were just out there, and we can tell you that no plow has been down Crooked Street yet. Two, if we wait until it gets darker the fire will be easier to see if someone actually does happen to go by."

Jack and Roger both looked like crestfallen children who dropped their ice cream. Jack pouted, "But with the way it's snowing, the hole we have worked so hard on will be filled up."

"Mark and I are back. Four people working at it will be faster and better than just two."

Roger sadly shut the door and leaned the shovel against the wall, "A'ight, Dad. I'll wait to go outside and play."

"Shit on it, anyway," Jack blew into his fingers.

Mark looked at McQueen and took a deep breath, "I found something for you, Mr. McQueen."

McQueen grunted.

Mark opened Alicia's suitcase and pulled out the shirts he had found, "Everything else of yours was soaked, but these were mostly dry. Thought you'd find these... uh... more comfortable."

McQueen had some flicker of emotion cross his face as he snatched the shirts from Mark, looked them over and said a short, "thanks," without looking up.

"You're welcome."

Jeremy left the fire and knelt down next to Hester, his knees popping loudly.

"You're not too cold, are you?"

"Oh, no. I'm doing okay," Hester sighed.

"I found something I wanted to return to you."

Jeremy reached into his pocket and brought out the ring he had pulled from Nate Maltby's burned finger.

Hester stared at Jeremy's open palm with wide eyes. Her mouth opened slightly and then closed again. She looked up into Jeremy's face with amazement, "That's Nate's wedding ring. But... how did you ever find it?"

Jeremy placed the ring in Hester's hands. She looked at it and then carefully closed her fingers the best she could, "Thank you. I am so... overwhelmed. It's just... wonderful, Jeremy. Really, thank you so much."

Jeremy wrapped his spidery fingers over Hester's closed fist, "You're welcome, Ma."

"So, genius, when the hell can the bonfire get started or are you two not finished sucking each other off yet?"

All eyes were now on McQueen. He had put on one of his shirts over the small, straining clothes of Nate's. Maria noticed beads of sweat popping out over stubble on his bald head.

Through gritted teeth, Jeremy managed, "I know that we are all under a lot of strain but adding to it isn't going to help anyone here at all, is it?"

Leslie stuck his head out from under the blanket from where he had been dozing next to Alicia. He didn't like the tone of Jeremy's voice.

"*Here it comes,*" thought Roger as he took a step closer to the gap between the couch and the chair. The only problem in the lifeguard's mind now was, if Jeremy started fighting with McQueen, whether or not Roger himself might take a swing or two at the fat man before trying to separate the two.

Jack asked a little too loudly, "Did either of you see a green suitcase out there? It's one of those old looking ones, hard covered... gold locks...?"

Mark took out one of his cigarettes, lit it using a twig from the fireplace after patting his pockets (*where the hell had he placed his lighter?*), and exhaled, "We didn't see anything like that, Jack. Did we Jeremy?"

McQueen and Jeremy were staring each other down, not paying any attention to the conversation that was trying to de-escalate the crisis that was brewing.

McQueen said, "With all that's going on around here, it's bad enough without adding more bullshit that we all have to put up with in this house. Why would you make the rules? Who put you in charge? I need to get out of here. I don't have time to wait for a signal to get going."

Surprisingly, it was Mark who calmly spoke first, "We need to get out of here. *We*, Mr. McQueen. We are all in this together whether we like it or not. You have done nothing to help the situation since we arrived at this house. So, if there's nothing you can-"

"You shut your cock-sucking mouth! There's a lot more going on in this world that's bigger than anything you are-"

"That's it!"

Jeremy leaped at McQueen from where he had been kneeling, tackling him hard enough to make the winged chair flip onto its back. Everyone was now moving and shouting at once.

"Get offa' *me*!"

"Stop it!"

"Gentleman, please!"

"What's happening?!"

"Jeremy stop!"

"No, no, no, no, no!"

Jeremy straddled McQueen's chest, pinning the fat man's large shoulders to the floor with his bony knees. Handfuls of McQueen's shirt were clutched in Jeremy's fists, which were now thrusting up into McQueen's sagging chins with each word Jeremy spat out, "Why? What is your problem? Why are you so fuckin' mean to everyone for no reason?"

McQueen's eyes opened the widest they had been in years. His face turning red and purple with hate, but he was too angry to speak. His pudgy hands slapped and flopped wildly at Jeremy's sides, but his power was much weaker than the younger man's.

Roger and Jack were on either side of Jeremy lifting him from under his armpits. Amazingly, Jeremy still pinned down McQueen, their combined strength useless against Jeremy's sudden burst of primal rage.

"WHY?!" Jeremy spat into McQueen's face.

Leslie ran in front of the four men and yelled out with all the power his little lungs had, "Jeremy, stop it, please!"

Jeremy broke his unblinking glare from McQueen's face and brought it up to the boy. The look in his eyes shook Leslie, and Jeremy melted a little when he saw that the little boy was close to frightened tears.

"Please?"

Jeremy dropped his fury back down to McQueen's grizzly eyes, and spoke in the tone of quiet anger, "Alright... alright, here's how it's going to be. You are going to keep your damn mouth shut unless it is to help out. You are not to name call anyone, ANYONE else in this house to make you feel better about yourself. If you so much as look cross-eyed at anyone of us, so help me, I'll throw you out and let you find your own place to stay. Is that crystal clear?"

McQueen's face only twitched.

"I'll take that as a 'yes' from you."

With that, Jeremy was up and off McQueen, making his way upstairs away from the rest of the survivors. Without thinking twice, Maria followed him.

McQueen was still on his back staring at the ceiling until one of the doors on the second floor slammed. After another moment, McQueen rolled off the winged chair on to his side and picked himself up with much difficulty. He righted his toppled throne and sank down into it heavily, his breath heaving. He then started speaking to those present, as all eyes were on him. In a very low voice he said, "We, and I do mean we, need to get far away from that man."

Mark grabbed Leslie by the hand and led the boy to the kitchen, sweet clove smoke trailing in their wake.

"He's out of his mind," McQueen continued, "I saw the

look in his eyes. None of you did. They are the eyes of a killer. A freak. A murderer. We have to leave here or find some way of restraining him."

McQueen continued murmuring, not really paying attention to the burning anvil in his chest or that Jack and Roger had followed Mark's example and followed him into the kitchen away from the sermon that was now taking place from an extremely angry man.

"You all should be listening to what I am saying. That bastard up there with that nurse is scary. He's going to hurt one of us really bad, and then you all will know that I was correct. McQueen was right, damn it. McQueen was right all along. I know that you will all be saying these words sooner or later to each other and thanking me for knowing and speaking the truth first. He probably killed that man downstairs. That silly dead man must have been in the accident with us and we missed him. He made his way to this house in the middle of the night when we were sleeping and then Jeremy killed him. He killed him right under out sleeping noses."

Alicia stood with her blanket wrapped around her shoulders and disappeared as quickly as she could through the swinging door to the kitchen without ever once looking at McQueen.

The grizzly eyes from the winged chair turned to the last occupant in the room. Hester was staring at McQueen without the gentle look of humor her eyes normally contained. One arthritis ravaged fist clutched tightly to her chest.

"You're a woman who has lived even longer than I. You'll listen to reason. He's all evil. He's not done one bit of good in his whole life, I'll wager. We are all done for if we don't do something to stop him now. Something must be done about that man. Maybe they will all listen to you, but you listen to me so that you know what to tell them. Do you understand, Mrs. Maltby? Do you follow?"

With as much care as possible, Hester opened her fist and slipped her late husband's wedding band onto the middle finger of her left hand, pushing the band over her swollen knuckle. Without making a sound or changing the expression upon her defiant face, Hester Maltby stood up to her full height, and with as much grace as her ravaged knee would allow her, she limped out of the room with her head held proudly high.

Now completely alone, McQueen gripped the armrests of his chair, his arms quaking from the effort. He continued talking quietly to himself. He didn't hear the pounding from upstairs. He didn't hear Hester collapse into Roger and Jack's arms with a sharp cry of pain. He didn't hear the fire crackling away. He didn't hear anything at all. McQueen just sat there shaking and muttering to himself in a chilly, empty room.

PASSIONS

Maria gingerly opened the bedroom door Jeremy had slammed at the top of the stairs. She watched him pace back and forth across the room, breathing hard and running his hands over his head, fluffing up his still wet hair.

Maria could hear McQueen's low tones floating up from downstairs as she stepped in the room and closed the door behind her.

"Jeremy?"

"I can't believe it. I can't believe I just lost it like that and tackled him. I tackled him! I've never done something like that before and I did that in front of everyone. I just don't get it. He's just a racist, bigoted, small-minded ass, yet all anyone is trying to do is help everyone else, except him. Why?"

Jeremy stopped pacing and threw a punch at the wall in front of him. Puffs of dust billowed off lazily.

"Saying those hateful things to Mark and Hester. They never, ever deserve...

Punch

"... the things that he's saying, and yet...

Punch

"There is no (*Punch*) way (*Punch*) in hell (*Punch*) I'd throw him out in the snow (*Punch, Punch, Punch*)!"

Jeremy continued punching the walls until his hands burned, knuckles scraped, and his fingers ached when he opened his fists.

He felt better.

"Fuck," he simply said looking down at his dirty knuckles.

Maria still had her hand on the doorknob. She stared at Jeremy, looking at him as a caged animal, and then watching him restore himself to his human state with each punch upon the old wall.

When his storm had blown out, Jeremy spread his arms

and leaned his forehead against the wall breathing hard. Maria let go of the doorknob now and stepped closer to Jeremy, reaching out a hand and placing it carefully between his tense shoulder blades, "I'm sorry, Jeremy."

He lowered his head and let out a tired laugh. He turned to her. He looked drained and bedraggled, his pant legs still wet after his trek to the bus with Mark, "It's... it's just been hard on everyone, and look," he pointed to his watch, "it hasn't even been 12 hours since the accident that tried to kill us."

Jeremy hung his head and closed his eyes. Maria stepped up to him and pulled his hanging arms around her petite body. His eyes opened and stared into Maria's soft, brown eyes, "I'm sorry, too."

She kissed him again, his breath tangier than before. She pulled herself up to lock her lips tighter on his.

She felt his hands run slowly up her back, pulling her into a tighter embrace.

He walked her backwards to the ratty, bare mattress that lay on the floor. Lowinger her gently, Maria felt an eager hand pulling at the waistband of her sweatpants. Jeremy broke the kiss and flushed, "Are we really getting to do this right now?"

Maria helped him open up his wet jeans and slid them down to his knees before she pulled her sweats down and then helped Jeremy plunge inside of her.

"Go for it," Maria whispered.

*****

Down in the kitchen, everyone was eating. While no one was particularly hungry, it was at least a distraction. The low mumbling from the living room had grown silent. Hester was seated in a dining room chair daintily eating some canned peaches. Alicia was looking out the kitchen window over the grimy sink when she said, "I just wish the snow would stop falling. I never in my life have wanted anything more than that."

Jack was popping olives into his mouth, "Sorry about

leaving you out there, Hester. We didn't mean to do that on purpose."

Hester balled up a paper napkin and touched the corners of her mouth, "It's alright. I think it makes more of a statement if a broken, old lady gets up and walks away unaided from a conversation."

Alicia turned from the window, "You sure are made of something, Hester."

The old woman paused for a moment and said, "I was a school teacher for forty-six years. I'd still be doing it if it weren't for my arthritis. I might be the world's oldest teacher and breaking a record every June 25th on my birthday. I suppose that's what I am made of."

Alicia moved closer to Hester, "What grade did you teach?"

"I taught kindergarten for the first two years and then third grade for forty-four years. I was lucky enough to have had a former student's grandchild in class, if you can believe it."

Roger smiled, "That's what's up. I wanted to be a teacher for a while because of my third-grade teacher. I liked her a lot. Mrs. Putman."

Jack raised his good eyebrow, "Mine was Mrs. Holman."

"Mr. Brigleb," Mark chimed.

"Mr. Turner. He was good. He was cute, too," said Alicia.

Leslie walked over to Hester and said seriously, "I'm only in the second grade. Her name is Mrs. Lioner. I don't like her. My friend, Jared Morgan, says that his mom says that Mrs. Lioner should have retired years ago."

"Do you remember your third grade teacher, Hester?" Alicia asked.

Hester sighed and looked up as she remembered, "Oh, yes. It was Miss James. She sure tough loved us children. She was one of my favorites, too. So smart. If we were really good all week, she would sing to us. She had such a pretty voice. We would all work hard all week just to hear her sing a song. Looking back on it now, though, I think she liked doing it so much, she would have done it whether we were good students or not. She was just a beautiful lady."

"Do you sing?" Leslie asked hopefully.

"No. Not me."

"I do."

They all turned to Mark. He blushed and looked at the floor, "I trained in New York. Then I got cold feet about auditioning and moved back home to Boston. I mean... I still do... sing. Just not where many people have heard me."

"Like what?" Roger prodded.

"Well, uh, I was trained in musical theatre, so I do those kinds of songs. Jazz, too. My voice isn't built for rock or pop songs, though. I would have been great in the days of vaudeville."

Jack popped another olive in his mouth, "Why don't you get back into it? Try again?"

"Almir really wants me to," Mark's eyes lowered to the floor again, "he's... uh... my boyfriend. He likes to hear me sing. Anyway, he wants me to give it another shot. He's always bugging me about doing it."

Leslie looked at Mark with a very puzzled expression, "Why don't you have a girlfriend?"

Mark shifted uneasily. He looked around for help and just met the same bewildered look in everyone's eyes. He looked at Leslie and carefully said, "That's... um... that's a very good question. You see... uh... Leslie, I never liked girls. I mean, I like them, but not in that very special way. They are great, but... I'm gay... you see?"

"Oh," Leslie said.

The boy thought for a moment while he looked at Mark. The singer suddenly looked sad to him.

"Mama says that gays are bad people, but you aren't bad. You have been very nice. I think Mama was wrong about that. I think Mama was wrong about a lot of things she said."

Mark smirked, "Another mind changed for the *Non-Judgement Day*! One more and I win a toaster."

Mark pulled a bent picture from the sweater pocket he was

wearing, "This is Almir."

Hester looked at the photo first, holding it carefully by the edges, "He's a good-looking boy. Does the family like him?"

"Yes, they do! He and I have been kinda' together for a year. I really can't wait for more."

"My Nate and I celebrated our 49th anniversary back in October."

Mark brightened, "October what?"

"The 25th."

"Really?! Ours is the 20th. It's a good month."

The picture passed around the tight group of people. Roger handed the photo back to Mark, "What's your man's favorite song that you sing?"

"'*One for My Baby*' by Frank Sinatra. Well, Frank Sinatra by Mark Navarette. He said he always liked the vibe of that one the best. The pictures in his mind, I guess."

Leslie sat on the floor, drummed his knees, and grinned from ear to ear, "Sing it! Sing it! Sing it!"

Mark looked down at their picture warmly and began the song, his eyes never leaving the creased photograph in his hands. His voice navigated the notes beautifully, like an ocean liner making its favorite routine voyage in calm waters. Mark's voice filled the old house, reaching into the dead man's ears that could no longer listen in the basement, to McQueen sitting quietly in the living room staring at the flames in the fireplace, to Maria who was being frantically thrust into, and to Jeremy, who hadn't felt such pleasures of the flesh in over three years.

Leslie watched Mark, swaying his tiny upper body to his voice, and loving every word that came from him. While Leslie may not have understood every single lyric, he certainly caught their meaning.

A quiet tear rolled down Mark's cheek, his voice tightened, but he finished each note on pitch for the largest audience he'd had since graduation day from his theatrical school.

The six sat quietly in the kitchen for a moment, when they all suddenly heard it. For an instant, everyone's heart filled with hope and happiness.

One entire instant.

It was a rumbling sound that thrilled each heart in the isolated group.

It wasn't until the rumbling didn't grow louder into the dragging, crunching noise of a snowplow that everyone's joy quickly turned to dread. It was a sound Roger Watson had thought he had wanted to hear during their arduous trek to their current location, but upon filling his ears, he hated himself for ever wishing for it.

Wind.

THE PIT

Jeremy lay on his side next to Maria breathing hard. It had been a long time since his sex muscles had been used. That effort combined with his walk to the bus and back had exhausted his thigh and stomach muscles in an electrically thrilling way. He stretched out a hand and touched Maria's tight stomach, "Are you okay?"

Maria was staring straight up at the ceiling. Her body exposed to the cold room from her breasts to her ankles. The nurse shivered slightly then said, "I... I feel... well... surprised... I guess that's the word I am looking for."

Jeremy rolled onto his back, his manhood finally starting to soften, "It's a different way to keep warm."

He laughed, reaching a hand down and stroking himself. Maria just smiled tiredly, "Maybe we should get back to the others."

Jeremy looked down at his exposed body, as if in self-congratulations. He pulled his jeans back up into position and leaped up off the mattress. Maria redressed and stood up much more slowly.

"Shall we, babe?"

"We shall," Maria said.

It wasn't until they were halfway downstairs when Maria noticed how dark it looked outside, "What time is it?"

Jeremy glanced at his watch, "Five after three. The storm must be getting worse."

"I didn't think that would be possible."

McQueen still sat in the winged chair, staring straight into the fireplace and beyond.

"Everyone else must be in the kitchen."

Maria stopped at the window closest to the front door while Jeremy went to look for the other survivors. Everyone except Leslie and Hester were staring out the back window above the old sink, each face as dark as the worsening blizzard.

Jack turned and flashed his lopsided smile, "Dark enough for 'ya, Sarge?"

"I suppose."

Roger turned and half ran by Jeremy, "I'll take the first shift of digging. Some of what we dug earlier must still be there."

Jack's smile broadened, "Alrighty then, let's do it!"

"Yay!"

Leslie stood up and grabbed one of Hester's hands, "Do you need help back to the couch?"

Before she could reply, Jeremy scooped the old woman up and headed for the living room, "Leslie, my boy, could you get the door for us?"

"At my age being a damsel in distress?"

Jeremy reassured, "No worries, Ma. You're doing just fine."

Roger, shovel in hand, opened the door and the wind ripped it out of his grip, banging it solidly into the wall, "Holy shit that's cold!"

As he tried to pull the door closed, Maria grabbed his strong elbow, "Ten minutes. I will be keeping time. I don't want anyone out there more than ten minutes."

"You got it," and Roger was gone.

Mark tossed another log on the fire. Alicia started going through the suitcase that she thought she had lost forever. She pulled on two heavy sweaters and a wool cap over her head, "I could go outside and dig next."

Jack's eyebrows raised in surprise, "Are you sure about that? It's mighty cold out there?"

"Yes. My friend, Stacy, is expecting me in San Francisco for New Year's Eve and I am planning on being there," she said, rubbing over the scabs on her left wrist, "And for Kim, too."

"Alright, that's five workers on that bonfire pit. We'll be done in no time."

"Want me to do something, Jack?" Leslie asked hopefully.

The banker smiled and answered, "Your job is to keep everybody happy. You think you can do that?"

"I can carry wood, too," Leslie said with confident dignity.

"We will be needing that soon..." Jack suddenly slapped the uninjured side of his forehead, "Shit on a stick, I forgot all about that. Excuse me."

Jack left the room and returned a moment later looking relieved, "Everything is okay. I left the shed door propped open so we don't have to dig to get back in again."

The front door flew open and Roger half fell in, "Someone tag my ass out... the shovel is on the porch."

Alicia was up and out before anyone could say anything else.

McQueen stood and plodded to the kitchen. The emotion in the room lightened considerably by the time the swinging door stopped moving.

Mark lit up a cigarette by the fireplace with another twig he pulled from the log pile. The flames gave him unique lighting in the darkening room. Leslie watched the way he smoked his cigarette. Two puffs, inhale and then exhale. Two puffs, inhale and then exhale. He somewhat reminded Leslie of the contemplating Caterpillar from Alice in Wonderland.

Leslie then looked at Jack. The swelling over his eye seemed better, but it was sure blackening up. The stubble on his face was long and Leslie wondered how long it had been since Jack shaved. Maybe Jack was like his daddy. Daddy just hates having to shave. He only did it once a week, but Leslie always thought he looked cool when he did it, standing next to his father at the bathroom sink and watching him in the bathroom mirror. Leslie couldn't wait to shave someday.

Hester and Maria sat together on the couch, with Maria gently rubbing Hester's hands. Leslie liked them. In fact, he liked everybody there, even mean ol' Mr. McQueen. Mr. McQueen was only mean because he was more scared than everybody else, which meant Leslie was braver than him.

Everybody here was everything different from what his mother had been. Maria didn't dye her hair; it was soft and silky. Mark's cigarettes smelled sweet, and he hadn't tried to burn

Leslie with them. Hester hadn't hit him when he had cried so hard. She even hugged him while it happened. Jack and Roger let him help with the wood hauling, not treating him like a burden. Jeremy made him feel important. Alicia made sure he ate something and stayed warm, and Mr. McQueen... Mr. McQueen had yelled at everybody else but him!

Not to say that Leslie wasn't worried. He had found something terrible in the house, even worse than that dead body down in the pool room, but he just couldn't bring himself to think about it, let alone talk about it with anybody. Not even Hester. Leslie decided to keep it to himself and just not think about his terrible find. He really wished he had never gone downstairs.

Alicia stumbled in and Mark left the room, his sweet smoke trailing behind him and out into the raging gale.

The wind howled outside, slamming 40 mile an hour gusts against the old, dark house, making it quake in fear.

Alicia sat shivering next to the fire, drinking a cup of water clutched between her trembling hands, "You... you know... you know, I've never... never had to shovel snow at the library."

Alicia couldn't wait until the only trouble she had was an argument about an overdue book from some grouchy patron who couldn't pay attention to dates.

Jack stood up from the blanket he was sitting on, "It's the waiting that seems to be getting to me. The crash was... what, only half a day ago? It feels like weeks. I just... I feel like we need to be saved as soon as possible before the person who killed that guy downstairs comes back here. We could be sitting ducks."

Leslie looked up at Jack, tilting his head, "I think we will be fine. We won't have to worry about that at all."

Jack stopped mid-stride and eyed the boy, "Is that so?"

"Yep! We'll be *just* fine. Safe and sound. I know it in my heart."

Jack continued at a slower pace, his lopsided smile slowly spreading back on his face. "I wish I could feel that way, Kiddo.

Maybe I'm just jumpy thinking about going outside in that mess again."

Right on cue, Mark sailed into the house, "Who's fucking next?"

Jack hung his head, "I'll go."

Jack took the shovel from Mark and forcefully closed the door behind him. Mark beelined it to the fireplace, sputtering as he went, "Sorry for swearing, Hester. The cold makes me say awful things."

He plopped down next to Alicia, "Girl, you're a... a better man than I am."

Roger brought Mark some water.

"Th-th-th- thanks. It's freezing out there. How on earth are we going to get a fire going in that hellacious wind? It's... it's just fierce out there."

Roger pulled blankets around Mark and Alicia's shoulders then sat down next to them, "Jack says he's got a plan. Says he'll get a fire going big enough to keep burning even when we are sleeping."

"That damn wind," Mark rolled his eyes, "the way it just knifes into you. I had no idea Mother Nature worked for the mafia."

Alicia simply blinked at Mark.

"I'm sorry. That terrible joke sounded so much funnier in my head. My audience up there *loved* it."

The house trembled as another huge blast blew over the land. Everyone sat silently listening to the wind batter and rattle their creaking sanctuary. Blow after blow, gust after gust.

Hester shivered and gripped Maria's hands tighter.

"Are you alright, Hester?"

"I'm not so sure. I just had a bad feeling land in the pit of my stomach." Her voice lowered to a whisper, "I think I am actually scared of something... I... I just don't know what it is. I can't seem to put my finger on it."

"That makes two of us."

Jack flew into the room with snowflakes billowing behind

him, "I'll give a thousand dollars to the person who takes this shovel out of my hand."

Jeremy grabbed it and he vanished out the door. Jack stumbled to the fireplace, his hands outstretched as if to strangle the very flames he desired, "Remind me later... to give him an extra fifty bucks... for not breaking my fingers off when he took the shovel."

Mark exhaled, "How are we going to get a fire going out there?"

"Two... seconds... please."

Jack rubbed his hands furiously in front of the flames. His teeth seemed set in a permanent, exaggerated grin. He blew into his fingers a few times and then shook his hands vigorously. He inhaled and breathed, "So, here's what I think... think will happen. Want to happen. There is a large, blue tarp in the shed out back. It had been covering the wood pile. A few of us pile, say, ten to fifteen logs on it and then carry the tarp out to the pit. There's a few dozen bottles of oil and lighter fluid out there, too. We pour the oil over the logs, light it, and presto! Instant bonfire."

Roger rolled onto his side, propping his head up with his hand, "Sounds like a plan to me. I only wish we weren't the ones having to do it. Man, I should be eating some of Aunt Vi's lasagna right now."

Leslie looked at Roger, "What's that?"

"Lasagna? Are you kiddin' me? Kid, you are missing out. It's Italian food."

"Is it good?"

"Aunt Vi's lasagna will make you cum in your pants."

It was a phrase Roger typically only used with his friends when he was describing something that was his favorite. He said it so often when describing the lasagna of his aunt's that he didn't even think twice. It wasn't until the phrase had left his lips that he realized he just said this in front of a seven-year-old boy and a sweet, old lady.

"Oops."

Then Roger started laughing, trying, and failing to apologize, unable to get the words out between his embarrassed guffaws. Soon, everyone was laughing. Howling. Their laughter bellowing out loud enough to cover the sound of the wind. It infected each person, bringing some relief to their tired spirits. Tears rolled down Hester's bright red cheeks as she daintily held her fingers up to her sealed lips. Maria tumbled to the floor, trying to cover her mouth. Jack doubled over, slamming his thawing fingers together in a spasmed clap. Mark was clutching one of Alicia's thighs, while Alicia had flopped back on the floor holding her stomach. Leslie, who didn't understand what was so funny but loved the moment, was wrapping and unwrapping his knees with a blanket between bursts of laughter.

The laughter was a small victory against the horrors of the past day of their lives.

After the laughter had died down to sighs and hushed gasps, Jack asked, "So is everyone required to always bring two pairs of pants to dinner?"

This sent everyone back into a frenzy as Jeremy came back inside, "I always seem to miss everything."

Roger stood up and crossed to Jeremy. Taking the shovel, he called out over his shoulder, "Ask Hester," and then closed the door behind him.

*****

Even with the raging wind, Roger could still hear the laughter from the porch. The pit for the bonfire should be finished in a few more rounds, if Mother Nature would kindly allow it. Snow flew in Roger's face like the world's smallest paratroopers, but he didn't care. Roger kept on smiling.

At 17, Roger Watson hadn't had much experience with sex. His first and only time with a girl had been this past summer under the boardwalk in Atlantic City. Her name was Jennifer Goff and she worked in her parent's clothing and souvenir shop not far behind Roger's watch tower on the beach. She had grown up a lot from the last time Roger had seen her, even though they were the same age.

After he got off duty on his last afternoon of the summer, Jennifer had led him under the famous boardwalk, with hundreds of feet stomping overhead into the muggy darkness. The act itself, with the humid air and the cold sand hadn't lasted very long, but it was enough for Roger to learn one thing: As good as his aunt's lasagna might be, he couldn't wait to get back to Atlantic City for more lifeguard duty.

"Save me a room in that condo, Aunt Vi!" yelled Roger as he tossed a shovel full of powder high into the air.

WINTER OLYMPICS

McQueen shoved another forkful of ravioli into his mouth. He had already gone through two cans of it and his stomach was calling out for more. The laughter from the living room made him smirk evilly, reminding him of board meetings when insults aimed at his assistants had made the other board members roar. McQueen had been through more assistants in one year than most have before retirement.

He never killed anyone, but he had murdered many a career from his office. It took a strong man to be in his position, and the people he was stuck with now just didn't understand, and never could. They weren't his kind of people. They probably never cared about getting to the next level.

The pitiful attack from Jeremy was now in the past and now it was time to look forward. Better things will be coming for McQueen. Just thinking about the money that he was going to make from suing TransCoach alone was going to keep good ol' Harold going for however long he was stuck in this goddamn house.

He tossed the empty can onto the counter along with the other spent ones. He had tried counting all the cans of food and gave up at 107. There was going to be enough no matter how much he ate. McQueen picked up another can, and a long receipt fell to the floor from where it had been wedged.

McQueen picked up the receipt, unfolded the long paper, and looked it over. Each can had cost 79 cents. Taking off a few bucks for water, utensils, and cups, the fact was clear that there were over two hundred cans of food in the house.

Everything in front of him on the counter had been purchased on the evening of December 23rd. The date seemed so much longer than four days ago. H. Ortiz was the name just below the timestamp and the store name in which everything had been paid for in Albany.

Ortiz?

Why did that name ring a bell? John Ruess' new account? No, that name was Orta.

Ortiz?

Then he had it. It's the name of the man downstairs. The colored nurse had said it.

Hector Ortiz.

"He obviously wasn't going to be needing food anymore, anyway," thought McQueen as he cracked open another can.

Was this Ortiz's house?

Nonsense. Why the hell did he bring so much food here at one time? How did he get here with all this food? Where was his car if he drove here? Was Ortiz hiding from someone?

If he was, indeed, hiding from someone, he didn't do a very good job seeing that his extremely dead body was lying downstairs.

So, who was this Hector Ortiz hiding from?

Ortiz.

The name seemed a little more familiar to McQueen than just Maria's saying it this morning.

Hector *Ortiz*.

McQueen had stopped chewing and watched the snow dance wildly outside the kitchen's darkening window.

*****

Mark slammed the front door shut, "That has got to be large enough."

Jack made for the door, but Mark threw his back against it with the shovel crossing his body like a spear, "If you even think of going out there to check if I am correct, I will insert this inside of you."

When Jack took one more exaggerated step closer, Mark raised the shovel slightly higher, "Test me."

"Alright," Jack smiled, "let's go fill a tarp."

*****

4:25 p.m.

Jeremy, Roger, Alicia, and Mark followed Jack through the living room into the kitchen, bypassing McQueen who was staring out the back window with a can of spaghetti in hand, and into the dining room to the glass-paned back door.

"Now, that shed is over 100 paces straight out this door. Be careful on the steps just outside, they are hidden by the snow. None of you want to be doing a comedy routine on them like Roger and I did this morning. It'll be hard to see out there in that mess, but we should be able to get this done in twenty minutes at the most if we really push ourselves. Ready?"

Everyone nodded and took a breath as Jack pushed on the door and then held it when it didn't budge.

An elongated '*daaaaamn*' tumbled out of Jack's lips as he pushed harder on the unmoving backdoor. It inched out slowly over the powdered drift that had built up along the back of the house. The door stopped opening after a foot and a half. Jack pushed a little harder on it until the glass cracked.

"I think that's good enough."

Each person slid through the half-open door into the hip-high snow drift.

"It's a good thing I never wanted children!" Mark yelled out over the wind.

The sight of the blizzard was confusing. The orange glow that comes with a heavy snow was back, but it was mixed with heavy white flashes of flakes and total blackness. Roger felt like he was trying to walk through a static television in flames on the sinking deck of the RMS TITANIC.

Once they all finally made it inside the shed, Mark reached into his pockets, "Damn, it's dark in here."

"Not too dark," said Roger. "Save your fire."

Jack handed one end of the old tarp to Alicia. They spread it out on the ground and folded it in half, looking as if they were preparing for the world's lamest picnic.

"Let's try for fifteen logs. That should do it."

Jack and Roger tossed log after log from the tall pile onto the middle of the folded tarp. Once there were fifteen stacked up, each person picked up an edge of the tarp off the cold, dirt floor. Jack and Roger were in the lead, Mark and Alicia in the middle, with Jeremy holding the back corners together.

"Here we go, gang," Jack hissed out threw his clenched teeth.

The group pulled and dragged the heavy load in the tarp through the snow. Grunts and groans musicalized their journey toward the front of the house where a quickly filling pit sat waiting for them. One murderous log kept bouncing heavily off Mark's right thigh.

"Hold it!", Jack yelled.

He handed his corner to Roger and went bounding back to the shed in the deep snow.

Mark yelled to Roger with his eyes nearly shut, "What the hell is he doing?"

"Maybe he's cold?"

"No shit."

A violent gust nearly blew them over as Jack came hopping back to the group, "Okay. Sorry about that. Let's get back at it."

As they began their formidable haul again, Mark called out, "Not to sound like a whiny bitch, but what was that all about?"

Jack reached around with his free right hand and pulled up his sweater to reveal a can of oil half stuck in the waistband of his sweats.

"I've never seen an ass run on that before," Mark huffed.

The walk up the slope and around to the front of the house was a long one. Each body part burned with cold, joints were freezing up, and every tooth was chattering off another. By the time the group reached the pit, it had gained nearly an inch of fresh powder.

Pulling the tarp into the pit and walking around it freely

was a relief to their frozen, flaming legs. Roger and Alicia spread the tarp out as flat as they could while Jack squirted oil all over the logs.

"O... kay. Let's have... the... light... lighter, Mark."

Mark stuck his hand into his right pocket to retrieve his Zippo like he had done hundreds of times in the past. It was an automatic movement. He started shaking harder as his eyes widened in horror, "I... I don't have it. I don't... I don't know where it is... I must have put it down somewhere."

Jack laughed wildly and pulled his hair, "What the fuck is this about? Wait... wait... how are you... how were you smoking earlier? We all saw you smoking just a little bit ago. How the *hell* did you light that cigarette?"

"I used a piece of wood... from the pile... by the fireplace... because... we..."

Jack grabbed ahold of Mark's shoulders in total desperation, "When did you last have it? Do you... do you remember where you were?"

Mark frantically searched his memory for when he last had his trusty Zippo, but failed miserably in the storm, "I... I... It was when..."

"I got this," Roger called and bounded as fast as he could back to the front door of the house.

Mark turned to Alicia, "Can we do rock, paper, scissors, to see who gets to run madly for shelter next?"

Although it was difficult to see, Alicia could just barely make out the front door being flung open. She hoped desperately that Roger had seen Mark's lighter somewhere in the house; protected, warm, and waiting to be reunited with its owner.

Jeremy stood looking at the other three shivering and shaking, wanting and wishing desperately that they were in the house, safe and sound.

"Look," Alicia yelled.

Roger came back even faster than he had left. He was carrying a log about the size of a femur, the top half of it on fire.

To Alicia, he looked like the first Olympic torch bearer, to Jack and Mark, he looked like relief, and to Jeremy, he looked just plain brave.

"*MOVE!*"

Roger made it to the edge of the pit and launched his improvised torch into the pile. Everyone held their breath as the flames died down. After several eternal moments, the flames caught on and spread quickly throughout, the oil turning low blue flames into taller, yellow ones. Cheers came from the frozen survivors as the wind gusted and blew but the flames held their positions.

Jack leaped into the air, "Let's get our asses inside. I'll bring some more wood around later."

The five of them trudged their way happily and quickly into the house. The rush of warmer air kissed their faces as they entered the living room. Leslie and Hester were on the couch together, McQueen was back on his throne, and Maria was putting another log into the fireplace.

Hester had been whispering something to Leslie when they all made it inside and closed the front door. Four pairs of warm, curious eyes met five frozen but victorious pairs.

"We got it going," said Jack triumphantly.

"Yay," Leslie leaped off the couch and ran to Jack, not caring at all to hug his snow-covered legs, when his little head suddenly recoiled and cried, "Ouch! What's that?"

"What the hell is that, indeed?"

Jack felt down his legs and stuck his hands into the forgotten pockets of his sweatpants. He froze harder than he had outside, his face a mix of horror and shock. He pulled his hand from a pocket and held up Mark's Zippo.

He stared at it in wonderment, "Son of a bitch."

Roger stepped up to Jack, glaring into his good eye, "What the fuck is that?"

"I... I forgot Mark gave it to me this morning. I had it in the shed earlier and you told me to put it out. I stuck... I stuck it in my pocket and just forgot about it. I'm... I'm so sorry everybody."

Mark snatched his lighter out of Jack's hand, "You, my popsicle friend, are an idiot."

"I'm *sorry*."

Jeremy started laughing, "Oh, brother. That's perfect. Just perfect!"

After explaining to the confused people who had been inside as the frozen five changed into dry clothes and warmed themselves up, nearly everyone was laughing at the little mix-up.

Eventually, Jack did, too.

THE SECOND NIGHT

11:00 p.m.

Everyone was in the living room and toasty warm near the fire. They had all had a filling meal in the kitchen and a mostly pleasant conversation all around. Even McQueen had politely exchanged a few words with Hester and Jack about 401ks.

Once everyone had retired to the living room, Jack and Mark had gone out to throw more logs on the roaring bonfire. They returned happily with Jack saying, "She's a-burnin' beautifully."

Mark then sang a funny song that Irving Berlin had released in 1913. He had learned it during his second semester at his acting school. Hester talked about the one time she had ever been on stage. It had been in a church play when she was four or five years old in the early 1930's. She was halfway through her part as a baker when she stopped and called out to the audience, "What do I say now, Mom?"

The entire audience had started laughing at Hester and she got so nervous she dropped her loaf of bread from the pan that she had been carrying. That performance was her swan song to the world of live theatre.

Now, everyone was sleeping in the same places as they had the night before. McQueen in the winged back chair with his feet propped up on the tired coffee table, Hester on the couch with little Leslie in her arms, Roger, Alicia, Maria, Jeremy, and Jack in a row with Mark lying just above their heads.

The fire in the fireplace crackled quietly, keeping a steady watch over the nine slumbering survivors.

*****

"We're losing him!"

Maria found herself running down the hall in her hospital

ward. She was pushing a wheelchair with a bleeding boy in it.

The boy's father had rushed him to her as soon as the accident had happened.

"Why was he in a wheel chair? Where the hell was everyone? Why was nobody helping her?" the nurse wondered.

She tried to pick up the little boy and put him on a bed, but he was too heavy, as if he was hiding weights under his clothes.

"I'll get up there myself," said Jack and he flopped from the wheelchair to the bed.

"Kid, you need to stay calm for the doctor. He'll be here any minute," said Maria as she pulled the bleeding flap of skin that had been his forehead back into place.

She turned to the boy's father, "What exactly happened? I'll need to put it on the doctor's passenger list."

Harold McQueen, awash in tears, his face white with dripping clown make-up, cried out desperately, "Your ex-husband, Dan, did it with a can opener. He thought the darling boy was a can of... a can of olives!"

Another nurse walked coolly into the room, smoking a clove cigarette, "So typical of ex-husbands, I'm afraid. Bastard, sons a bitches. I have four bastard sons a bitches myself," said Hester dropping ash onto Jack's face.

"We need to get a CT scan done as soon as possible. We need to make sure that there is absolutely no frostbite on his skull."

Maria had been a pediatrician long enough to stay calm even in the most hopeless of situations.

"We should wait for the damn doctor, anyway," Hester tapped a few more ashes onto Jack's face, "He always knows what to do in situations like this."

"Just, please, hurry and save my beautiful boy," McQueen wailed as he dropped to his knees, *"Please!"*

"Keep an eye on him, nurse, I'll go get the doctor."

Hester pulled the flap of forehead down hard over Jack's eyes, inspecting the wound and tearing a little more skin, "You got it."

Maria turned to leave, stepping over the sobbing mess that was McQueen, and heard a quick, sharp hiss as Hester put her cigarette out on Jack's exposed bone.

Maria found the good doctor in room 204. He was actively screwing the patient in bed number one while another patient slept in bed number two.

"Doctor?"

"What is it?" snapped Jeremy.

"I need a CT scan done to the patient down the hall in room 200."

"Can't you see I am busy assisting another patient at the moment?"

"I thought you'd like to tend to this one first. He's just a little boy."

"Fine."

Doctor Jeremy gave one last, rabid thrust, leaped from the bed and woke the patient sleeping in bed number two. "Could you fill in for me?"

"Sure," Roger said.

He stripped off his hospital gown and climbed on top of the patient in bed one.

"Just keep a good rhythm going and she'll be fine."

The good doctor watched until Roger's tight buttocks found an easy, steady beat.

"Excellent work. Just excellent. How does that feel, Miss?" Jeremy asked.

Mark pulled the blanket away, revealing a face covered in blood, "It's just fine. You do it better, but thank you for asking just the same."

Mark turned his gaze back to the patient from bed number two, "Are you qualified to do this?"

Roger's shoulders had built up a fine sheen of sweat, but he kept thrusting away, "Of course, ma'am. I do this every summer in Atlantic City. It's my job."

"Well, I think you're doing just fine. Thanks again for the recommendation, Doc," Mark said with a squeal.

"That's my girl."

Maria followed Jeremy down to room 200, his erection bouncing and drooling the entire way, "Before we do the CT, did we try flaming fire on him yet?"

"I thought a CT scan would be more beneficial to him."

Maria turned into room 200's doorway and stepped into the basement pool room of a lonely house in upstate New York. A light shown from above brilliantly in the space and fresh, blue smoke hung in the air. Hector Ortiz lay in between the bar and the pool table clutching his stomach and making gurgling sounds.

"Good God, what happened?"

Maria pried his hands away from the wound.

"Can you help me, Mami?"

"I think so. What happened?"

Hector's face contorted, "He did it. I don't think he meant to, but I am hurt so bad, Mami."

There was some movement behind Maria as a chilling voice said, "He did it. He knows so much more than you do. Beat it out of him. If he cries, he's bound to tell you. Just get by her and you will be fine. Beat him. Beat him to death if you have to. Eventually this bad boy will tell you everything that you need to know."

Maria turned and looked at Alicia standing protectively over Leslie. Snowflakes and ice hung from her hair and eye lashes like garlands of frozen, blue death. Leslie stretched out a fractured, crackling, purple hand to Maria, "Don't let her do it, Mama."

"Oh, please don't!" Maria cried.

"Don't what?" asked Alicia as she raised a burning log above the boy's head, smiling a wicked smile full of rotten, black, sharp teeth as she did so, "Don't what, darling?"

"*NO!*"

*****

Maria's eyes fluttered open. She was staring at the ceiling of the old house and she was shivering. It felt colder in the room, but the fire still burned away in the fireplace. She closed her eyes and demanded her brain to let her get back to sleep. A moment or two later, the nurse did just that.

*****

Mark sat straight up, shaking from his spot on the floor, "Damn, it's cold."

He blinked several times trying to get the blur to clear from his gummy eyes. The fire had died down some but not enough to be this freezing in the house. Wrapping the old blanket tightly around his body, Mark stood carefully and stepped as quietly as he could manage over the sleeping bodies to the small pile of wood and tossed two more logs onto the low, glowing flames in the fireplace.

A sudden bang behind him made him twirl around, the hair all over his body standing on end in an instant. The front door was hanging wide open, snow billowing in furiously onto the old wood flooring. There was a solid coating of white where it had been falling carefree into the living room.

"What the actual fuck?"

The door must have blown open a while ago and was letting the storm get comfortable in the living room with the sleeping survivors.

Mark hurried over to the front door, slamming it shut, while the accumulated snow on the floor burned agonizingly into his bare toes and arches. He backed slowly out of the little snow drift, listening carefully. Inside the house, aside from the snores, wheezes, sighs of sleep, and crackling of the cozy fire, it was silent. Outside, the wind howled in freezing agony.

Mark half walked and limped back to his spot and laid himself down. He was sure he had just seen something odd, even more odd than the door standing open, but it must have been a trick his tired and cold mind played on his eyes. It didn't make sense what he saw on the porch. The room was slowly gaining in temperature again, and Mark's eye lids grew heavier with it. Just before he fell asleep, he thought about what he had seen on the porch. It just didn't make sense, and it was unfortunate that he wouldn't remember it in the morning. As sleep took the failed singer back into her comforting arms, Mark whispered one word to a room that wasn't paying any attention to him:

"Footprints."

*****

Jeremy kept waking every twenty minutes or so. Each time he fell asleep, he dreamed of the bus.

Sylvia Pink's body curled up in the aisle, the final embrace of the McPike's, Nate Maltby's crusty fingers, and the driver's dislodged flask clanging noisily to the floor with the teeth still embedded in the half tarnished metal.

Each time the jarring noise of the flask clanged in his mind, Jeremy woke up.

The corpses weren't coming back to life, trying to grab him or anything, he just relived his journey through the burned half of the bus over and over again.

"Would the fire have happened with TransCoach's new bus design?" Jeremy wondered.

While most bus engines are in the back of the vehicle, TransCoach had developed a bus with two engines, the usual one in the back and a totally separate one in the front under the spiral staircase and the driver's seat. This enabled the buses to continue if something happened to one of the engines.

Therefore, there were fewer delays and transfers, with the driver easily switching between engines as they would gears on a stick shift.

TransCoach had quickly become one of the top lines in the Eastern states, easily beating out the competition the company had. Larger, more comfortable seats, more travel time options, and buses that couldn't break down without the intervention of a volcano.

Jeremy guessed that the driver had been using the front engine when he plowed it into the guardrail. If he hadn't, Leonard the Lush would probably still be dead, but would Nate Maltby? Sylvia Pink? Dylan and Libby McPike?

Jeremy's feet still felt the sheer cold from the day's work. If only he could get a good night's sleep to keep his hope up for another day.

The tussle between him and McQueen really bothered Jeremy. The sex with Maria did not. It was the warmest he had felt since the accident and (more than likely) since his girlfriend broke up with him back in the autumn of 2003.

All of this must have been happening for some good reason, Jeremy Henderson wasn't trying to figure out why, just how? How what, though? Maybe his brain was just fried. Too fried.

Jeremy closed his eyes and opened them twenty minutes later.

*****

Leslie Pink sat in a small chair in the middle of a large, yellow room.

His mother stood in front of him, leaning her back on the wall, the ever-present cigarette sticking out of her mouth, "I'm very pissed at you. Keeping secrets like that. You know better. I raised you better."

Sylvia took a step closer, exhaled smoke, and tilted her head at the boy, "Well?"

"I don't know, Mama. I'm trying to be good."

"You have a dick, that is impossible. Dicks aren't made for good."

She inhaled and smiled. Leslie always thought his mother had a pretty smile, even when she was angry, but he never told her that.

"You know I wanted a girl, right? A beautiful girl to dress

up and take shopping. That's how you got the name Leslie. Your daddy hated that. That's why he called you Les. He got me stuck on calling you that stupid name, too."

"*That's not true,*" thought Leslie, but he knew better than to correct Mama when she was like this.

"But I wasn't gonna let you turn into some fag. Naming you Leslie was just a bad idea," Sylvia inhaled, "So, when are you gonna tell them or are you gonna keep lying to their faces?"

Leslie stood up and walked toward his mother. He knew he was dreaming and also remembered that she was never going to be able to hurt him again. He knew what he was going to say wasn't going to make a bit of difference, but he still wanted to say it. Just do like Hester said and let it out.

"Mama?"

"What?"

"I love you."

Sylvia let out her throaty chuckle and stuck her cigarette into Leslie's forearm. "I thought I raised you better than that."

Leslie sighed and looked down at the small, round burn. It didn't hurt this time. It would never hurt again.

He went back to his little chair and sat down. His mother wasn't standing there anymore. It was just Leslie in a chair in an empty, yellow room.

"At least I tried," Leslie Pink said and then waited for someone to wake him up.

*****

Roger's bladder poked him awake and let him know that he had to take a wicked piss as soon as possible.

He stood up as quietly as he could and walked carefully to the bathroom through the kitchen. It was pitch black in there, but he found the toilet with little difficulty. Not taking any chances in the dark, though, he sat down and waited for his semi erection to subside. The flow that finally came felt heaven sent and Roger was convinced that he was taking the best leak of his entire life.

After giving his proud member a satisfying shake, he flushed and went into the kitchen for a swig of water.

"All of this will be over soon," he whispered to himself.

He looked out the kitchen window and felt his heart skip a beat. The flakes of snow seemed to be falling in fewer numbers.

"This *will* be over soon," he said a little louder than he meant to.

He walked with a happier step back into the living room. Everyone seemed at peace in their sleep. However, if their dreams were as bad as the one that Roger's bladder had just saved him from, peace wouldn't be the correct word.

Before he put himself on the floor again, Roger just had to see the weakening snowfall again, just to make sure that he was right.

He looked out the middle window into the front yard of the house and smiled. The wind still shrieked, but the snow fall was finally diminishing. He turned to go back to bed, stopped and looked out the old glass again, the realization hitting him hard.

"No fuckin' way."

His heart now felt a thud of disappointment smother his happiness. He blinked several times, stared again, but there was no mistaking it.

The bonfire had vanished.

PART II

December 28th, 2006

MISSING YOU

7:58 a.m.

Everyone looked as if they had just lost a loved one.

"We'll just do the damn thing over again," Jack said, his voice tight with emotion. "It will be better this time. I can promise you all that."

The survivors were silent for a minute or two.

Hester spoke up with attempted enthusiasm, "The snow *has* let up some."

Jeremy added, "And I highly doubt a plow went by last night which means nobody missed anything. No harm done."

"Surely someone is looking for us," said Mark, his eyes in a near squint, "We've been missing for over 24 hours now."

McQueen rubbed his chest.

Roger stood up, shaking his legs awake, "When do we get started again?"

"We should all eat something first," Maria stretched herself, "then we can worry about getting another bonfire going. We all need to keep up our strength."

Leslie ran for the kitchen, "I want some olives for breakfast!"

Hester looked after the boy lovingly, "I wish I could have a touch of his energy."

She gingerly put both feet on the floor and stood up by herself while Maria kept a close eye on the old woman. It took two attempts, but Hester stood on her own, "My knee does feel a little bit better. It still smarts, but it's better."

Maria took Hester's left arm and the two started for the kitchen together.

"I just don't get how it completely covered up," Jack said, still staring out the window. "If it had stopped snowing so much last night when we were sleeping like Roger said, it shouldn't be filled in like that. We should be able to see at least something of our firepit."

"Maybe the snow drifted," offered Jeremy, "Don't sweat it."

Alicia stood and pulled her blanket over her head like a hooded cape and started for another canned breakfast, "I'm not excited about going out in that wind again. It didn't feel as cold when it was just the snow attacking us."

Jack and Jeremy stood silently together looking out the front windows at the missing bonfire.

After Mark and Roger had left the room, McQueen hefted himself up and approached the two men, "Listen..."

Jeremy turned to McQueen, taking in the large man's image. His huge button down was stained in sauce and juices from whatever he had been wolfing down in the kitchen the night before. Ugly, dark circles hung under his hard, grizzly eyes. It appeared that the business man's dreams had been as bad as everyone else's.

"Yes, McQueen?"

"There's something bothering me since the... since Maria.... since Maria said it yesterday."

McQueen stood solidly with his hands clasped behind his back, looking out the window to where the bonfire should have been, "The name Hector Ortiz. Does that name sound familiar to either of you?"

Jack took his eyes off the dead bonfire and turned to McQueen for the first time since the large man had left his throne, "That's the guy downstairs."

McQueen sighed heavily, a flash of irritation rippling across his face, "I know that. The name, though. I'm sure I heard it before yesterday. In fact, I feel as though I had read it."

Jeremy shrugged, "I never heard it before."

"Nor have I," Jack quickly added.

McQueen snorted, "Well, I am sure I have. What's more, it wasn't connected with anything good. Something very bad. I... *we* need to get away from this house and very quickly."

Jack and Jeremy exchanged glances before Jack asked, "Any suggestions?"

McQueen shook his head, "Nothing more outside of what we have been doing. I will help with the next bonfire."

McQueen turned and waddled off to the kitchen.

"Well, well, well. Someone wants to change positions halfway through the game," Jack laughed as the kitchen door finished swinging.

Jeremy smiled and leaned against the wall, "Glad to have him here."

Jack rubbed his nose and snuffled, "Fuck, I am so sick of being cold that I can't even see straight. The wind out there is murder... murder on us... this... this..."

Jack turned quickly around and began kicking the wall beneath the middle window. His teeth were gnashing and breaths coming out in storms. The sudden outburst made Jeremy step back, taking in the assault.

Jack growled out with spit flying from his mouth, "I'm so fucking sick of this house. I just wanna be somewhere warm, soaking in hot water, far away from this goddamn, fucking house!"

Jack's foot kicked a hole in the old plaster. Jeremy grabbed Jack by the shoulders and threw a punch to the uninjured side of Jack's face as hard as he could. Jack fell backwards against the banister and crashed down to the cold floor.

Jack let himself lie there for a minute panting while Jeremy stood unmoving from where he had hit the banker, neither looking away from the other.

Jack rubbed his cheek while he stared unblinking up at Jeremy, "I guess I needed that."

Jeremy's stone face broke into a nervous grin as he bent toward Jack with an outstretched hand, "No problem there, brother. Welcome back."

Once Jack was up and steadied on his feet, he studied Jeremy's face. Jeremy seemed to be studying Jack just as closely. Jack flashed his lopsided smile in the awkward moment, "We're in fine shape, aren't we? How about, after breakfast, I start humping McQueen's leg as I really go barking mad?"

Jeremy hmphed, "You do that, and I'll be there to smack you again, too."

"Thanks," said Jack, throwing an arm around Jeremy's shoulders, "always good to have someone who is looking out for your best interests."

Just as they started toward the kitchen, Jeremy pointed at the new hole in the wall with his foot, "You know you're going to have to pay for that, right?"

"What? That little hole? Forget it. You can afford to have it repaired. Remember, I still owe you a thousand dollars."

The two men walked into the kitchen and were greeted by silence and several pairs of guilty looking eyes.

"So… everything cool?" Roger asked, a hunk of tuna waiting to be consumed, floating before his lips.

Jack smiled, "You mean that little cluster fuck I just had in there? Yeah, I'm fine. Just blowing off some steam. Jeremy here got my gasket back on tight, though."

Everyone smiled nervously and relaxed their shoulders as tension released its grip for the moment.

Jeremy cracked open a can of pears. He forked a large slice into his mouth, loving the sweet and mushy moment his tongue was having. Perfect.

"Who's missing you?"

All eyes turned to Mark as he carefully ate his cold ravioli.

"Who are you talking to, hon?" asked Hester.

"Anyone that would want to answer. Right now, I am living for the fact that there are people out there looking for us. Also knowing that there are people out there cheering on the people who are looking for us... It just makes me feel better. So, I ask again to anyone who cares to answer the question, *who* is missing *you*?"

Everyone stopped picking at their cans and thought for a moment. Leslie beat everyone to an answer, "My daddy. He was gonna meet me and Mama in Buffalo."

"Stacy is probably wondering why Kim and I haven't let her know where we are in our travels, but she wouldn't be expecting us for another two days. I wish I hadn't left my cell in my coat pocket when I left the bus. Maybe I could have gotten a signal out here. If it wasn't totally ruined by the water, that is," Alicia said.

"Mine came out with me after we crashed but it was totally useless," Mark said sadly. "I just loved that old flip phone. I can't wait to find out why insurance won't cover an accident like that."

Hester wrinkled her nose as she giggled shyly, "You know who will be missing me soon? Doctor Donegan and Nurse Dixie! Nate had an appointment for me at 10 a.m. this morning. Our daughter will want to know why we haven't called her yet... oh, and Brownie."

"Who's Brownie?" asked Leslie.

"She's our elderly, overweight wiener dog. Our neighbors have been taking care of her while we have been gone, but I know Brownie's missing me. I'm the only person she likes. She's a mean little thing and I just love her to pieces."

"Aunt Vi will be pissed that I haven't shown up yet. She'd be callin' my moms, and I know my moms would be raisin' some hell to anyone who would listen," Roger said with all seriousness.

"My Almir," said Mark. "He probably told his twin that I haven't shown up yet. He'd have Aram call Mother and Dad. That would get things going on my end. If he has said anything yet, that is."

McQueen was inhaling his second can of spaghetti."My firm. I'm supposed to be in a meeting in Chicago tomorrow at 8 a.m. sharp. I have never missed a minute of work in my life. All of them will be wanting to know where I am."

Jack laughed. "With a worried firm behind you, McQueen, that ought to get everybody out of here on their own private jet when they find us. Say, why didn't you simply fl-"

"Airsickness," McQueen barked out before Jack could finish the question.

Jack watched the way McQueen shoveled the food into his mouth and almost laughed again at the idea of McQueen losing his lunch all over the unlucky passenger that happened to be sitting next to the McQueen. In first class, of course. That made it funnier.

"I wish airsickness was my problem," Maria said, "I haven't flown since the attacks. I tried once. I sat on that plane for nearly ten whole minutes before I got up and walked off. My luggage flew to Orlando for a friend's wedding, but I am still too scared about it. I haven't admitted that to anyone until this very moment. My friend sure wasn't too happy with me after that weekend."

"Who's missing you, Maria?" Leslie asked.

"My sister, Luisa, will be the one on it for me. I was supposed to be going to Buffalo for a job interview at St. Paul's. Luisa always calls me just before she goes to bed no matter where I am."

Mark straightened up. "St. Paul's? The hospital?!"

"Yeah, why?"

"That's where Almir is. Room 511. What a coincidence that we'd both be going to the same place and not knowing each other before."

McQueen snorted loudly and plodded out of the room, tossing his empty can onto the counter without another thought.

Maria asked quickly, "Is that the two of you in that picture on the mantle above the fireplace?"

"Yes. I put it there because I didn't want to ruin the picture more than it already has been when we were out there working on the bonfire yesterday."

Jeremy was scraping out the last of his pears and said with a mouthful, "He promised to bring Almir that picture."

The nurse touched Mark's arm and smiled, "That's so sweet of you!"

Mark's cheeks flushed and he looked at the floor.

*****

If he wasn't in the spot he was in right now, Mark would have traded places with Almir in a heartbeat.

Almir Leon had taken Mark's breath away the first time Mark had lain eyes on him. Mark was on a break with his best work pal, Tracy. They went to the coffee shop across the street on every work break they shared together to talk about men, home, work, whatever was on their minds.

It was a late July afternoon in the coffee shop. Tracy and Mark had just been venting to each other about a new assistant manager at the movie theater while they waited in the long line to put in their caffeine orders. Mark stopped mid-sentence when he looked up and saw *him*, this tanned God of Love steaming a pitcher of milk at the bar.

He was shorter than Mark, which didn't bother him at all, as the singer liked a man who could climb him. The man behind the bar had beautiful, satin-walnut skin, a perfect growth of black hair on his forearms, brown pools of beauty for eyes, and a set of perky, red lips that Mark wanted to recline on. Just a gorgeous, gorgeous man.

Mark made his drink extra complicated that day in Wilson's Coffee Shop, just so he could stay longer and chat with this new beauty at the bar. This guy appeared just as nice as he was pretty and had a smile that could melt butter a mile away. "Pretty" was only skin deep, but "Nice" would always be radiantly beautiful.

Mark was soon going over to Wilson's a little more often, most of the time without his "Lady Tracy," although he always ordered something to take back to her so he could gain a little extra time with the sexy barista amongst the aromas of coffee and high-pitched whining of the milk steamers.

After a month of hanging around Wilson's, Mark boldly asked Almir out to a movie.

It was a lovely little date until Mark tried kissing Almir as they sat in a park on a secluded bench underneath a flowering cherry tree.

"Whoa! You know I like girls, right?"

"Yeah," Mark said in the most embarrassed tone he had ever had in his life, "I was just trying to make you laugh. Didn't work, did it? I'm sorry. Really."

They still remained friends, however, and continued hanging out. Things were getting weird between them, and it all came to a head on that fateful night of October 20th when Mark told Almir that he couldn't be around him anymore. He had fallen too hard for Almir, and it just tore his heart out every time he had to listen Almir talk about the ladies that he was interested in.

Almir got angry. Very angry. He started yelling about how he couldn't lose Mark's friendship over something so stupid; they had become so tight. It actually scared Mark the way the barista was carrying on.

Almir threw himself down on a bench in front of Mark's apartment building. Mark sat carefully next to him, placing his hand on his strong back and rubbing warm circles there, listening to him breathe hard. Mark's eyes scanned the area to make sure they were alone so that he didn't add to Almir's already strained level of comfort.

After a moment or two, Mark quietly sang 'One for My Baby' for the first time to Almir. When he finished, he noticed that Almir had tears running down his cheeks. Almir then suddenly grabbed the back of Mark's head and kissed him violently and deeply, nearly pulling the singer's hair off in his tight fists.

Almir pushed Mark away from him as forcefully as he had pulled him to his lips, "I can't fucking be this way."

"What way?"

"Ay! You're a guy! I'm a guy! I... I think about you all the time... I think these things about you... *you-*"

Almir bared his teeth and scrunched up his face for a moment. He sighed deeply and then said in a voice that was just above a whisper, "I think I love you, Mark."

Mark felt thrilling tears welling up himself, "Well, you know how I feel. I... I loved you from the moment I first saw you steaming that milk."

Almir laughed and rubbed his wet nose on the back of one of his strong hands, "Even though I kept fuckin' up your drink?"

"You know I did that on purpose."

Almir pulled out one of his famous cloves, "You're a bitch, you know?"

Mark leaned over and tenderly kissed Almir's cheek, nuzzling the tip of his nose carefully over the barista's light stubble, "I know it can be scary out here in the world, baby, but I'm here. I'll always be here to help you."

They sat in silence for a moment before Almir asked, "So, what do we do now?"

Mark stood up and let his eyes wander up the facade of his moonlit apartment building, "I'll tell you what. You ever feel like making a man out of yourself, why don't you come up? I'm home every evening."

Almir smirked at Mark, "You got it, Miss West."

Mark placed his hands on his hips and swayed towards the front door, "Oh, for you sailor, anytime!"

Almir then followed the singer up to his apartment, to his living room, to his hallway, to his bedroom, and stayed all night.

And the next three.

After a year of being together, Mark was impatient about wanting to tell everyone that they were boyfriends. It was difficult to understand where Almir was coming from. After all, aside from his twin brother, no one had ever given Almir a lot of affection.

It was all still new to Almir. Some days, Mark wondered if he should move on and try to find someone who would be out and proud of himself, and be unashamed of their relationship with Mark, no matter how much it would hurt to lose Almir.

But then, Almir would say something like, "Someday, Miss West, you'll be married to me," and then Mark knew that he was really trying, and Mark knew in his heart that he could wait.

*****

Leslie asked excitedly, "Who's looking for you, Jeremy?"

"Just my job, I guess. I manage Goodman's Pizza on Ellicot Street in Buffalo. It's actually right next to the bus station. I'm pretty sure my absence isn't sinking the business into the earth, though."

Maria nudged him, "You never know."

Roger banged his empty can down on the counter, "And you, Jack?"

"Me what?"

"Who's out there looking for your sorry ass?"

Jack Doll smirked and sucked his teeth, "I'll be honest with you, Roger. It's either hundreds of people or none at all."

A gust of wind rattled the house and brought the conversation to a full stop. The house shook and shuddered. All eyes drifted up the ceiling, half expecting it to peel off and expose the survivors like weary sardines to the freezing grey sky.

"I'll tell you all one thing," Jack said looking out the dirty window. "I'm not looking forward to going out there into that frozen hell again."

HESTER

"I'll go first," said Roger. "Is the shovel chillin' by the front door?"

"Yep," Jack moved to follow Roger to the living room, "Put on extra layers. It's going to be a bitch out there."

"Get the show on the road," Roger strutted out of the kitchen with Jack imitating the strut close behind.

Alicia followed them, as did Leslie. Hester stood slowly from her chair and limped toward the bathroom.

"Need any help?" Maria asked.

"Oh, no. I'll be fine. I can't believe how much better my knee feels today than it did last night."

"That's great," said Jeremy. "I'll sign us up for the next Boston marathon."

"Please make it for the following year."

The rest of the survivors left the kitchen to give Hester some privacy. With the door standing open, there was enough light so that one could see what they were doing in the bathroom.

When she finished her business, Hester limped back into the kitchen. She picked up the empty cans on the kitchen counter and placed them in a discarded grocery bag. She then lined the remaining cans of food in neat rows and stacks, then made neat piles with the plastic forks, spoons, cups, and napkins.

Once this was finished, she limped to the rusty sink and looked out the window. It was the first time she could see the shed everyone had been talking about. It seemed like the tree line was twenty feet behind the shed. It was a typical New England forest. Mostly bare deciduous trees with a handful of evergreens mixed in.

Hester startled herself for a moment but calmed down when she realized it was her faint reflection in the glass of the window that had scared her.

Her permed hair was in loose tangles and sticking out in odd places. Every wrinkle on her withered face seemed more pronounced and the skin from her neck seemed to hang a little lower.

"Oh, Hester Maltby, what have you done to yourself?"

She had aged a lot in the six years since her retirement. She had substituted for the first three years after, but her body couldn't handle a full day like that anymore, even on a temporary basis. Standing for hours, holding the chalk, managing student behavior, monitoring the playground had all become too much for her aging body.

She still got calls once in a while, because she was very good at what she did.

Just this last September, she had spent two hours in Mrs. Monroe's second-grade class reading stories to the students of her old friend.

Because, even at 78, Hester Maltby still had what so many teachers longed for. She could still hold a child's attention. Command it. In an age of technology taking off into the stratosphere, Hester could still excite a child about reading, challenge them to do addition and subtraction, and push them to think and ask questions for themselves.

Sure, Hester had her failures, the children that never had an interest in learning, but she could count them without using all her arthritis ruined fingers. Even those children at least liked her better than the teachers that they would encounter later in their schooling career, because, through it all, Hester still cared. A child could feel her love and respect, which is so much more than what some teachers even did for their fellow staff members.

Hester looked toward the dining room of the house and then limped to the archway to have a good look around. She could picture a family sitting around this great table, having a nice dinner, then listening to Jack Benny or George and Gracie on the radio, laughing and enjoying themselves before a good night's sleep.

Hester walked slowly to the basement door, opened it and looked down the stairway. It seemed so dark and unwelcoming. Maria had told Hester yesterday that she hated basements and the old woman had agreed. There was something deathly terrifying about basements that always got under one's skin, especially if you were the one who had to turn the lights off for the night.

Even if Hester had the strength, she had no desire to go downstairs, dead body there or not.

She closed the door and shuffled over to one of the other dusty dining chairs and sat herself down to give her knees and joints a rest. Hester's thin, tired body ached all over, but she wasn't through yet. Aside from the last week, she hadn't felt this much pain since the last month she taught regularly. She hadn't complained to anyone but to Nate, so it was a surprise to the entire staff that she planned to retire.

On the last day of the school year at Mount Mission Elementary School, Hester arrived and began the long walk to her classroom. She was stopped by the principal halfway there and he asked if Hester would join him in the multipurpose room.

A colorful banner over the entrance read 'MRS. MALTBY DAY' and inside, packed wall to wall, were five hundred former students and colleagues. Nate was there, having kept the secret from his wife for over a month.

So many people said kind words, and her current class sang her a special song for the occasion arranged by the music teacher, Mrs. Krebs.

By the end of the surprise party, Hester was crying. Not because of how touched she was, and not from the mountains of flowers, cards, and gifts. Hester Maltby cried because her body was hurting her so badly. She was glad that she was the only one to know the true reason for the tears on that special day, not even Nate.

Hester snapped out of her thoughts and rubbed her knee. She had no idea what time it was. She was aware that it had been nearly 36 hours since she had last spoken to her husband. His health had declined some over the last few years, but he was still a sprightly man for being a month shy of 80 years old. The way things were planned, Hester was going to go first. After her death, Nate would sell the house and move closer to their daughter in Boston. Hester had planned to at least see 80 herself but didn't expect to live much longer after that, not with the way her body had been treating her as she aged. That's when the Maltby Plan would go into action as soon as her funeral was over.

She let a few private tears fall now for Nate. Why had she woken up and gone to the bathroom at that moment? Why hadn't she asked Nate to help her to the back of the bus and down the narrow aisle? Either way, they would be together right now.

"General, I wish I knew what on earth I am supposed to do now."

That made Hester smile in spite of herself. She hadn't called Nate "General" for a few years. Of course, it had been the same amount of time since Nate had called her "Hester Williams."

"Who's General?"

Hester jumped in her seat and looked up to see Mark leaning in the archway to the kitchen.

Hester felt her cheeks burn, "I... you must think I am crazy talking here by myself. I was talking to Nate. I used to call him 'General' and he called me 'Hester Williams.'"

Mark smiled, "I call Almir 'Baby'. He's the first person I have ever been able to call that. It just thrills me every time I say it."

"Does he have a pet name for you?"

"Now it will be your turn to think that I am the crazy one. He calls me 'Miss West'."

Hester angled her head, "Why is that, hon?"

"Well, one of my heroes is Mae West. I imitate her a lot. So, when I do, he calls me 'Miss West'."

Hester smiled and shook her head, "How does someone

your age know who that is? You're too young to know Mae West."

Mark pulled up his sweater and displayed an Al Hirschfeld caricatured tattoo of Mae West on the right side of his ribs.

"Is that her signature I see there underneath?"

"Just her first name, yeah. And on the left side is…"

Another caricature danced before Hester as the singer turned his body and this was one she knew really well.

"Lucy! As in '*I Love*?'"

"The one and only," Mark said, pulling his sweater back down into place. "Those are my girls. Of course, they are both dead, so they can't possibly do anything to piss me off now and make me regret getting that ink therapy done."

Hester shook her head again in disbelief, "Well, I'll be. Sometimes the youth of today just surprises me. Um… Mark… can you give me a hand up?"

Mark offered his arm, "Are you going back to the couch?"

"That's the destination. Although, it was nice to see a different room today. I'm being a regular world traveler."

Hester stood and tried to keep her balance. She would have fallen had Mark not been there with her, "I am sorry. I guess I pushed it a little too hard today. I'm glad you came along when you did."

"I'll be outside digging out the new pit next. I just wanted to check on you first to see if you were okay."

"Well, if it gets too cold out there and you need to warm up," Hester really went for it as best she could, "come up and see me sometime."

Mark let out another large 'Ha' that filled the whole house and then said to Hester in a near perfect imitation of the 1930's silver screen siren, "That's my line, dearie."

They giggled together and made their way through the swinging door. Jeremy looked up and smiled when he saw them, "We were wondering where you had gotten to, Hester. I thought maybe you had gone out back to make a snowman."

"Well, you know me."

Mark helped Hester sit down on the couch and stretch out

her aching legs, "I was just having myself a look around. I've seen less of this house than the rest of you. It must have been a dream home fifty or sixty years ago."

"It's in pretty good shape now. Doing a good job of keeping us safe," Jeremy said.

The front door opened, and Alicia stepped through. Only a few flakes were falling now, but the wind still blew with mighty fury. Alicia silently handed the shovel to Mark.

"You alright, Alicia?"

She only nodded and held up her trembling hands to Mark's eyes. They were nearly purple, with a few knuckles cracked and bleeding.

"How encouraging," Mark shivered, "Does anyone have any nice and kind words of hope for me?"

There was a pause, then Roger smiled and shot Mark finger guns from his place on the floor near the fire. "Stay white."

Mark 'Ha-ed' again and was out the door into the howling wind.

A CHILD'S TENT

Roger glanced over at Jack sitting on one of the arms of the couch, "What's the plan for this fire?"

Jack rubbed the scruff on his chin, "Hell, I don't know. I was wondering if there was maybe something in the basement, we could use to haul wood around like we did with the tarp, but I am afraid I don't want to go down there."

Maria was holding Alicia's hands and blowing on her fingers for her, "The snow covers the windows down there, but there should still be enough light to see by."

Roger stood up, "I'll help you, man."

Jack smirked, "Roger and Jack, together again. Let's do this before I lose my nerve."

*****

The workroom of the basement was darker than it was the day before, but there was still enough light to have a look around. Roger started with the dirty boxes closest to the stairs on the workbench that wrapped around the room while Jack opened a large box that filled one of the forgotten chairs.

"Hey, Roger? You ever watch *Gilligan's Island*?"

"In reruns, yeah, and only if there wasn't anything else to do. Why?"

"With all of the tools that I am looking at right now, I was wishing the Professor was here right now to build a radio, because these aren't going to do us a damn bit of good."

"Forget it, Skipper. He couldn't even patch up a boat in three years. Keep on looking, though. There's gotta be something."

Roger pulled out his third box. There were old clothes in there that looked too small for anyone, even Leslie. They looked molded, anyway.

At the bottom of this box, there was an old picture album. Mostly filled with black and white pictures, the newest looking one in the back containing a young woman in a poodle skirt.

The next box had more old, rusty tools, as did the next. Roger coughed as dust billowed up into his face and he wiped a hand across his mouth, feeling grit as the back of his hand passed his chapped lips.

The next box he pulled out had been hidden by other boxes under the work bench and having been pushed up against the basement wall. It was more rectangle than the others and seemed to be in a little better shape. It had red and blue line drawings on the side of children playing a stereotypical game Cowboys and Indians around a small tent. It must have been from the 1950's as old as it looked.

Roger opened the box flaps and found that the little tent and poles were still inside, "Hey, Jack!"

When he didn't respond, Roger looked up and saw the banker standing completely still staring at the closed door beside the boiler. It was apparent that Jack's mind was somewhere else.

"Yo, Jack! You still here, man?"

Jack shook a little and turned his gaze to Roger, "What... Sorry about that. Just knowing that room... it... it makes a person's morbid curiosity want to go in and have a look to see if... to see what it looks like in there."

Roger sucked his teeth. "Come on, try not to think about it. Come take a look at this. I got an idea."

*****

Mark walked in and tossed the shovel down. "Can I go home now?"

"You are home," Jeremy smiled.

Mark looked at his surroundings, closed his eyes and sighed, "Shit."

McQueen stood up, "I'll go out there next."

As he stomped towards the door, Mark picked up the shovel for McQueen. The businessman grabbed it without even a glance at Mark and slammed the door as he went outside.

"*He's* helping?" Alicia asked in surprise, "What god did we please?"

Jeremy sat in the winged chair, crossing his legs, "I guess he finally realized that we are one unit and each one of us needs to function together to keep the machine running."

After flopping himself near the fireplace with the balls of his bare feet flexed as close as possible to the hearth, Mark opened up his pack of cigarettes, and counted them before he stuck one between his lips. He tried to light his Zippo, but his frozen fingers were failing him. After a few failed attempts, he gave up and used another twig from the woodpile like he had done yesterday, "I am getting pretty good at lighting these damn things without my lighter. I must be turning into a mountain man. I sure am starting to feel like one," he said, rubbing the little stubble on his cheeks.

Leslie sat down next to Mark, "I sure like the smell of those."

"Don't you ever start smoking when you get older. It's so bad for you. It even says so right on the box."

"Why do you smoke then?" Alicia asked.

"Reading was never one of my stronger subjects, and, right now, it makes me feel closer to Almir. Oh, Almir-" Mark sniffed, turned to Alicia and abruptly changed the subject, "Do you have a man in your life?"

"I did. We broke up this summer."

"Mutually, I hope."

"Not really. I think he was tired of dating a librarian. He didn't think it was exciting enough. Kim helped get me through that break-up. In fact, it was her idea to go to San Francisco to see our friend for New Year's."

Alicia absentmindedly stroked the scabbed lines on her wrist, "You know, I just can't get it out of my head. Kim just staying under the water like she did. I think it's going to haunt me forever."

She started to tear up and brought her hand to her mouth. Leslie stood and walked over to her, "Would you like a hug?"

Alicia smiled at the boy, "I can always use a hug."

Leslie wrapped his tiny arms around Alicia's shoulders. Mark rubbed her back, turning his head so he didn't blow his sweet smoke into her face.

Hester folded her hands on her lap and sighed, "This will take a long time for any of us to get through, hon. Life has a way of doing that to us. My mother always used to say: 'what doesn't kill you makes you stronger.'"

Maria sat carefully on the edge of the couch next to Hester's out-stretched legs, "I think it's every mother's job to say that. Mine did when my father went back to Mexico, leaving Mom to raise Luisa and me all alone. She's almost as tough as you are, Hester."

The six of them sat in silence for a moment. The wind beat on the house, not allowing anyone to forget its presence. Leslie was sitting on Alicia's lap while she stroked his hair, "You know, as much as I hate the snow, listening to that wind makes me want it back."

Jeremy uncrossed his legs, "I agree with you there. It's a little warmer when it's just snowing."

Footsteps were heard coming from the kitchen. Roger's back opened the swinging door. He was carrying a long, filthy, white box with Jack holding up the other end. They brought the box behind the couch and dropped it heavily to the floor, a hollow tinkle of metal sounding.

Jeremy was up and crossing to them, "What's that you have there?"

Jack arched his back, cracking it, "It's a kid's play tent. Roger found it and came up with a beautiful idea, I think."

"See, we set this up in the pit outside. We build the fire inside of it. It'll be easier than trying to fight the wind out there. Let it burn up as the fire builds," Roger said with pride.

Jack winked at Roger with his good eye, "You're brilliant,

my dude."

The front door of the house flew open, and McQueen stormed in, wheezing, dropping the shovel in the doorframe as he came. He waddled over to the winged chair, poured himself into it, pulled off his black leather shoes, and buried his stocking feet into a blanket.

"Guess it's my turn," Jack said, heading for the shovel.

"Be careful, Jack," Leslie called.

"Nay, young child! The wind should be careful of me!" he cried as he closed the door against the wind.

Roger had opened the box and was pulling out the poles to assemble the tent. Leslie walked to the lifeguard's side to watch him work and wrinkled his nose, "It stinks wicked bad."

"Yeah, bet, but this here is gonna help us make a nice bonfire so we can get rescued."

Maria pulled out the rough, tan canvas and started unrolling it, "I hope it's not too wide to fit through the door."

"That's what I am hoping, too," said Roger, "Anything that we don't have to do outside is fine by me."

"Damn it," McQueen said and started rubbing his chest.

Maria eyed McQueen carefully, "Are you feeling alright?"

"*Stop asking that stupid question!*"

"I'm fuckin' fine! Just tired," McQueen snapped from his throne.

Maria made a choice to treat McQueen as if Hester was speaking to her, "Take a nap then and have someone get you some water."

Without looking at the nurse, McQueen growled, "Sure."

Jeremy's eyes burned into the back of the huge man's head. Everyone stiffened, ready for Jeremy to say or do something, but they let themselves relax a little with each second when nothing happened. The only sounds were the wind, the crackle from the fireplace, and the sounds of Maria and Roger working on the little tent.

Leslie quickly walked over to Jeremy and timidly asked, "Could you please take me upstairs to go to the bathroom? I like that one better, but it still scares me up there."

After a moment, Jeremy blinked and looked down at the boy and smiled, "Sure, son. Follow my lead."

Mark and Alicia watched as the two disappeared up the stairs. Alicia leaned over and carefully whispered, "That is one of the smartest seven-year-olds on the planet."

"Tell me about it," Mark said, "The government should hire Leslie Pink for every tense negotiation."

Alicia and Mark laughed together, Mark laughing a little extra harder when McQueen glowered at them.

The tent was ready by the time Jack came shaking back inside. It was definitely a child's play tent, standing almost four feet tall, five feet long, and just over two and a half feet wide.

Jack smiled and leaned the shovel up against the wall, "That looks great, Roger. The pit won't have to be as big this time around, I think. Not with the snow not coming down."

"Great," Roger flashed his perfect teeth, "Maria helped me put this beautiful baby together. I'll go out and dig another round and then maybe we can get the party started."

*****

Leslie flushed an empty toilet and went out to Jeremy in the hallway. He was leaning up against a closet door, staring into the open bedroom across from him.

"Whatcha' looking at, Jeremy?"

"Nothing. Just studying that room. I think that's the master bedroom because it's bigger than the other two."

"I do like this house," said Leslie, "I always wanted to live in a house with stairs in it."

Jeremy ruffled Leslie's hair, "You know something, I like it here, too. Nice and quiet and there's some good people here."

"Even McQueen is nice when he wants to be," Leslie whispered, "but I think he's just scared."

"You may be right about that."

"I mean, he has done nice things. He helped Hester get

here on the suitcase and he's been outside digging to get a new fire going."

Jeremy looked towards the stairs, losing some of his smile, "Ulterior motives."

"What's that mean?"

Jeremy's full smile came back, "Ask me again someday and I'll tell you, you smart, little boy."

Jeremy swiftly picked Leslie up under his arms and swung him back and forth in the narrow hallway, "Look at this smart, little boy fly!"

Leslie laughed as Jeremy piloted him up and down, left to right until they were standing at the head of the stairs. Jeremy put Leslie down and knelt to his eye level, "How was your first flight with Air Henderson. Are you a satisfied customer?"

"That was wicked," Leslie squealed and wiggled. "You have to do that again when we have more room to play in. Will you?"

"Anytime you want, son."

Jeremy took Leslie's hand and guided the boy back downstairs, their smiles leading the whole way.

AND THEN THERE WERE EIGHT

"Here's the plan," Jack had the floor, "Roger and Maria will take the tent out to the new pit. Mark, Alicia, Jeremy, and I will be bringing the logs around the house up to you two to place in that little tent. McQueen will bring a couple of bottles of oil out with us. Then, wham-bam-thank-you-ma'am, we have ourselves a new distress signal. Are we ready?"

"As we'll ever be," Mark said.

"Then let's get to it."

"What do you want me to do, Jack?" asked Leslie, not wanting to be left out of the big plan.

Jack kneeled and placed his hands on the boy's scrawny shoulders, "Your job is the most important. You have to make sure Hester isn't left here by herself, so she isn't lonely."

Leslie swiveled his head and looked at the old woman. She beamed and stretched her arms out to him. Leslie beamed back and ran to her, hugging her tight, "You got it. I can take care of Hester."

Jack straightened up, "Now are we all ready?"

Everyone nodded in agreement and then set about their business.

Roger and Maria picked up the tent, Roger feeling some relief that the poles should be heavy enough to keep it from blowing away easily, especially when the wood was placed on the floor of the tent. The fire could start up easily and they could get the hell out of this wind.

There was a panic moment when the frame got stuck in the door, but a good shove from Maria got it out into the freezing air on the porch. Leslie closed the door behind them wishing them luck.

The snow was waist deep on Maria and the wind tore at her wavy hair. She had never felt such cold in her life, even after being submerged in the river, and she suddenly felt more admiration for the ones who had been outside digging in this mess. The color of her hands had gone from soft caramel to lobster red in a matter of minutes. Her grip was nearly lost on the tent a few times from the wind trying to snatch it up for its own use.

"How the hell did you guys dig in this?"

"What?!"

She couldn't believe how hard the wind blew. Maria yelled louder, "How the *HELL* did you guys dig out in this?"

"We're into S&M!"

Maria smiled at this and then felt her bottom lip split in the middle, and her smile vanished instantly.

Once they were in the new pit, Roger held the tent while Maria crouched down to get herself inside it, she and Roger's combined weight battling to keep it from the gale. This pit was about twenty feet farther away than the last one, closer to the tree line, and directly in front of the house so that the fire could be easier to keep an eye on from the living room.

Roger knelt and stuck his head through the flaps, "You... you know.... It's not so bad when the wind's not hitting you."

Maria looked at Roger seriously, "You've been out in this more than anyone else. You will always be a hero to me, Roger Watson."

He smiled, "No problem. I'm just glad that the wind didn't blow this tent out of our hands and off into the trees. There were a few times there that I thought we were going to lose it."

Maria nodded, "If you had let go, I would have sailed up there with it."

*****

A group of five were assembled in the dining room, looking out of the cracked glass door.

Alicia shivered, "I swear this will be the last time I say this, but I really don't want to go out there again."

Jack placed his hand on the knob.

"WAIT!"

This was a command from Mark. He quickly stuffed his hand into his pocket and rummaged around for a moment, then he pulled out his Zippo with a flourish, staring and grinning at Jack, "Just making sure."

Jack sighed heavily and said, "I know, I know. Here we go."

He pushed open the door, letting the bitter wind come inside. They trudged out single file into the waiting drift.

The sky was still overcast, but it had stopped snowing. McQueen loudly guessed the temperature to be around 15 degrees with the wind chill. Everyone wished he had kept this guess to himself.

Inside the shed, Alicia grabbed three logs, Mark and Jeremy four each, while Jack managed five.

McQueen bent over to grab the oil cans after the others had left with the wood when two metal cans of paint thinner caught his eye. They had screw tops and warning labels claiming to be highly flammable. He smiled to himself as he picked these up, knowing that they would probably start a fire much easier than oil in this shitty weather. He twisted hard on the cap of one of them and the fumes hit him immediately. He twisted the other lid in the relative shelter of the shed. He smiled to himself, thinking about how clever he was to be doing this now instead of out there exposed in the deadly cold. The little whiff of fumes seemed to make him slightly dizzy, while his heart skipped a beat. He screwed the caps on tight enough to not spill anything on him as he made his way around the house to the fire pit and then off he went to follow the others.

*****

Hester asked Leslie to carefully put another log in the fireplace. She wanted to be sure that the room would be as warm as it could when everyone returned.

"How long do you think we will be here, Hester?" Leslie asked staring at the wood he had just added to the flames.

Hester sat up with a little struggle and stretched her legs to the floor, "I wish I could tell you, hon. I don't wish us to be here much longer than we need to be."

"Yeah. Me, too."

Leslie walked over and sat next to Hester, "I don't like feeling cold all the time. The fire helps, and you guys are so nice, but I really want my daddy."

Hester smiled and took one of the boy's hands, "I want my daddy, too, sometimes."

Leslie's little eyes widened, "Wow! He's still alive?"

"Oh, no," Hester laughed, "he'd be well over 100 years old if he was. He and Mother both would. No, hon, my daddy died the first year I was teaching. He was really sick. Mother died about twenty years ago after she fell and broke her hip. I still miss them very much."

"But you're an old lady and a teacher. Why do you miss them when you're so smart?"

Hester put her arm around the boy, "You'll hopefully understand someday. You only get two parents in life, and sometimes, if you are lucky enough, your parents grow into being good friends, too. Mother, Daddy, and I were good friends. Maybe someday, you will be friends with your daddy, too."

Leslie thought about this for a moment and then looked at Hester, "Are we friends?"

"When a group of people go through what we have been... what we *are* going through right now, it binds you together for the rest of your life. Yes, Leslie, you are my friend."

"Good, because I like you a lot."

"And remember, hon, you're going to take me swimming in that park of yours someday."

"Hester Williams?"

"That's right," Hester sighed, "I think I can be Hester Williams one more time."

Hester felt tears welling up. She looked down at Leslie and tried to smile but faltered. She took a breath and was trying her best not to upset the boy. "I'm sorry. I guess I am just having a weak moment."

Leslie smiled up at her, "It's okay. It's your turn to be brave now."

"Oh, Leslie."

Hester hugged him tight and cried into his dirty-blonde hair, "You are such a darling boy. I can't wait for you to have a happy life. A long, long happy life."

Hester sat up after a minute and rubbed the tears from her eyes with the backs of her thumbs. Leslie took hold of one of her hands and said, "I'm sure doing good at my job."

Hester inclined her head, "What job, hon?"

"Keeping you company and safe and I don't even feel like I am working!"

She smiled with the corners of her mouth and squeezed Leslie's hand. They watched the fire in peaceful silence together, waiting for the others to return.

*****

Maria hopped quickly back to the porch with Alicia and McQueen. The boys were still standing around the firepit. Alicia had wanted to be out there, but the paint thinner's fumes were flushed into her face with the hands of the wind, and she was getting a headache.

Mark kidded Jack about his lighter while McQueen had finished his task of adding his fuel to the wood pile in the tiny tent. Jack had clenched his teeth at Mark and begged him to forget about the lighter incident while Roger and Jeremy laughed about it. The mood was almost pleasant.

McQueen and Alicia trudged into the house while Maria stayed on the porch watching the boys. Mark held his lighter up triumphantly while Jeremy and Roger clapped, and Jack just hung his head. She could not hear what they were saying to each other, but the four seemed very happy out there. It was like watching a silent picture.

A violent gust of wind battered Maria's face which made

her bow her head against the breeze. She was squinting down at her feet when it happened.

Everything brightened for an instant. A muffled bang rattled Maria's ears. She heard Leslie yell "Whoa!" from the house while Hester and Alicia screamed.

Maria looked up and saw a plume of black smoke being smeared up into the sky by the wind. The tan tent was being replaced by a block of flames as it was consumed. She saw Roger stand up, holding the side of his head.

Maria immediately leaped off the porch into the snow, her legs churning toward the scene, not feeling the cold or the wind.

Jack came running around from the other side of the bonfire. He yanked on an arm sticking out of the snow and Jeremy popped up to his feet.

Maria reached Roger first, his face blackened and eyebrows singed, but he was okay.

Jack and Jeremy half limped toward Maria. Their faces were darkened. The left half of Jack's head looked burned.

"What the hell happened?" yelled Jeremy. Beads of sweat were popping up on his forehead and stinging his wounds.

Maria looked to what had been the front of the tent and saw Mark lying on his back. His legs were pushing and kicking the snow as if he was trying to backstroke away from the fire.

The nurse leaped over to help him up and froze for a moment when she really got a good look at Mark.

The singer's right hand still clutched his Zippo, but his hand was burned up to the elbow. The maroon sweats he was wearing were burned in several places, most no bigger than a quarter. Surprisingly, his hair wasn't touched but the lower half of his face was baked.

His left hand was pressed up to his neck, Mark's blue eyes rolled around wildly, not focusing on anything at all.

Maria was over him instantly, "Mark! Mark let me see."

Blood oozed between the fingers he had clasped to his neck, dripping down into the snow. Maria pulled on his arm to try and examine the wound, "Mark, please let me-"

A jet of blood shot into Maria's face and mouth as his fingers were pulled away from the hole in his neck, with more bubbling out from his mouth and nostrils. She placed her hand over the wound, feeling something stick into the tips of two fingers.

"Mark!" Maria spat, spackling Mark's face with his own blood.

For a moment, his eyes focused on Maria, recognition passing over his face.

"Cold," Mark Navarette burbled and then died a moment later.

The blood flow slowed out of his neck and continued to trickle out one side of his relaxed mouth. Maria stared hard into Mark's eyes and watched his pupils dilate.

"Is he okay?" Roger asked in a pleading, tight voice.

Maria took hold of the hard piece in Mark's neck and pulled, feeling the object grind against his jawbone as it dislodged.

She stood up slowly and turned around to face the three waiting men. She held up a bloody piece of a paint thinner can that had turned into shrapnel, the shredded and curled shard no thicker than a razor blade and shorter than a sewing needle.

"He didn't make it."

Maria turned and walked towards the house slowly, barely picking her feet up as she pushed through the resisting snow. Jeremy dropped to his knees and sobbed, leaning against Jack's thighs. Roger sat down holding his head, while rocking back and forth.

Maria stepped up onto the porch, trying to twist the knob, found that it wouldn't turn when she commanded it, and not understanding why. Her fingers just couldn't seem to hold onto the cold metal. When someone inside opened the door, Maria dropped her hand and shuffled in.

It was Alicia standing there. She took in the sight of the nurse, covered in blood from her mouth down to her hips. Tears leaped to Alicia's eyes as she cried out in near hysteria, "What happened?!"

Maria walked beyond her into the living room. McQueen, Hester, and Leslie were standing in the middle of the room looking at her in horror, Hester doing her best to block Leslie's view.

"Jesus," McQueen wheezed.

Hester's voice was teetering on panic, "Maria, hon. Tell us what happened out there."

The nurse stopped and stared at Hester. With no emotion in her voice, she said dully, "Mark's dead."

"Oh... Oh, no," Hester collapsed onto the couch, pulling Leslie along with her.

Maria walked to the fireplace to warm herself, stumbling through the blankets on the floor. She held up her hands to the flames and noticed that they were both solid red in Mark's congealing blood. She saw that one hand still held the projectile that had ended the singer's life. She opened her hand and let it fall to the floor, tinkling onto the hearth.

"Close the door, Alicia," Maria said, "it's awfully cold outside."

Maria brought her gaze up, away from her hands and found herself looking into two smiling faces on the mantle. Mark holding his Almir close with one arm, the other extended out to take a picture of them both on a beautiful spring day in Boston. The vision of smiling faces and a sunny day gave way to a clouded grey and then total blackness as Maria's knees buckled and she slipped silently to the floor.

ASHES TO ASHES

The room spun before Maria's eyes as she came to. Hester was rubbing a folded wet sock on the nurse's forehead. Leslie sat on the couch behind Hester, squeezing his hands between his knees.

"Oh. Sorry about that," Maria said, trying to sit up.

"Lie still," Hester commanded, and Maria obeyed.

Maria glanced down at herself and saw that she had been changed into different clothes. She brought her hands up and saw that they were mostly clean, just a few bits of blood caked around her fingernails like the remains of an odd manicure.

"Hester, can you please tell me that it was all a dream," Maria said, closing her eyes.

"Jack says that there was nothing you or anyone could have done. Mark probably didn't even feel anything."

"But he had to have felt something, Hester. He looked right at me and said '*cold*'. He was feeling something. That piece of metal I pulled out of his neck must have severed his carotid artery. He was going to die, but it still took some time. At least a full minute for him to know that something was terribly wrong."

Hester smoothed Maria's hair back and continued rubbing her forehead with the sock, "We will never know what thoughts he might have been having in the end. If anything, he saw that you were right there with him, so he did know that he wasn't alone."

Maria had said those same words not so long ago. It was to Alicia, that's right. The librarian's friend who was under the water in the back of the bus during the accident. Kim. That was the friend's name, Kim.

"And he died knowing he was loved. He knew his Almir loved him, and he didn't die alone. That is so much more than too many people get in the end."

Maria noticed McQueen sitting in the winged chair. He was looking down at his feet, breathing heavily.

"Where is everyone else?"

Hester hesitated just long enough to raise the nurse's suspicions, "You just try and rest yourself some."

"Where are they, Hester?"

She stopped rubbing Maria's head for a moment, "They are out burying Mark in the drift next to the house. Jeremy was worried about any animals that might come by. Jack says it will only be a temporary resting place until we are rescued."

A gust of wind made the house shudder in a way that seemed to work its vibrations into Maria's intestines for a brief moment. Hester looked up to the windows, "It seems as if another storm is moving in. They wanted to have it done before more snow comes."

There was silence for some minutes before Maria said, "I saw right away that there was nothing that could have been done. I would have given anything to save him, though," she wrapped her arms around Hester and buried her face into the old teacher's slender body, "There wasn't anything... He was just so torn up. I was completely useless to him. He looked to me for help and then he watched me let him slip away."

Hester held Maria and stroked her hair. The old woman had lived through enough loss in life to know that this is one of the times to be silent, as there was nothing to be said right now that was going to fix this mournful, broken heart. Hester let Maria pour out her loss, anger, and helplessness into her weary body.

"All he wanted to do was go to Buffalo and be with his Almir. To sit in a stinking hospital room, hundreds of miles from home to hold his hand and tell him that 'everything's going to be okay' and now he can't because of some... some fucking shard of metal."

Maria said other things but it was lost to sobs in Hester's body. When Maria's private storm calmed a little, Hester said in a voice that had an iron edge that none of them had heard from the woman before, "It is all unfair, what things we have had to live through these last few days. It has been so trying on all of us. Mark's passing just adds to the horror and hopelessness of it all, making us all feel so much more desperate. His will to survive was very strong. His will to leave this place was even stronger. We should look to his strength and use it as fuel for our own spirits."

Leslie slid off the couch and put his arms around Maria and Hester. He didn't know what to say. A hug was all he could think to do at the moment.

Maria hiccupped a few times and said, "I'm sorry, Leslie."

The boy hugged the tearful nurse tighter, "It's okay. You're just being brave."

"Yes, she is," said Hester, "Maria is being very brave."

Maria leaned back onto the floor again, massaging her temples, "I am so exhausted."

"You just lie still then." The motherly warmth returned to Hester's voice. "A good cry can take it out of you."

Maria closed her eyes and laced her fingers together over her stomach. Hester continued rubbing Maria's forehead with the sock. Leslie put one of his hand's on top of Maria's, he was gently rubbing her knuckles with his tiny, warm finger tips.

Maria's eyes popped open, "How's the knee, Hester?"

"It's doing fine enough for you not to worry about it. You just rest a while."

Maria closed her eyes again. The damp sock was bringing some comfort and relief to the tension in her head. Little Leslie's hand was soft and warm. Maria breathed in deeply, letting her chest rise slowly and then letting it fall just as slowly with each exhale.

The wind gusted.

Deep breath

The house groaned.

Long exhale

The fire crackled.

Deep breath

Footsteps on the porch.

Long exhale

Stomping.

Deep breath

The front door opening.

Long Exhale

Maria could hear whispering and sniffles. She heard the door squeak closed and the grit of the shovel tip hitting the floor as it was leaned against a wall.

"How is she?" Jeremy asked.

"She's fine," Maria said, "You all just missed the fit I threw. Definitely one for the record books. How's the fire outside?"

"Great," Jack said without much enthusiasm, "just great. Burning beautifully."

Maria let out a laugh that even frightened herself, "Sounds to die for!"

She shook off Leslie and Hester, standing up. Alicia was taking off her shoes, Roger was on his way up stairs. Jack and Jeremy stood facing Maria. The soot had been washed off the three men making their fresh burns stand out brightly. Jack looked the worst of the three. A boiling was building up quickly in Maria's gut. Even as pathetic as the men looked facing her, she knew it was all going to come out.

"What the hell happened out there? It didn't happen the last time."

Jack's shoulders somehow sagged even lower, "We aren't so sure. Jeremy and I were talking about it, but we think it was the paint thinner."

"Explain."

"Maria, it's hard on all of us. Maybe you should lie back down."

"I said, *EXPLAIN!*"

Jack shifted, "Well... we were guessing the fumes maybe. The tent held them in and that caused the explosion. We should have just used oil instead."

"Alright then. Who brought the paint thinner? Who left

metal cans full of fumes into what was to be a bonfire?"

"It was I," said McQueen, "I knew it would light up better in the wind out there. I didn't think it would go up like that. Nobody would."

Maria turned to McQueen. She looked at his enormous girth filling up the winged chair like a massive bowl of spoiled pudding. Her boiling point had been reached, "Of course you didn't think. It wasn't going to be you out there when the whole thing went up. Unless it was about you, you couldn't give a shit! You lazy, selfish bastard!"

McQueen stood up faster than anyone could have imagined, "That's enough out of you. The fire is going. What happened, happened, okay? Being a nurse, you should have the brains to know by now that you can't win 'em all!"

"*Can't... can't win them all?*" Maria raged in disbelief, "That didn't have to happen out there. We should all be sitting in here right now, instead of one of us being buried out there in the snow next to a dilapidated house!"

"It's over now. It's not like someone important was lost. If you expect me to worry about some faggot that had been flitting around here..."

"You watch your damn mouth, McQueen," Roger hissed, glaring at the fat man from under his eyebrows like a lion sizing up his prey.

It was McQueen's turn for disbelief. He stared back at Roger with his grizzly eyes burning brightly, "Just like you to stick with someone like that. You think I give a damn about what some colored kid thinks about-"

"Mr. McQueen!" Hester stood, "I've had just about enough of your attitude and prejudice. You're an appalling man for the day and age that we live in. Not to mention the fact that you are completely ignoring our broken hearts over this loss of that sweet, young man. You just don't care!"

The old teacher's cheeks filled with red as she spoke. Her hands were trembling, but her stance was firm. Hester Maltby was angry.

McQueen was turning to look everyone in the eye, rubbing his chest with one hand and wiping his brow with another. McQueen thought to himself, *"These people just don't understand. They aren't on the same level as I am, and they never will be."*

"Listen to me... I've-" McQueen exhaled and sucked in air fiercely, "You people just don't understand a man of my position. Where I am coming from. This world doesn't have... have time..." He breathed heavily. "You all... have no idea... at all!... You... you just keep... fuck me!"

The heart in McQueen throbbed for all it was worth. He gritted his teeth and hissed, "Nothing beats.... me... you can't-"

"Just sit down, McQueen," Jeremy commanded.

"NO!" McQueen gurgled, his face turning purple with clanking rage, "I make the damn... damn rules... nothing and nobody... I mean, NOBODY.... Nothing will ever... Christ!"

McQueen crashed face first to the floor; his huge body flopped and twitched a few times and then he went still.

For a moment, no one in the room moved. They all just stood there, blinking, and watching, as if they had all been frozen into statues.

Roger was the first to break out of the spell, leaping over the handrail of the stairs and landing on McQueen's right. Roger pushed on McQueen's heft trying desperately to flip the businessman onto his back.

"Help me, damn it!"

Maria snapped to attention and rushed to Roger's side while Jack dropped to McQueen's left, pulling while the two pushed. Ever so slowly, McQueen rolled over, exposing his contorted face, broken nose, and blue lips.

"He's not breathing. Can you do compressions and I'll do the breaths?"

Maria nodded, her expert hands following the huge ribcage, finding the right spot and she began pumping. After fifteen pumps, she yelled out, "Blow!"

Roger blew two puffs of air into the cold thin lips, the spittle McQueen had raged out of his mouth with his last words still there, making them colder.

Maria compressed; Roger blew.

Maria compressed; Roger blew.

Maria's hands felt familiar crunches as three of McQueen's ribs popped and dislocated beneath her thrusting palms.

In between Roger's fourth go around of breaths, McQueen coughed up into the lifeguard's mouth with a breath that had the flavor of spoiled milk. Roger covered the gag in his throat as he crawled away from McQueen's quaking bulk.

The large man's eyes were open, his mouth turned down in a deep, exaggerated frown. His breaths coming in and out shallow, wet, and labored.

"We have him back," Maria said simply, crouching back onto her heels.

Roger stood up calmly, walked at an even pace through the swinging door to the kitchen, into the bathroom, and promptly dropped to his knees and vomited into the toilet.

Once the waves in his guts calmed down and the kaleidoscope of colors stopped flashing in his eyes, Roger rested on the cool bathroom tiles and cried.

The angry tears flowed down his cheeks and flowed into his pink palms. McQueen, the bigoted bastard, just had a black man save his life. Roger had put his lips to those that had let slurs drip from them as easily as water spattering from a leaky faucet. Lips that had said those ignorant, hateful words with such force for years, and Roger had just breathed more life back into them to go on, for however much longer, saying the same disgusting slurs.

People like Harold McQueen aren't changed by situations like this. Roger could save him one hundred times and Roger would still be that "*colored boy*" to McQueen.

So, why had Roger saved someone like him? Why did he leap first when everyone else froze? For an instant, it seemed as if the rest of the survivors were content to let McQueen die right then and there, but Roger leaped to him, ran to him, and gave life back to him.

Roger Watson had saved a bigot.

Why?

Because, at the end of the day, when all was said and done, Roger still gave a damn, even about people like McQueen. Life still mattered.

Roger grabbed the toilet bowl and pulled himself over the edge of the seat just before he vomited again.

*****

McQueen lie sleeping as Maria and Alicia covered him in blankets. The wool cap Alicia had been wearing was now on his head. Maria would have laughed at the sight of McQueen wearing a pink cap with white puppies on it if Alicia hadn't placed it on him out of pure kindness.

Maria had been closely watching McQueen and relaxed some when his breath had found a steady rhythm, "He'd be better off in a hospital. He just needs to lie down and stay where he is until someone comes along."

"*If* anyone comes along," Jack grimaced. "I'm getting pretty close to the end of my rope here."

"I think we all are," Alicia said.

*****

The librarian had shoveled out the snow next to the house while the three men brought along Mark's body. The sight of him had been so horrible, yet she couldn't bring herself to look away. Picturing him laughing, grasping her thigh, and smoking one of those damn cloves less than an hour ago before this moment was almost too much for Alicia.

Her father had been a sergeant on the police force, and he said that he dealt with death by separating the person from the body. The shell was left to say what had happened but whoever the person had been was now long gone and out of any pain.

Alicia couldn't do that.

Just thinking that Almir wasn't going to hear *'One for My Baby'* again had sent Alicia over the edge and crying into Roger's shoulder as they stood next to Mark's primitive, shallow grave. Jack had placed a hand on her shoulder while Jeremy began covering the shell of Mark Navarette.

*****

"He needs to stay warm," Maria said wrapping the last of the blankets tightly around McQueen's legs, "The rest of us should do without blankets tonight."

Hester stood next to the couch and asked, "Should we move him up here?"

"No. We shouldn't move him," Maria said, not so sure they even could.

A massive gust blasted the house. Jack shifted his gaze from McQueen and out the window, "I'm going to toss a few more logs in the bonfire."

Alicia stood up, grabbing her shoes, "I'll go with you."

She followed Jack silently into the kitchen.

Leslie stood up and walked to the couch. He took one of Hester's hands, "Let's go get something to eat."

"Sure, hon. That would be nice."

Maria found her place on the floor and closed her eyes. She heard Leslie and Hester make their way slowly to the kitchen. The nurse felt exhausted to her core. She just wanted to sleep until help finally arrived. Strike that, she wanted to sleep until she woke up in a warm bed in a hospital a month from now.

The sweet smell of spice suddenly invaded Maria's nostrils and her eyes snapped open. She spied Jeremy staring onto the depths of the flames in the fireplace, leaning up against the dusty bricks and smoking a clove cigarette.

TENSIONS

Jack picked up a log and threw it as hard as he could across the shed. The last week had been rough. Too rough. The plans he had set into motion several months ago were shot to shit. The only plan that had worked out in his favor at all recently was him having a canned fruit cocktail for breakfast. He hurled another log at the wall in full force.

"Fuck!"

The shack shuddered in the wind, its tin roof rattling right along with the thin wooden walls.

"Jack?"

Jack turned to Alicia standing in the frozen doorway. He had forgotten about her following him outside. The way the wind caught her hair and tossed it around her face made her suddenly look so mesmerizing to Jack. A gorgeous dame lost in a frozen, arctic hell.

"You sure are beautiful, Alicia."

She stared at Jack and half smiled at him, inspecting his face carefully to see if he was joking with her or not, "Thank you, Jack." She decided he was telling the truth and just speaking what was on his mind. "I think I actually needed to hear something like that. I didn't realize it until you said that. That's funny, isn't it?"

"If you think so. I was just looking at the way the white snow showed off your black hair. It's really a pretty color."

"I think it is pretty good for the price I pay," Alicia laughed, "It's a mousy brown but I always thought it looked better black."

"You have everybody fooled. It looks natural. Do you have any other secrets that we should know about?" Jack asked through his lopsided smile.

"I don't think so," Alicia smiled back and then playfully asked, "Do you?"

Jack picked up two logs and handed them to the waiting young librarian, "We've all got secrets, little lady. Someday, you'll know about mine. You probably all will. Isolation has a way of bringing out all secrets."

Alicia held the logs tight against her body. The expression on Jack's face startled her more than his words had. His black eye, singed hair, and burned places on his face adding to the horror of the secret stuck in his lopsided smile.

Jack cocked his head to one side, "Ain't I a pretty picture? I must look like the goddamn Phantom of the Opera."

He laughed at this, and Alicia managed a weak smile. Jack turned back to the wood pile and picked up two more logs for Alicia's arms, keeping that weird smile on his face, "I'm just so damn tired of this place. Tired, tired, *tired*! There's just been so much that you... what's wrong, Alicia?"

"You're kind of creeping me out to be honest, Jack. All secrets out in the open, right? Are you okay?"

Jack's smile widened, "Sorry about that. I don't mean to be creepy or scary. Just letting my crazy ass thoughts fly out into the free air instead of keeping them locked up in my brain. Your own thoughts just might scare you if you ever let them loose and fly free."

Alicia backed up against the door frame, a branch stub on a log digging into her left breast as she squeezed the wood tighter to her body. Jack almost seemed like an entirely different person than this morning. Maybe they were all different people now.

Alicia herself certainly felt like a marked woman since the explosion in the bonfire pit. While Mark's violent passing had been awful enough, now McQueen's heart attack made it all seem so near. Death had never been so close to Alicia Brooms in her life. He was stalking them all with his scythe, lurking around the woods just out of sight and ready to dance on their graves as they all joined Mark in the snow around the house.

When you're as young as Alicia, Death shouldn't even know your name. Twenty to thirty should be the invincible years, right? The only people that die around you are the ones you were vaguely familiar with from high school. No one you knew really well, of course. *"Oh, that's too bad,"* you'd think as you wracked your brain trying to remember the person's face clearly.

Now, Kim was dead. Kimberly Such was dead. Lying in the back of a bus, staring into dark, icy water. Alone. Mark was dead. Mark Navarette was dead. He had snow packed into his staring, lifeless eyes and around his torn throat. Kim, she had known since the 7th grade and Mark she had known since Kim died... when was that? Had it been a month? It couldn't possibly be two nights ago. She met Mark the day Kim died. He was dead now...

"Are you going to answer me?"

Alicia began trembling and looked up to meet Jack's eyes, "I'm sorry. What did you say?"

"I asked if you wouldn't mind taking those into the house for me? You should stay inside. I think the cold is getting to you."

Jack was right. She was having crazy thoughts and she needed to keep them locked up tight in her mind so she wouldn't scare him like he had done her.

"Everything is getting to me!" she yelled a little too loudly, as she turned and hurriedly made her way to the back door in the deep snow.

"Great, you moron. Just great," Jack thought defeatedly, *"I wonder if I can frighten the rest of them before the day is out."*

*****

Alicia walked through the kitchen, passing Hester and the boy in the dining room. She opened the swinging door and dropped the logs to the floor, one smashing the toes on her left foot when the scent assaulted her.

Clove.

Her eyes widened as she scanned the room and then narrowed when they landed on Jeremy, "What do you think you are doing?"

Jeremy looked up at Alicia casually, "I am obviously smoking."

"Those aren't yours. They are *his* cigarettes."

"I wanted a cigarette, and these are the only ones around."

"But they aren't *YOURS!*" Alicia seethed.

Jeremy tossed the remainder of the clove into the flames, "Okay. Is that better?"

Alicia picked the wood up and stalked over the fireplace. She threw her load down at Jeremy's feet, "Thank you ever so much."

She turned and left the presence of Jeremy and Maria for a bedroom upstairs.

"Jesus," Jeremy said after a door slammed overhead. "I just needed a smoke."

Maria said from the floor as she gently closed her eyes, "I know you can understand where she's coming from. She's just hurting."

"We all are, Maria. You think I liked going out there and burying him? You think I enjoyed staring into that look on his face as I shoveled snow on top of it?"

Maria opened her eyes, sighed, and then closed them patiently again, "And I suppose you must think I liked seeing that look form on his beautiful face. I was over him while he died, Jeremy. I watched him slip away, his eyes pleading for help, and no one was answering."

A single tear escaped Maria's closed lids and rolled into her right ear.

Jeremy sighed and laid himself down next to Maria, taking her in his arms and kissing her check, "I'm sorry. This shouldn't be happening in this house. I guess we're all a little on edge. I really am sorry."

Maria wrinkled her nose at Jeremy's breath. The sweet smell that lingered on his lips made her stomach turn. It was a scent that was coming from the wrong person. It should be coming from Mark.

Maria suddenly wanted to be away from Jeremy, the arms around her making her almost as sick as his breath. She could feel his erection stiffening and poking into her thigh. Between the throb of Jeremy's penis and McQueen's labored breathing, it was all just too much for Maria.

She got up from the floor, quickly slithering out of Jeremy's embrace, "I'm going upstairs to talk to Alicia. I think she just needs someone to listen to her right now."

Jeremy looked up at her in surprise but he didn't move from his spot, "Alright." His voice sounded hurt, "I hope she's doing okay."

Maria turned and walked up the stairs, fighting the overwhelming urge to vomit.

*****

Hester and Leslie were sitting next to each other at the old table in the dining room. Leslie didn't like to hear Alicia yelling, so Hester had asked Leslie to show her the dining room as a distraction from the argument.

Leslie hadn't said much since the tragic accident with the bonfire and Hester was beginning to worry about him. It was never good for a child to keep their emotions bottled up, although the boy seemed used to it. That idea bothered Hester even more.

Leslie slowly ate another peach from a can, its juices making tiny sticky rivers down his chin. He didn't seem to notice or care at the moment, so Hester didn't bother to clean his face as he ate.

As she looked at the silent boy, she noticed a few round scars on the base of his neck. She reached out her left hand and touched them tenderly. "What are these, Leslie?"

Without breaking his gaze from his can of peaches, Leslie simply said, "Mama's cigarettes. There's a few more on my arms and on top of my right foot."

Hester drew her hand away as if the scars burned her fingertips. The old woman was filled with overwhelming relief and then guilt. Relief as she knew that Mrs. Pink would never be able to hurt little Leslie again, but guilt because she had to die to make that happen.

As if reading her mind Leslie spoke again, "You know I loved her, right?

Hester looked at the boy, "Your mama?"

"Yeah. She was burned before, too."

Leslie speared his plastic fork into the can and turned to face Hester. His face seemed to wizen beyond his seven years as he spoke, "Her daddy used to hit her. She told me one night when she came home late wearing sunglasses. I wanted to know why she was wearing them at night and then she showed me. One eye looked really purple, like Jack's does. She said a guy gave it to her at a bar after she said she wouldn't blow on him in his car. I tried to hug her then but she didn't want that. That's when she said that her daddy used to hit her, too."

Hester just stared at the boy, amazed by his indifference to what he was talking about.

"That was the only time I ever saw Mama cry. She said she was so mad at him and so glad when he died. Then she laughed. She laughed that her daddy was dead.

"I liked Mama's smile. She could be pretty when she smiled. I told her that I was sorry he hurt her. She laughed and stuck her cigarette on my arm. She told me that it's what love really feels like, that it hurts, and then she slapped me when I was trying not to cry. 'Real men don't cry, Les. You shouldn't, either if you want to be a man.'"

He turned back to his peaches and picked up his fork, "That's why I still love her and wish she wasn't dead. I don't want to be like her. The way she was, happy that her daddy was dead. I won't ever be like Mama."

Hester put her hand gently back over the scars on the boy's neck, wishing her touch could dissolve them. She wanted to erase the marks from a woman who never appreciated what a darling child she had.

Leslie was eating his peaches again, "When we get back to Buffalo, you can come stay with me and Daddy when you get lonely. You can bring Cookie, too."

"Cookie, hon?"

"Your dog."

"Oh," Hester smiled, "Her name is Brownie, but she sure looks like she likes to eat cookies."

Hester hadn't really thought about what was going to happen to her once they were rescued. She could always go with the Maltby Plan that Nate was supposed to do after she died and go live near their daughter in Boston, but it felt awkward that it would be she and not Nate going to live near her.

Hester loved her daughter more than anything, but their only child had always been Daddy's Little Girl. How Hester was going to break the news about Nate was another matter entirely. Naturally, she should be the one to tell their daughter about her father's passing, not some policeman who wouldn't be as gentle about it as Hester. She should also tell her in person, but that could be days after they were rescued, and that could make it all the more hard for her darling child.

Hester touched Nate's wedding ring and trembled ever so slightly.

Leslie looked up at her, "Are you okay?"

"Yes. I just had a little bad feeling inside me again."

"Like you forgot something?"

"Yes, hon. It was just that thought. I forgot something."

What Hester kept to herself, for the second time in as many days, was that she had the overwhelming feeling that she was never going to see her daughter again.

"Just a really silly feeling," Hester said.

"What's going on?"

Roger had walked into the dining room. He pulled an old chair up to the other side of the table and faced the boy and the old woman but kept his eyes down at his hands. He casually wiped some drool from the side of his mouth.

Hester smiled warmly at Roger, "You sure did a good job in there."

Roger only shrugged silently, keeping his gaze on the table top and his long fingers.

Hester couldn't pinpoint the emotion surrounding Roger. She said hurriedly, "You have no idea how lucky we all are that you were on that bus. I can't imagine what things would have been like for our little group if you hadn't been here."

Roger looked up into Hester's withered face. She was smiling her little, sly smile at the corners of her mouth. Roger felt his own smile growing when he noticed a blush rising in Hester's cheeks. People like Hester would never truly understand what Roger had been thinking about after he saved McQueen, but seeing her smile, her attempt, flooded Roger with affection for the elderly teacher.

He spoke before he realized he was doing it, "You sure are a beautiful lady, Hester."

Hester's eyes widened and more color leaped into her cheeks, "Oh, Roger... I... you need to meet more women."

For the first time since the bonfire accident, Leslie smiled over a peach slice, "You're right, Roger, and I think so, too. You are a very pretty lady."

Hester swiveled her eyes from Roger to Leslie and back again. Her hands raised to her face, "Well! Two compliments on my looks in one day. Aren't I a lucky one? If you two think I look good now, you should have seen me in my twenties."

"You must have been the finest teacher in Buffalo."

Some starch entered Hester's arthritic spine and she seemed to grow in her seat, like an old flower finding its way back to a sunbeam to bloom one final time, "I did have the most apples on my desk and they weren't always from students."

Hester said this with pride as she thought back to some of her fellow teachers who had made polite passes at Hester in the early years. There was only one man that Hester ever dreamed of being with intimately and she had been lucky enough to marry him. However, it was always nice when someone had looked her over and it was at this moment, in this cold and dilapidated house, sitting with strangers who could be her grandchildren, that Hester ever allowed that fact to enter and make a home in her mind. It was wonderful to have people think that she was nice to look at.

She shook herself out of this thought when the back door creaked open. A freezing blast assaulted the three dining room occupants, as Jack stepped in and closed the door, one arm cradling three logs, "Afternoon," Jack managed through wildly chattering teeth.

"Oh, Jack," Hester stood and limped toward him, "I forgot you were out there."

Jack involuntarily dropped the wood and began shaking violently, "F-freezing…"

Hester reached him and brought her hands up to his face. The cold nestled deep in his skin, stinging Hester's palms. His scruffy cheeks felt like prickly moss-covered marble in a forgotten cemetery.

"You come and sit down."

"I… don't think… so… might break in… half…"

"Everything alright?"

Jeremy was standing in the archway to the kitchen looking at Jack and Hester with raised eyebrows, "I heard a crash, just making sure everything is okay in here."

Hester continued to hold Jack's damaged face, "He's frozen. He was gone so long that I forgot he was out there."

Jeremy walked over and took hold of one of Jack's arms. Without a prompt, Roger was up and to the other side of Jack to steady him. The two men half carried Jack through the kitchen to the living room.

Roger smiled, "Let's get you to the fire, Georgie."

Jack could feel the joints in his shoulders and hips creak with every movement. Just before they reached the other end of the kitchen, it hit him, "Who… the hell… is Georgie?"

Roger shrugged, "I have no idea. My moms always calls me that when I was being dumb."

Jack managed half of his lopsided smile, "Are you calling me dumb?"

"You were the one trying to warm yourself up in front of an old lady."

"You... got me there..."

By the time the three reached the fireplace, Jack's knees gave out. His weight fell into Roger's strong arms and the young man managed to put him down by the fire as gently as possible with Jeremy's assistance. Jack's back was to the flames, and Jeremy began rubbing the banker's hands, "What were you doing out there for so long?"

It took a minute for Jack to warm up enough to answer, "After I put more logs... in the bonfire, I went back to the shed... to... to do some counting and thinking. I think I scared Alicia earlier. I hadn't meant to. My nerves seem to be more frayed than... than I thought."

"That explains a lot," Jeremy said, his gaze drifting overhead.

Jack continued, "There's at least fifty logs still in there. We'll be fine for a while longer, but I'd rather use that broken coffee table as firewood than go back out there. Also, did you fellas notice that... it's starting to snow again?"

Jeremy followed Jack's humorous gaze out the window. Fat flakes were fluttering to the ground, "Indeed it has."

The floor quaked as McQueen broke wind and sighed in his sleep.

Jack smiled, "What a romantic scene. A warm fire, snow fall, someone holding my hands, and McQueen on the woodwinds."

Jack looked at Jeremy and noticed he was straining to hold in a laugh.

"Kiss me, beautiful."

At that, Roger ran snickering for the kitchen door, "I'm outta here, man."

Jeremy bellowed a bark of laughter as Jack thought, *"Great. I might be teetering on the edge of complete madness, but I still got it!"*

THE THIRD NIGHT

Terry Sorenson felt sleep tugging at his eyelids. It was almost 10:30 p.m. when he pushed himself away from his desk.

It had been a long couple of days for the middle-aged state trooper. The winter storm that blew through New England and the Tri-State area less than 24 hours ago was being replaced by another one. New York alone was a freezing, tattered mess. Power was out in three of the city's boroughs, half of the highways were closed and at least 75 people were reported dead or missing in the Empire State alone.

Sorenson had been a trooper for 26 years and never ran across anything as bad as this from a winter storm.

He walked into dispatch for a cup of much needed coffee, even if it was old and lukewarm.

The dispatcher on duty swiveled away from her console and faced Sorenson. She narrowed her eyes, frowned comically, then flipped him the bird.

"How goes it in here?"

"It's all tits up, Junior."

"You said it there, Mom."

Patricia Selleck was the only person in Livingston County who could get away with calling Sorenson "Junior." When they first met, she had already been a dispatcher for five years, and the fresh, young officer had no idea what was in-store for him. Being the newest, youngest, and the shortest on the force, Pat gifted Terry with the nickname "Junior" and that's what the dispatcher had called him for 26 years and counting.

Aside from her four grown children, Pat was also "Mom" to every rookie, trooper, dispatcher, and any other emergency worker she ever encountered. She was a whiz on the radio, with her wit being sharper than a butcher's knife. When it came to an emergency, though, there was no better person to have on the other end of the line.

Pat stretched her legs out in front of her padded seat,

"How about things on your end?"

Sorenson walked over to the map on the old brick wall, "Found a couple frozen in their car on Resa-Anne Lane around noon. I'd already been here two hours when that came in. There are at least seven or eight vehicles full of people unaccounted for and that's with only a third of the phone lines working. People are missing all over the state, not to mention the ones freezing to death in their own homes without any heat."

"I'm guessing you haven't heard about this yet," Pat held up a yellow report, "This fax came in from Buffalo a few minutes ago. Seems that TransCoach is missing one of its buses."

"Stolen?"

"Nope. It departed Boston at 1700 on the 26th with 13 people on board, that includes the driver. When another bus got stuck near Albany, this now missing bus picked up two more passengers in Saratoga Springs around 2130. It was heading on 29 when the driver last radioed that he would be taking a detour to I-90 around midnight to avoid an accident blocking the roadway. That's the last that anyone has heard from them."

Sorenson ran a dry hand down his face, sighed heavily, and drained his cup, "I'll make sure the boys know to keep an eye out. How could a whole bus simply disappear?"

"Like I said: Tits. Up."

Sorenson crumpled the empty paper cup and tossed it in the trash, heading for the door, "I've got one more report to finish and then I am heading out. Enjoy the night, Mom."

Pat gave him the finger again and turned back to her console.

The trooper called out playfully over his shoulder, "And thanks for keeping me up on my sign language."

*****

10:47 p.m.

Jeremy stood in the living room, looking out the front window. He watched Roger toss more wood on the bonfire.

He could just make out the young man's figure through the billowing storm.

Hester and Leslie were asleep on the couch. McQueen still wheezed away from the place on the floor where he had collapsed.

When it had been suggested that more wood be put on the fire outside, Jack had started to get up, but Roger restrained him. Jack was back to sleep on the floor again before his head touched it. Maria was lying close by.

"Jeremy?"

Alicia was standing behind him, her eyes cast down to the floor. It was the first time she had spoken to him after the outburst about the cigarette earlier. He turned fully to the librarian and Alicia shivered, "I'm... I just wanted to say that I am sorry... about before."

A silence hung between them for a moment or two. Alicia finally brought her eyes up to meet Jeremy's through her black hair. He smirked and said, "Thank you. It's alright, though. We've all had to blow off some steam."

"I mean," Alicia lowered her voice, "Jack kind of gave me the willies earlier and then smelling that stupid cigarette and all... well... it was just too much, and I am sorry for yelling."

Alicia's talk with Maria earlier had soothed her fears for the time being. She liked Maria. In fact, she liked all the other survivors except for McQueen. She had learned to tune out people like him, though, so he was just a talking slab of meat that she didn't pay much attention to. She did not, however, wish for McQueen to die in this house. She didn't want to wish that on anybody, except maybe people who willfully banned or burned books.

Alicia shivered again. "Anyway, I thought I'd... are you alright, Jeremy?"

Jeremy raised his eyebrows and felt the sting on his forehead as his skin protested the movement. He put a cool palm to his head to relieve the heated itch, "I'm doing as good as anyone else. I'm sorry, too, Alicia. I should have taken your feelings into consideration."

Alicia shook her head, "It's so stupid. It was just a cigarette. I was acting like I had caught you robbing me. It's just that... I smelled it and expected to see Mark. Like, I had made the whole thing up, and he was going to say that he was alright. It's amazing how fast thoughts can form in your head. Before you know it, A is somehow connected to D in a huge leap."

Alicia squinted through the dark window, "I hope Roger is okay out there."

"He's fine. I've been keeping an eye out just in case. He'll be along in a moment."

"How much longer do you think we will be stuck here?"

She looked up at Jeremy. He was looking out the window and smirking. "That, my dear, is a question I don't want to answer."

*****

"Ouch, motherfucker!"

An ember had landed in between two fingers on Roger's left hand. The snow and wind licked his face, and, until the ember, he hadn't been paying attention to how his body was feeling. He could barely see the poles from the tent, warped and twisted from spending hours in the fire. At least the idea of his worked. The tent had made restarting the fire easier.

He wished he was at Aunt Vi's house right now. Under twenty blankets on a soft, warm bed, with a space heater going full blast, and a cup of hot chocolate clutched between his hands. He didn't even like hot chocolate, but it sounded damn good right now.

The wind barely let the fire's heat kiss Roger's outstretched hands. He turned and faced the house. A strong feeling of foreboding washed through to his bones and made Roger want to turn and walk the other way, taking his chances out in the empty country instead of going back into that damn house.

He dejectedly began trudging back through the snow. He could see two figures standing in the center window watching him. Though the light from the fireplace danced inside, the glow wasn't bright enough to make out who was standing there.

He stumbled on his next step, and he sprawled out into the snow, his right knee suddenly singing in hot, white pain that shot up through his thigh.

Gritting his teeth, he picked himself up and limped back to the porch, almost slipping when he stepped up onto the old boards.

Roger slammed the front door shut and leaned against it, raising his right leg slightly out in front of him, "Sure feels better in here."

It was Alicia and Jeremy standing at the window.

Alicia stepped toward him, "Are you alright, Roger?"

The lifeguard bent his injured leg for the two witnesses of his fall, ignoring the pain, and then began batting the snow off of his lean body, "It's not too bad now that I'm not out there wading in that shit. I just need to rest."

"You need some help to the fire?" Jeremy asked.

"Naw, I'm good."

Roger sucked up his pain, limped to his spot, and threw himself down on the floor.

Alicia stifled a nervous giggle and then took her own place in front of the fireplace for the night.

Jeremy sat down quietly and listened until the survivors were all fast asleep. His eyes roaming over each member of his group tenderly.

He sighed sadly and thought to himself as he looked them all carefully over again, *"There should be nine of us."*

Still sitting up, he closed his eyes for a moment, dreading sleep and the dreams that might be there waiting for him. He didn't want the clang of a burned, tooth encrusted flask to wake him up again.

*****

Jack Doll found himself standing in a black space, a single light coming from straight overhead. He took a few tentative steps and discovered that the light followed. Looking down, the banker saw that he cast no shadow, as if the light was shining brilliantly through the banker's body.

"That's odd."

His voice sounded muffled, like trying to talk through a pillow. Jack started walking again. Faster. The eerie light keeping pace with him as he moved.

"Jack..." a distant voice to his right called out, "*Jaaaaaack...*"

The voice was as muted as his, but it had an almost hollow ring to it.

The walk had become a jog. Jack took off his heavy, leather jacket and discarded it in the direction of the voice. His footsteps sounded dully on the black floor. Its surface looked like polished tile, but his foot falls sounded as if he was marching on dead, whispering grass.

"Jack... it's of no use to run. We are all on to you," said the voice calling from his left this time.

His pace quickened. Jack felt like he should be deathly afraid of running into a wall or falling into an abyss lurking up ahead, but that fear wasn't there. The only thing to fear was the voice.

Heavy breathing suddenly came from behind Jack, and he was running for all he was worth now. He turned his head but could see nothing in the cavernous space. If the light were a little brighter, he might have been able to tell who the voice was coming from.

"On to you, Jack. We are *all* on to you."

"You have no idea," Jack yelled, choking on the words as if he were trying to exhale soft cotton, "I've been through too much shit to be doing this now."

"What did you expect? You knew that you were going to be running for the rest of your life if you wanted to stay alive. It was the choice you made that brought you here. Not *his* choice. Your choice. Isn't that right? It was your idea, wasn't it? Not his."

The voice cackled wildly directly in front of Jack. He stopped running long enough to pivot in another direction but went tumbling to the tiled floor instead when his feet collided with each other.

"I had no other choice," Jack wheezed.

He stood and began running in the direction he had come from, "No other choice! Do you hear me?"

Jack was screaming now. The breathing had moved back over to his right and the wild laughing seemed to be coming from all around the darkness.

"Just keep up that useless running, Jack. After all, what else could you possibly expect to do?"

Jack stopped, fell to his knees, and rolled on to his back, totally drained of energy. The tiles began melting into his body, fusing and chewing on his skin.

"You don't understand. It was my life that was being taken from me. Then I had a way of keeping some scrap of it, preserving something of what I had been. What I worked for. Then... then he tried to take it all away from me. After what I had done to help him out and everything!"

The tiles nibbled away on Jack's flesh. When he raised an arm, chunks of skin were pulled away, being devoured hungrily by the tiles.

The pain was almost too great to bear.

"Make it stop. Please! PLEASE!"

"Run! Run, Jack. Start running and don't stop. You stop and you die. It was the choice you made. Go," the voice said simply.

Jack pulled himself to his feet. The back of his scalp remained on the tile, a hairy, bloody glob sinking into nothing.

"*RUN!*" screamed the voice.

Jack took off in a full sprint, leaving the pieces of himself behind in the dark. The light continued burning brightly from above, "It's unfair. It's so unfair."

"That's it, Jack. Don't. Stop. *Running!*"

*****

Hester waded through the waters to the front desk of Dr. Donegan's office. She found it odd that there should be ankle deep water in an office on the 3rd floor, but she was only a teacher. What did she know?

The old, owlish looking nurse behind the front desk didn't look up from her mystery novel until Hester was right in front of her.

"Dixie?"

Nurse Dixie looked over the top of her book and smiled at Hester, "Mrs. Maltby," Dixie's baritone voice shook the desk, "you're here for your 10 o'clock aren't you?"

She smiled and pointed toward a row of chairs, "Dr. Donegan is busy with that actress, Vicki Michael. You know, she had work done on her ticker last year and he's just making sure it keeps ticking and not tocking. The doctor shouldn't be too long now, unless Ms. Michael has gone off on another tangent about costuming again. You just wait over there until Dr. Donegan is ready to see you."

The old nurse turned back to her book and seemed to forget about Hester.

Hester waded to a seat and sat down carefully. Her joints didn't feel so bad now, which made sense as her pains always seemed to diminish just before she saw her eccentric doctor.

"It's too bad Nate can't be here," someone said.

There were three occupants in the waiting room. One occupant Hester couldn't see properly as he sat with his legs crossed, his face hidden behind a magazine. The other two she knew as Maren and David. Lovely, beautiful people that she has seen on the stage in Buffalo many times, but they were fast asleep. The one with the magazine must have been the one to speak up.

"Nate's parking the car. Sometimes he waits for me there

and sometimes he comes in to wait with me. He was in an accident you know."

Hester tugged on her skirt and put her purse down in the seat next to her. The water had crept up to just below her calves, "Dear me. This water... have you been waiting long, young man?"

"Why do you ask?" the man said from behind his magazine.

"It's just that the water is blue now. I think it was green when I first came in here not five minutes ago."

The man behind the magazine laughed, "It's when the water is purple that you need to be afraid."

There was silence for some minutes, as the water steadily crept up Hester's old legs and began soaking the seat of her chair.

"Oh, this won't do," Hester looked for the watch on her small wrist and saw that she must have forgotten to put it on, "Excuse me. I am sorry to bother you, but do you have the time?"

The man tossed the magazine on the coffee table in front of him and looked at his watch, "It's 78 minutes after two. I don't know if it's a.m. or p.m., though," Mark Navarette sighed.

Hester gasped and brought her hands to her face, "Why Mark?! It's so nice to see you. I didn't get to say good-bye before you died."

"I am aware of that, my dear woman. You must know, however, that I had to die in a very quick fashion."

"That's what we were told," sighed Hester, "Jack and Maria told me that you went really fast. I am just a little unclear as to what happened."

Mark stood, walked to the front desk and picked up a pen, "May I borrow this, Shari?"

"It's Dixie. Yes, you may use that, but I want it back. It's my favorite."

"Dixie. Of course, how silly of me. Shari must be your beautiful granddaughter that I went to acting school with."

Mark splashed back to the row of seats and sat down next to Hester with the pen, "I'll show you what happened, but bear with me. I might not do this correctly."

Mark shoved the pen deep into his neck and pulled it out quickly, leaving a nice, neat hole.

Hester bent forward and inspected the wound. "But Maria was just covered with blood. There's nothing coming out of you."

"See, I just knew I would do something wrong," Mark said, throwing the pen back to the desk. Dixie caught it and placed it back where it belonged without even looking up from her mystery.

Mark strained and grunted with only a little trickle of blood coming out of the hole in his throat, but nothing more, "Hm. Maybe it's because I'm dead."

"That may be. I hadn't thought of that. I should have asked you something else."

Mark lit up a clove cigarette and inhaled. A small trail of smoke seeped out of the hole he had poked in himself. Hester looked up to see if Dixie had noticed, then she pointed at her neck and then to Mark's.

Mark looked quizzically at the old woman and then noticed the smoke trail, "Now that is just silly," his words taking on a faint whistle. "Thanks for catching that, Hester."

He plugged the hole with a finger and continued smoking. When he inhaled, the hole puckered around the tip of his finger, when he exhaled, it sounded like comical flatulent noises. This made the snoozing David giggle childishly in his sleep while Maren only frowned and nudged him. Hester tried not to laugh at this sight of the three waiting room occupants, but it really was just too much.

The slopping water had now filled up the room to her waist and threatened to turn purple from a deep crimson.

"You know," Mark whistled, "why don't you go on ahead of me? Dr. Donegan won't be able to help me out very much today."

Hester frowned, "Now, don't say that. He's been my doctor for years. He's very good. I know he could help you."

Mark let out one of his large barks of laughter and said, "I'm dead, darling. Remember?"

"Oh. That's right."

Nurse Dixie stood up and called out, "Mr. Navarette?"

Mark looked at the nurse, "Hester's taking my spot. I want her to do so."

"As you wish. Mrs. Maltby? You may now follow Nurse Gunkle to your examination room."

"I'm coming, Dixie."

Hester stood and collected her purse, turned to go into the office, stopped, then turned back to Mark, "May I ask you just one more question?"

Mark smiled, "As long as it isn't a piece of metal from a paint thinner can, shoot!"

Hester clutched her hands together, afraid to ask but more afraid to hear what the answer would be, "Mark... did it hurt?"

"Did what hurt, darling?"

"Dying?"

Mark smiled and exhaled a plume of his sweet smoke, "Our beautiful Hester. I am going to let that be a surprise. We all have to find out sooner than we think."

Hester straightened up, satisfied with that answer, "Alright then."

Dixie buzzed Hester through to the back office as Mark was swallowed, still smiling, into the deepening purple waters in the waiting room.

*****

The bus driver's flask clanged to the floor.

Jeremy's eyes snapped open as he lifted his head from his knees. He had dozed off in his sitting position, watching over the other survivors, the sting of tears in his eyes. The very same, damn dream from last night not leaving his mind, jarring him awake again. Why couldn't he just get some relief from this dream? If only it would just leave his mind in peace.

He stretched, feeling the aches and pains that his body never dreamed of feeling before, the utter weariness settling into his bones along with the cold. He was so fatigued from everything. Was it possible to die from being so exhausted?

Jeremy stood, arched his back, and flexed his knees. The ever-present fire had lessened some, so he moved to throw two more logs into it. He froze mid-stride when he heard Jack whimper.

"Jack?" Jeremy whispered, "Are you awake?"

Jack trembled and was biting the skin on the back of his right hand. Jeremy touched him, carefully pulling his hand from his gnashing teeth.

"Unfair," Jack said to whoever was tormenting him in his dreams and he rolled over.

"Yes," whispered Jeremy standing up, looking at the shuddering banker on the floor in the flickering firelight, "it would be very unfair."

MCQUEEN

"Almost had you beat, didn't I, Harold?"

Katie McQueen was sitting in her ex-husband's office, staring at the businessman from the other side of his gigantic desk.

She was 47 and just as beautiful as the day Harold McQueen asked Katherine Cockrum to be his wife. Sure, there were now the faintest of wrinkles around her mouth and near her eyes, but it just added to her natural beauty.

Katie McQueen was a strong believer against unnecessary plastic surgery and was the envy of not only the few friends that the McQueen's had but of anyone who looked at her. Her long, blonde hair never out of place and she looked like royalty, even when working in her garden clad in faded jeans and a sloppy flannel shirt.

"My dear, Katherine, you never stood a chance of beating me. You seemed to forget who you were dealing with in that courtroom."

Katie stood and walked over to the windows of McQueen's spacious corner office, "How did you do it, Harold?"

McQueen swiveled in his chair, watching her, his stone-faced expression never changing, "Do what, Katherine?"

"Come off it," Katie snapped, "and don't call me Katherine. You know how much I despise that."

"Alright then, Katie, what did I do?"

"You know damn well what I am talking about. Fake the prenuptial agreement. You and I both know that I never signed anything like that 19 years ago. So, now that it's all over, the divorce finalized, and you have won in life once again, how did you do it?"

McQueen didn't flinch. Katie smiled her award-winning smile and a dash of color flared in her cheeks, "I'm not wearing a wire or interested in opening up another case in the courts. I just need to know. For my own knowledge. My own peace of mind, shall we say, and no one else's."

McQueen stared at her for quite some time. The ticking from the huge grandfather clock the only sound in the room. Katie stared right back. She was the only person who never seemed afraid of McQueen's grizzly eyes. He hated that.

McQueen coughed and snorted, "Do you remember Clifford McFann?"

Katie's eyes narrowed, "You fired him three months ago if I remember correctly. He killed himself a few weeks after that."

"Not surprising," said McQueen, "Once I terminate someone, they rarely get a job in this cushy line again. Knowing how many bills he had from his private life, spending all of that money on his schooling. What a waste, am I right?"

McQueen smiled at this.

"What are you made of?"

"He was weak."

"You killed him."

"I did no such thing," McQueen slammed his fist on his desk, "He put the noose around his own, worthless neck."

Katie crossed her arms, "Well, what about him?"

"He did have a talent for artistry. He could imitate the greatest artists in the world. It was a little private hobby of his, reproducing famous works in his garage. Of course, I knew about it. I know everything about anyone who dares to work for me. He may have added that artistic touch of his to a particular document. Paying off a few witnesses that could testify what we were like in the early years at parties, and it didn't take much to convince anyone, especially a judge, that you must have signed the document after a particularly long and eventful night *before* we were married."

Katie smirked and paced the length of McQueen's office. After another moment of silence, she asked, "And how much to really convince the judge?"

Now it was McQueen's turn to smirk. "Around $50,000 give or take. A fraction of what you were trying to wrench away from me. Everything that I had worked for when you were just the pretty little figurehead that I could flaunt at any time. You do know me so well, Katherine."

"You must excuse me when I say, 'fuck you,' but I think you deserve it."

"And why is that?" asked McQueen.

"It's more than just calling me Katherine again, although that really helped with the motivation," Katie smiled, her circle of pacing growing smaller as she spoke, "I did live with you for over twenty years. I watched you rise to the top. Of course, I have been grateful that I was by your side, giving me the life that I once had. I was with you when you put on the weight and even let you touch me when you could get it up, but I just hated watching the person you were becoming inside. The person that you currently are."

"What I am is tough, Katherine," McQueen hissed, rubbing his chest.

"No, I am tough, Harold. I'm the one that's had to put up with the increasing jokes and snickering behind our backs. I heard every word of it and put up with it. Listening to it become all the more vile as the years went along, and you drove people away that I truly cared about."

"Then, pray tell me, what am I?"

McQueen's newly minted ex-wife stopped pacing and stared hard into his grizzly eyes with her pale, grey ones. In this moment, she looked absolutely radiant to McQueen, just as she did the first time he saw her.

"You're vicious," she said simply with a smile, "You're a vicious, unfeeling, callous, little man."

Her eyes were on him and unblinking, "You don't care about anyone anymore, least of all yourself. Any caring human being that used to be inside you died a long time ago. It just wasn't until this last year that I finally accepted and mourned that death and decided to move on without you. Yet, for some damn stupid reason, it still saddens me to know that I am most likely the last person in your life that will ever feel any kind of love for you."

With that, Katie McQueen turned on her heel and walked out of the spacious, corner office, never to lay her eyes on Harold McQueen for the rest of his life.

*****

"Katie," McQueen croaked out over his dry lips.

He was looking up into an unfamiliar room. It was chilly here and his chest hurt like a bitch.

"Fuck me," McQueen said, and began remembering with a sickening creak of his ribs.

The room glowed from the fire in the fireplace. He felt clammy and his tongue cried out for a drink of water.

Trying to sit up pained McQueen's chest in ways he never experienced. He rolled onto his side and used the back of the couch to stand up on the legs and feet that didn't seem to want to support him anymore.

He coughed shallowly, and carefully cradled his chest, trying to keep the pain away.

He looked at the sleeping figures on the floor.

Something was missing from this picture and didn't look right.

Then he had it. The fag had died, and that spic nurse tried to blame him for it, just like Katie McQueen had tried to blame him for the suicide of Clifford McFann seven years before.

"*Weak victims of circumstance,*" thought McQueen, "*mere steppingstones to get to the next level.*"

No, there was something else missing from this picture, but McQueen's fuzzy mind couldn't quite place what wasn't there.

A huge wind gust made McQueen look out the front windows. He saw that snow was falling again and what was left of McQueen's damaged heart sank.

Lumbering to the window closest to the front door, he watched the snow fall and cursed every damn flake that hit the ground. Seeing the bonfire, however, did lift his spirit some.

Those flames were going to be his ticket out of here, and into a lawsuit that would bring him more money than he ever dreamed of having for himself.

"I'll fill a hot tub with cash and roll around naked in it," McQueen rasped to himself, turning to get a glass of water for his sand filled throat.

Something registered in his mind very slowly, as he turned back to the window again to have another look at the bonfire.

"What...?"

He shuffled toward the front door and opened it. The arctic blast nearly made him close it again, but he had to be absolutely sure. You don't get to be a man like McQueen without being absolutely sure.

He stepped out onto the worn wood of the porch, automatically pulling the door closed behind him. He moved to the very edge of the porch, snow and wind whipping his jowls, and he squinted hard at the bonfire again.

"No!" he hissed.

McQueen saw a dark figure shoveling snow onto the burning pit, watching sparks fly up, die out, and then blend in with the billowing flakes. He blinked and rubbed his eyes, but the figure and its horrible act remained in motion.

"No. Stop!" McQueen wheezed out.

He stepped off the porch into the drift. The icy flakes melted quickly into his socks. He lurched toward the fire as fast as his broken bulk would allow.

"*You're built for luxury, not speed, Harold,*" McQueen could hear his ex-wife giggling evilly in his ear as he plowed on.

"Shut up, you abandoning, weak-willed bitch."

He couldn't feel the pain in his heart or feel the creaking and groaning of his dislocated ribs. On he marched, to save the fading beacon that was going to get him out of here and away from these filthy low lives.

"No, please!" McQueen pleaded.

The figure stopped moving, the shovel held in mid-air,

watching the sad spectacle of McQueen moving for all he was worth.

McQueen stumbled beyond the figure and onto the edge of the fire pit. He dropped to his knees and began grabbing at thick clumps of snow that hadn't melted into the glowing coals yet. The dying fire bit back at McQueen, burning his hands, melting the hair on them, and singeing the cuffs of his shirt.

"No, no, no, you stupid bastard. I'm trying to save you," McQueen mumbled.

The shovel cracked McQueen squarely in the back of his head. His entire bulk crashed into the remains of the bonfire. Again, the shovel came down, crushing his face deep into the coals that he had just exposed.

"*This is a mere steppingstone to get to the next level,*" Harold McQueen thought, as the shovel came down again.

PART III

DECEMBER 29th, 2006

THE TRUTH WILL SET YOU FREE

7:10 a.m.

Leslie's eyes fluttered open to morning light. The boy smiled and hugged Hester's arm a little tighter as he whispered excitedly to the dully lit living room, "Today's the day!"

He just knew that today was the day that everyone was going to be saved. Naturally, he would have to talk to Jack alone before they all went off to the hospital. It was going to be a hard, very grown-up-talk, but that talk had to be done.

Leslie pictured his father arriving with the ambulances and firetrucks. Crowds of people showing up to look at the heroic survivors. Daddy would push his way up through the crowd of people and pick Leslie up in the air and cry for all present to hear, "This is my boy!"

Then, he would have his daddy meet Hester and the party of three could go home together.

Leslie couldn't contain his happiness anymore and just had to get moving. He carefully moved Hester's arm and sat up. He looked at the sleeping old woman. Her face contorted, and filled with confusion. She must be having a very weird dream.

"It's going to be okay, Hester. You'll see," he whispered as quietly as he could.

Her face cleared some, and he knew he had gotten through and made her dream better.

Today *was* the day! It just had to be!

No longer were they going to be cold and scared all the time, and he was going to have his new friend come and live with him so she wouldn't be lonely in Buffalo.

He got quietly up off the couch and wiggled with excitement. He half skipped to the swinging door to use the bathroom.

*****

The patter of little feet woke Alicia. She rubbed her eyes and inhaled deeply through her nose, allowing herself to inflate her stiff muscles, "Ouch."

Her back and hips hurt from lying on her side all night long. She stretched her arms out above her head as far as they would go. Relaxing onto her back, Alicia felt a strange giddiness building up in her chest. She nearly felt like laughing out loud, "It's today!"

She just knew it. Today was the day she was leaving this house. Alicia Brooms was going to go out that front door on this very day and never come back into this frozen prison ever again.

"That's wonderful," she said happily.

Alicia stood up, shook some more stiffness from her body and went to the kitchen. She picked up one of the gallon jugs of water and brought it to her lips. She was drinking it as if water had never tasted so sweet or delicious in her life. It dribbled out of her mouth and on to the front of her shirt, which made her spray a fine mist of water all over the old counter and cans of waiting food. Food she knew that would go uneaten after today.

She laughed to herself, not feeling a bit sorry for what was now going to be wasted cans, that would most likely rot away along with this house as there would never be anybody else here ever again after they all left. It was the most joy she had felt in her heart after purchasing the bus tickets to San Francisco.

"Whatcha' laughing at?"

Alicia whirled around and faced little Leslie. He was standing in the bathroom's doorway smiling a mischievous, little smile. That smile made Alicia laugh again, spilling a little more water from the jug she was holding. She simply didn't care.

"You... you scared me, Leslie. I'm just so happy!"

"We're leaving today, Alicia!"

The librarian dropped to her knees and threw her arms out wide, not a care in the world, with the boy running into hug her tight, "I know! I feel it, too. There's something about today that makes it true. We all know that it's almost over."

They were both laughing wildly together in the cold kitchen.

*****

One of Jack's eyes popped open. He could hear laughter coming from somewhere.

He reached up and gingerly wiped sweat from his sore and scabbed forehead, relieved to find that his dreams were finally over.

There was still a small, irritating throb above his left eye, but it wasn't singing like it had before. He was slowly healing.

Jack propped himself up before rolling over to the fireplace. He picked up the last log available from the vanished stack and threw it in the crackling coals along with the last of the newspaper for good measure.

He watched the paper blacken, crumple, and curl into ashy oblivion in the belly of the hungry fireplace.

"Feeling better?"

Maria was propped up on an elbow watching Jack feed the fire, "I wonder what the fascination is in the human mind that makes them enjoy watching a fire build up? I have always enjoyed that myself."

"There is something satisfying about it, isn't there?"

Maria let her focus drift to the kitchen, where there seemed to be a lot of giggly, happy noises, "Sounds like a fun tea party going on in there."

"Wanna see what's going on?"

"Why not?" Maria stretched, "I could use a laugh."

Maria stood and assisted Jack into a standing position, "Jesus, just call me Jack Maltby."

Together, they found Alicia and Leslie, laughing and digging into a large can of ravioli without a care in the world. Maria couldn't help but laugh out loud seeing the pair's happiness.

"Fill us in, would 'ya?" Jack said, leaning against and then pulling disgustedly away from a moist counter top courtesy of Alicia.

"We're getting out of the house today!" Leslie shouted happily.

"Come again, Kiddo?"

"Can't you just feel it?" Alicia gushed. "It feels like we are leaving today!"

Maria couldn't help her grin. The nurse felt it growing with the enthusiasm in the kitchen looking at the two happy survivors, "What are you both talking about?"

"Look!" Alicia exclaimed, pointing out the window with gusto, "It has stopped snowing and listen, listen, listen!"

The four were silent for a moment.

"I don't hear anything," Jack said.

"That's right! You don't hear anything!" Leslie leaped up and was tugging at Jack's shirt with so much excitement, "That means there's no wind outside! We're going home today!"

Jack allowed himself to smile and feel the happiness in the room for the first time, "I'll be damned. We *will* be getting out of here soon."

The banker stared at the ground, as if in reflective prayer.

"Aren't you excited, Jack?!" Alicia bubbled.

"Well, sure... It's just..."

Roger pushed through the door, his eyes still half hooded with sleep, and he was favoring his hurt leg, "S'cuse me. I gotta take a wicked piss."

Leslie marched up to Roger and blocked his way to the bathroom. He jumped up and down, patting his tiny hands on

Roger's abs. "The storm's over, Roger. We're going to go home today. Just listen!"

Everyone stood still and let Roger listen to the quiet for himself. The lifeguard's eyes opened fully, and a large, goofy grin showed off his pretty teeth, "Hell, yeah... we are!"

Alicia squealed with glee again and headed for the living room, "I'm going to get some shoes on and go throw more wood in the firepit. People are going to need to see it. That plow will come down Crooked Street at any moment and they will see the fire and *then* we will be saved!"

Alicia ran to her damp shoes and nearly woke up Jeremy and Hester to join in the celebration. She decided that they would be up and finding out soon enough and headed for the kitchen before it hit her. She stopped and turned around, scanning the sleeping area.

"I wonder where McQueen went?" she thought.

"The upstairs bathroom," her mind answered back with a matter of fact tone.

That made sense. It was the only one he ever used before. Why he would tackle the stairs in his condition stupified Alicia, but she was beyond caring or worrying anymore about anything as trivial as McQueen's bathroom habits.

She walked through the impromptu party in the kitchen and to the glass door in the dining room. Alicia only pushed hard enough to get an opening that she could easily slide through.

The air was thin but didn't feel as cold on the skin of Alicia's hands. She was even sure she felt the slightest sensation of warmth on her cheeks from the morning sun.

She happily trundled to the shed for the wood waiting inside. She had a hell of a time squeezing through that door with four logs, but squeeze she did and didn't care in the least that the left elbow of her sweater tore on the door frame. In fact, she laughed at this tiny misfortune.

Two sparrows flew over the house, above Alicia, and then away over the treetops in the woods behind her.

"Be joining you soon!" Alicia called happily after the birds.

The still and quiet air seemed to make Alicia feel drunk, an experience she had only had twice in her life. She was giggling at this fact, too, when she came around the house and faced the firepit. The giggle quickly disappeared into a half choke.

"Oh, don't tell me."

She hugged the wood against her body tighter and lurched toward the bonfire, a dark cloud rolling in over the happiness in her heart that was trying to sing.

"It can't have been covered up again. Not ag-"

Alicia dropped the logs and screamed at the pair of snow covered, stocking feet that were sticking out of the drift where the bonfire should have been.

*****

Roger and Hester held Alicia as tight as possible on the couch to try and get control of her shivering. She was too stunned to tell them that it wasn't the cold that was making her shake.

Leslie sat in the winged chair, staring at the blankets that had encased McQueen on the floor deep in thought. He looked like he had the weight of the entire world on his little shoulders.

Maria, Jack, and Jeremy came in from the cold after inspecting the body of McQueen. The look on all three of their faces was unreadable.

Roger stood slowly, trying not to startle an already rattled Alicia. He wasn't sure she could handle even the smallest of shocks at the moment.

"What happened to him?"

Jack sat on the stairs, draping an arm over the banister while staring at his feet, "Looks like he got it with the shovel."

"How so?"

Maria cleared her throat, "His head has been caved in. Whoever was out there putting out that bonfire must have killed him and buried most of him along with it."

Hester looked over Alicia's head, her eyes as wide as

saucers, "What?"

Maria leaned up against the front door, her eyes cast down to the bottom step of the staircase, "His face and hands were burned. That tells us the fire was still going when he died. It stands to reason someone was putting out the fire with the shovel. It makes no sense that he would go out there in just his socks just to warm his hands. So, the three of us reached the conclusion that someone must have been putting out the fire. McQueen must have woken up in the middle of the night, saw what was happening and went out to stop whoever it was."

"When?" asked Hester.

"It's hard to tell," Maria said, "from the stiffness in his shoulders, I would guess he was killed around midnight or one o'clock this morning. Give or take an hour. Like I said before, that isn't my specialty."

The elderly teacher shifted and let her thoughts drip out from her lips as her mind processed the horrific information, "Killed McQueen... and put out the bonfire that killed Mark..."

An overwhelmingly loud silence and heaviness settled into the living room. The same thought hanging over six of the survivors' heads: Which one of us?

"Well," Jeremy said, breaking the silence and making everyone jump, "guess where that leaves us?"

Alicia shook harder, making Hester draw her arms away from the librarian, "It can't be one of you... I refuse to believe. I just can't believe!"

"Who else could it possibly be, Alicia?" Roger said, his voice with an edge of hostility.

"Shut up!" Alicia covered her ears and folded herself in half to her lap.

"It's true, Alicia," Maria said through her tightening throat. "No one else was here last night except the seven of us. There's no other way. It's one of us. We have to face that."

"I SAID *SHUT UP*! *Please*! I simply can't think about that right now. I want it to be this morning again when everything was okay and we were all going to be alright. Don't you understand? It... this can't be real!"

Alicia kept sobbing into her knees, but no one moved to comfort her as everyone began eyeing someone else.

"I'm so sorry," Leslie yelled out quickly, tears dripping from his eyes, "I'm sorry. I'm sorry. I'm *SORRY!*"

All eyes went to the crying boy. Jeremy shifted nervously, "Sorry for what?"

"I know who did it. I should have said something when I first knew... but it was all going so well, and everybody was getting along... I'm sorry."

Maria hurried to the boy and knelt in front of him, "Leslie, what is it you know?"

Leslie jammed his hand into the pocket of the oversized hoodie that had once belonged to Nate Maltby. Leslie hadn't taken it off since the first night in the house. He pulled out what looked like a card and handed it to Maria.

Maria's face was a ball of confusion as she held the card, "I don't understand, Leslie. Where did you find this?"

The boy wiped his nose on the sleeve of his huge sweater and sniffed, refusing to look the nurse in the eye, "I found it downstairs that morning. You know, that morning in the basement when we found Hector Ortiz? Remember? I thought everything was going to be okay until we were saved, and everything would then be alright. I'm sorry."

Maria's face had drained of color as she whispered, "Son of a bitch."

"What is it?!" Hester asked in near panic.

Maria held up the pinkish, plastic card for the rest of the room to see, "It's your driver's license, Jack."

JACK DOLL: BANKER

All eyes turned slowly to Jack sitting on the stairs. The smile that had scared Alicia the previous afternoon was back on his face. He laughed and shook his head, "I was wondering what happened to that. I had looked all over for it."

"Why did that Hector Ortiz guy downstairs have it?" Roger asked coldly.

Jack stood up and walked to the fireplace. The snap of the fire was the only sound in the room for a moment or two. He turned to Alicia and said, "You remember in the shed yesterday when I told you that I had a secret?"

Alicia nodded once.

"Guess it's time to tell you all about my sad, little life. Get this secret out in the open for everyone to hear. I told you that one can't keep secrets when you're isolated, didn't I?"

Jack turned back to the fireplace and gently tapped on the side of Mark and Almir's picture on the mantle, "Damn it, all."

He leaned his back against the wall and slid down it into a sitting position, letting his feet slide out in front of him, "I was hoping that I wouldn't ever tell this story to anyone, let alone you all. That none of you would know about who I am and what I had done until we were all out of here and back into our normal lives again, whatever that is for me now. None of my plans seem to be working out, though. Not a one. I'm just destined to be screwed until there's nothing left of me. You all might as well make yourselves comfortable."

Roger and Maria sat on the couch with Hester and Alicia. Jeremy crossed to the winged chair, picked up Leslie and sat down, cradling the boy in his arms.

"I sure hope some of the hate I see in all of your eyes fades a little bit by the time I am done telling you about this, but, like I said, my plans...

"Hector and I worked together at Atlantic First Bank, the branch located on 59th and Columbus in Manhattan. I'd been there for over fifteen years when we were all notified back in June that the bank had been sold to Empire's Common Wealth Bank. Starting the first of the year, we would all be brand spankin' new employees there.

"Common Wealth is a great place to work, so I hear, but the big wigs were making everyone staying on from Atlantic First start all over again as far as payroll and benefits go. Like I hadn't just spent a good chunk of my life surrounded by those walls. Hector had been there eight years, himself, and he was not too happy about it, either. It didn't matter if we tried to go to a new bank, either way, we were going to be starting over.

"Anyway, a couple of weeks after the happy announcement, Hector and I were splitting a beer at some joint in midtown when we came up with a beautiful idea. We were going to rob the bank. Rob from the rich and give to the poor, the poor being ourselves. We decided to do it on December 23rd. It made sense since the branch would be closed for Christmas Eve and Christmas Day. The money we took wouldn't be noticed until the 26th, you see.

"Hector was working the closing shift of the 23rd. I would be off, having to call in sick if I had to. He would have a suitcase with him, explaining to anyone who asked that he was flying to D.C. to see his ex-wife and three kids right after work. Since he had been working at the branch there for so long, no one even questioned him about showing up with a suitcase to work. The story for the suitcase now being a waste of time, but we had all the bases covered. It really was a solid cover story.

"Now, where do we go after we have the money? I had been scouting around for a place to hide since August. I just happened to find this very isolated house by accident back in early October. That's how I knew that there was nobody within ten miles of here."

"So, you didn't grow up around here?" Jeremy asked with contempt.

"I am coming to that part," Jack said, rotating his ankles, cracking them, "The day of the robbery, Hector jammed as much cash as possible into that old, green suitcase that he bought at a secondhand store just before the main vault closed at 4:30 p.m. I picked him up an hour later on the north side of Central Park in a car I rented, and we were on our way across the George Washington Bridge by 6 p.m.

"We stopped in Albany and bought that shitload of canned food, water, and toilet paper. He paid for it with his credit card, and we made a big show to anyone paying attention that we were heading on up to Maine. We figured that Hector would be pinpointed as the thief first, so we wanted to leave a paper trail that we were heading north and not west. We even stopped in Saratoga Springs and bought some liquor there, once again on his card.

"The plan was, we were going to lie low for a month in this place, then head to Mexico while all the attention was being paid to the north. Of course, by then, my name would be attached to Hector's so the both of us would be on someone's most wanted shit list.

"We were hiding out here by midnight going into the 24th. We counted all of the cash in the suitcase and came up with a grand total of $623,000. Hot damn for us, right?

"The next morning, I drove into Springwater alone to get some toothpaste. You can never remember to buy everything at the store at one time, can you?

"That's when I found out that the shit had already hit the fan. The story was right there on the front page of the paper. It seems that some helpful employee had gone into work on his day off and discovered that the money was missing just after the end of the business day. That vault should have been locked up tight after Hector closed it at 4:30 but this extra, hardworking employee was somehow in there after 5 o'clock. My guess was Scott Allen. He doesn't get along with his wife and will do anything to get away from her. Since the other four people who had been on duty were accounted for, only Hector was left to find. His picture was plastered on the newspaper, anyone knowing his whereabouts was to contact the police."

"So, that's what McQueen was talking about yesterday, when he felt like he had read the name Ortiz before?" Jeremy was rocking Leslie, the boy's eyes unblinking and watching Jack closely.

"That's right. That scared the shit out of me when he brought that up. I forgot all about the toothpaste and tore ass back here. Hector was so pissed when I told him about the newspaper article. I calmed him down by saying that our plan just started a little early on the man-hunt end of things, but we were still going to hide out here. I wasn't going to be going into town anymore, just in case my name and face made it into the papers, too.

Maria's glaring eyes never wavered from Jack, "Why is Hector dead?"

"I'll tell you, but I can use some water first."

"Don't you dare move. I'll get it for you," Roger stood and went quickly to the kitchen and instantly reappeared carrying the jug Alicia had been celebrating with earlier. He forcefully shoved it into Jack's hands and took his seat on the couch, putting a protective arm around the librarian's sagging shoulders.

Jack laughed to himself again and took a large swig. He sat the jug down and cleared his throat, "It turned out I hadn't calmed Hector down as much as I thought. He sure put on a good show of it, though. On Christmas night, all he did was talk about what we were going to be doing down in Mexico, all the ladies that we would be getting down there. How we were going to be having so much fun in the sun after just a month of waiting.

"I woke up around 9 a.m. on the 26th, with one hell of a hangover. I was right there on that very couch. I went to the bathroom and heard a noise downstairs as my flow was just finishing up. I found Hector in the pool room down there with the suitcase of cash open. He still seemed plastered. He was raving about the money, saying that it was all his, that he was the one who had taken all the risks. I could get off scot-free if I wanted to. That's when he pulled the gun from under his jacket and the scattered cash on that rotten pool table."

Jack suddenly threw his head back and guffawed, scaring the audience before him.

Jeremy held Leslie tighter, "What's so funny?"

Jack looked at Jeremy, his good eye wild with glee, "The whole thing makes me laugh. It's that tired old story of the struggle for the gun. It went off and he just dropped on his ass. His head bounced off the pool table a couple times as he tried to sit up and then he just stopped moving."

"That's not funny," Hester said through thin, pursed lips.

Jack calmed a bit after a moment, "No. No, I suppose it isn't or it's one of those moments where '*you should have been there.*' Anyway, I was in shock. I remember having the gun with me then. I lost it somewhere between it going off and tossing my cookies out that window."

They all turned and looked at the faint pink marks running down the wall that Jeremy had pointed out to them on that first morning.

"You said you did that during the night when I found it," Jeremy said.

"No, I didn't. I said I had done it yesterday. I didn't say at what time. I'm still happy that I got most of it outside."

"How the hell did you wind up in Saratoga Springs again? I remember you getting on the bus with me, and I remember that damn green suitcase now," Roger seethed.

"After I calmed down somewhat, I grabbed the suitcases of clothes and cash, after I wrapped the money tightly back up in a trash bag, and threw them in the trunk of the rental. I found my wallet and its contents spread out all over the pool table next to the cash. What he was doing with that, I have no idea. I don't know if he was going to kill me or just leave me here. Either way, I would have been screwed. No car, no wallet, hundreds of miles from home. Christ, was I scared. I still am, to be honest.

"I got in the rental and took off. I just drove and drove. I ran out of gas in Saratoga Springs. I ditched the car, leaving Hector's suitcase in the trunk. Had a hell of a time finding the bus station, seems no one in Saratoga Springs knows how to give directions to anything. Once I got to the station, I flipped a coin to decide where I would be going. West won the toss. It was when I tried to buy a ticket, that's when I noticed that my license was missing. I had to bribe the attendant with an extra hundred to book me a seat with no ID. So, that, as Paul Harvey says, is the rest of the story."

"How could you?" hissed Alicia.

"It's not like I haven't suffered, too, little lady. Look at me! I could be an extra in a zombie flick."

"That ain't what she's talkin' about, and you know it," Roger snapped, "Why the fuck did you kill McQueen and put out the bonfire? In fact, it's a bigger insult that you put out the one that Mark died for. You might as well have killed him, too!"

"I'm sorry to tell you, gang, but that wasn't me."

All icy eyes remained on Jack.

"You expect us to believe that after everything you just told us?" Maria huffed.

"Nope. Not at all," Jack said. "After the story I just told you, I'm not so sure I would believe me, either, but that's the truth. It wasn't me."

Maria stood up, balling her hands into tight fists then slowly releasing them, "You knew about this house, you knew about the food, and you knew about the body. What about the wood in the shed?"

"Who do you think put that cord of wood in there, my dear? I had those old newspapers stacked up at my apartment for months and they were just aching to be used as kindling. I wish I hadn't tossed my book of matches into my suitcase when I took off. I should have just left them here, otherwise, Mark... Damn it all, who knows? It's just my luck all around."

Maria stated in a low voice, punctuating each word, "And you said nothing about any of that to *any* of us."

Jack shook his head, "Look, I was asleep when the bus crashed. It wasn't until we were halfway across the bridge that I even realized where we were, don't you remember?"

"I remember," Hester said bitterly, touching her knee.

"Not exactly the best way to introduce myself to a bunch of strangers, don't you think? 'Hi, I'm Jack. I robbed a bank and accidentally killed my drunk best friend this morning, and what's your name?'"

"When we tried to start that first bonfire, you had Mark's lighter with you the entire time." Jeremy said.

Jack sighed heavily, "I seriously just forgot that I had the damn thing in my pocket. Mark had given it to me earlier to use while you two went to the bus. I put it there when Roger told me to put it away and forgot about it, that's all, that's the whole story," Jack's gaze lowered to Leslie on Jeremy's lap, "You really had my license this whole time and you didn't say anything to anyone, Kid?"

Leslie nodded slowly.

"You weren't scared of me?"

"No," Leslie said, "You were helping and being so nice. I thought maybe the man downstairs was a bad man and that's why you killed him. I was going to give it back to you after we were saved."

"Hector wasn't a bad guy, Leslie. He's like me. He's a good guy who just did some bad things," Jack shook his head and looked back at the boy, "Just out of curiosity, where did you find it?"

"It was on the bottom step of the stairs in the basement."

Jack flashed that lopsided smile of his, "I even had it in my hands at one point when I was rushing outta here and dropped it myself. It figures. I guess I'll always wonder what the hell he was doing with my wallet down there. I guess I'll never get to know."

There was silence for a few minutes before Jack said, "It's kinda' funny, you know? I feel better now. I just hated keeping all of that in. Wish I had told you all sooner before the really bad shit hit the fan."

Jack slowly looked at each one of his fellow survivors in the eye with all seriousness and then said, "I did not kill McQueen and I did *not* put out the bonfire. Jail would be better than this, having to be stuck here and watch you all suffer. Not one of you deserved this, not even Mr. McQueen."

Jack sighed and tilted his head back against the wall and closed his eyes. He let out another little chuckle, "The irony of it all. Just my luck."

He stood up and shook his legs, cracking another smile, "However, until I am proven innocent, I'll show myself to the basement, safely away from you all."

He picked up a blanket and headed for the swinging door. Jack turned around and faced the stormy expressions in the living room and said in his casual Jack fashion, "Catch you on the flip side."

The banker let out another dry chuckle and then disappeared through the swinging door to the kitchen, heading for the gloom of the basement below.

THE BEAT GOES ON

It was five minutes before 1 p.m. when Sorenson felt an arm wrap around his back and a head rest on his shoulder. He turned his eyes from the map he was studying to the familiar head of dyed hair, "You know, I am going to tell your husband about us someday."

Pat threw her purse on the desk, "Thomas knows all about us. He's been hoping for a threesome."

"That's a picture that will make me wake up screaming for the rest of my life."

Pat laughed and tapped the dispatcher on duty, "I'm on in a few, Misty."

"You got it, Mom."

Sorenson had turned back to the map, "While we're all lucky and honored to be in your presence, what on earth are you doing here so early? Aren't you on graveyard tonight?"

Pat put her lunch in the crowded mini fridge, "Renea had switched with Linda, but she's snowed in at her house, so I am doing a little extra because my heart is so kind and caring," she looked at the trooper, "Are you trying to find your house on the map, Junior?"

Sorenson smiled, "Saw another report about that missing bus. I'm just trying to figure out where the hell it could have gotten to."

Pat put on her headset and reading glasses, "I'll keep my ears open and see if anyone has heard anything. Maybe we got lucky, and they all went to the Radarstation to watch the Radar Dames burlesque troupe take it all off."

"That reminds me, they called to say that they couldn't accept your application."

Pat flipped him the bird, "That's because I'm overqualified."

Sorenson snickered and shook his head, "Please do keep your ears open, though. That missing bus has been bothering me since you told me about it. If you get the chance, call Buffalo and ask if that bus had been given any specific detours to take during the blizzard."

"You got it," Pat said, plugging into her console.

Just as Misty was about to sign off, she called out, "Sorenson, there's an accident reported on 29 near the turn off to Crooked Street. Appears that alcohol is involved."

"Alcohol by 1 o'clock on icy roads? Why not? Radio Ramirez and have him meet me there."

"Be careful," Pat called over her mouthpiece.

"Always," Sorenson said over his shoulder on the way out of dispatch.

*****

The mood in the house felt oppressive and sickening.

No one in the living room had moved or said anything for a quarter of an hour after Jack had taken off for the basement. The idea that he had murdered Ortiz and McQueen was unbelievable.

Alicia suddenly said, "It doesn't make any sense."

"Tell me about it," Roger replied glumly.

"I mean, why wasn't there any blood on Jack's clothes?"

Maria shifted, "I was thinking about that, too. My guess is because of the wool cap you put on McQueen. There was a little bit of charred band left when we uncovered his body, otherwise I would have forgotten about it. That cap would have limited a lot of blood spatter during the attack."

Alicia nodded, "I did forget about it. I had that stupid hat for years. I only put it on him to keep his head warm."

"What's bothering me is why he would admit to killing Mr. Ortiz but not Mr. McQueen? That just doesn't seem logical to me," Hester said.

"Because he was caught with the license, he has no other way to explain it being there with Ortiz's body. He must be trying to buy time to find the cash in that suitcase. For all we know, it burned up in the accident or it's at the bottom of that creek," Jeremy concluded.

"Besides, if he didn't kill McQueen, that means…" Maria let the rest of the sentence trail off as the remaining survivors began to eye one another again.

Jeremy put Leslie on his feet, "I need to get some fresh air." He walked out the front door, closing it a little too hard.

Maria took charge, "We need to eat. Even if you don't feel like it, we have to get something in our systems. Everyone to the kitchen."

Hester tried to stand and then yelped, falling back onto the couch. Alicia took one of her hands, "Are you okay?"

"Yes. Oh, something in my back pained me. Just hurt me… a little. I need to lie down."

Hester stretched out on the couch, facing the swinging door. After some reassurance that she was fine and was just needing to rest her back, Roger and Alicia left the old woman and went to the kitchen.

"You just rest, Hester. I'll bring you something to eat," Maria said.

"May I have some peaches, please?" Hester asked, "With a baked potato, sour cream, and lots of melted butter."

"Bacon bits?"

"No, thank you. My teeth don't like to handle bacon anymore."

"Can I have some pears, please? I want to stay with Hester," Leslie said without raising his eyes.

"Coming up," Maria said.

Alicia and Roger were picking at their cans when Maria walked into the kitchen.

"We're never going to get out of here," Alicia stated, "It's all over."

"I'm wondering," Roger said, "maybe there are houses closer than we were lead to believe. If Jack was hidin' the truth this whole time about everything else, why not that? Maybe we aren't as isolated and far away from help as he let us all think this whole time."

"What if he did lie about how far away we are from civilization?" Maria asked, picking up the food order for the living room.

"Then maybe I should start walkin'. Try and find somebody out there."

"No, Roger. It would be too dangerous. We need you here more than we need you freezing to death out there," Maria said, "Could you open a can of spaghetti for me, please? I'm taking these to Hester and Leslie."

Maria left with her freshly opened cans of fruit with plastic forks sticking out of the tops.

Roger tossed his empty can into a bag and headed for the dining room door and out to the shed beyond.

Alicia began cracking open something for Maria when she stopped and thought about the water she had drunk that morning, letting it spill out of her mouth and even spraying it when she laughed. What a waste that had been. How careless of her!

Alicia was surprised that she didn't want to cry. Maybe she couldn't. Maybe she had used all of the tears she had left in her lifetime, and she would never be able to cry again. No more tears for romantic movies or sappy card commercials.

Maria pushed through the kitchen door, "Where's Roger?"

"He's bringing in some wood from the shed, I think."

Alicia handed over the can she had opened for Maria and faced the nurse, "You know, Maria, I have just had it. I simply can't do this anymore."

The nurse just looked at Alicia, holding her can of food, "Yes, you can, Alicia. You have to. We all have to."

"How? How are we supposed to sit and wait like this anymore? I'm just starting to accept the fact that this is how it's going to end for all of us."

Maria put her can down, "But this is not the end! We are still alive. Jack's done some really, really ugly things, but now he's downstairs, away from us. Now that we know everything, he won't try to hurt us anymore."

Alicia slammed her hands on the countertop, "How do you know? Maybe when we are asleep, he'll come up and kill us all. He said he doesn't know what he did with the gun after he killed Hector downstairs, but we don't know if he's telling the truth. He could be down there right now taking it out of its hiding place and just waiting to start picking us off one by one."

Maria calmly lifted her can up, took a bite from its cold contents and chewed. She swallowed and said firmly, "I just know he won't."

*****

In the living room, Leslie and Hester were eating their fruit in silence.

When Leslie finished his pears, he tilted the can up and drank the juice. The rim tasted awful, but he wanted to finish it properly for Maria.

Hester forked a peach and decided to address the elephant in the room, "Why didn't you tell us about Jack's ID, hon?"

The boy shrugged, keeping his eyes on his empty can.

"Did you think we would be angry with you if you told us?"

Leslie placed his empty can on the uneven top of the coffee table, "He was helping us and everything. I liked him. I still like him. It scared me when I found it, but it felt like the right thing to do."

He turned to her, "What would you have done?"

Hester opened her mouth and then closed it. The thought hadn't occurred to her. She allowed herself to think for a moment before she spoke, "You know, I have no idea what I would have done. I guess I would have tried to talk to Jack about it alone, making sure that help wasn't too far away if I needed it. Then I would have tried to talk him into telling the others."

Leslie looked back at his empty can, the sadness and guilt on his little face were overwhelming. Hester could have fallen off the couch when he asked, "Are you mad at me?"

"Oh, no, hon. That's the truth. Don't you think that. I am surprised that you were able to keep that to yourself for so long, but I am not mad at you."

"Are you mad at Jack?"

Hester pursed her lips, "Very much so. He lied to us. There's a lot of things that I can forgive about a person's character, but lying isn't one of them. That's something that no one can forgive so easily."

Maria walked into the living room with Alicia.

Hester straightened up, "You both aren't angry at Leslie, are you?"

The women stopped and both looked at the boy.

Maria spoke first, "No, Leslie. I'm not. You were just trying your best with a big adult situation."

"We *might* wish that you told us sooner, but nobody here is mad at you," Alicia said.

In truth, had it been anyone else other than Leslie, Alicia would have been furious. She couldn't very well be angry at the boy. Frankly, she was amazed that he never let on at all.

Maria picked up Leslie's can, "It was a tough lesson for you to learn, Leslie. It can be really difficult to keep a secret when it could start hurting others."

"I just didn't think he would do it. Mr. McQueen could have gotten nicer. Jack just didn't know," Leslie said.

Hester sighed, "It reminds me of '*In spite of everything, I believe that people are truly good at heart.*'"

"What's that from?" the boy asked.

"*The Diary of Anne Frank*," the librarian said quickly.

Hester smiled, "That's right. It's a quote to live by, albeit carefully."

"Do *you* really believe that?' Maria asked.

Hester looked into the nurse's eyes. The old woman flashed her sly smile, "I am trying desperately to believe."

Roger came in with a load of wood in his arms and stopped when he saw the ladies and the boy. He looked them over and then went to the fireplace to make a neat pile of firewood, "We discussing something new? Find out that Jack is an actual drug kingpin in Hell's Kitchen?"

"We are talking about good hearts," Hester said.

"Sometimes I wonder," Roger said as he put a log on the fire.

Alicia pointed at the firewood with her foot, "I'll go get more of these for later. It'll save us the trouble if it gets colder."

Alicia walked through the kitchen to the dining room. The back door was still open a few inches. The cold air caressed her hands, sending a tremble through her body.

She stepped through the doorway and walked to the lonely little shed in a half daze.

On her way back, with her arms heavy with firewood, she froze just outside the open glass door when she heard someone singing faintly. It sounded like Jack, and he sounded drunk. A moment later she recognized the tune.

"*One for My Baby.*"

Alicia put one foot in the house and felt relieved to find that she was still capable of producing tears.

*****

Jack had placed himself in one of the dusty chairs, having tossed out the old boxes that had been sitting there, adding the pile to the floor in front of the workbench. He had wrapped himself in a blanket and was taking shots from a bottle of Everclear. He wanted to drink himself into a blackout stupor. He thought he had earned it after his performance upstairs.

After getting into the dreaded basement, he had gone straight to the alcohol stash that had been in a box under the pool table behind his friend's body. After removing the cap from his bottled prize, Jack toasted Hector's body and took a healthy swig, the sweet burn in his throat worth every drop.

Once he was in the chair and covered in the blanket, the alcohol could flow more freely into his gullet. He wished he had raided the stash days ago, but back then, he didn't want his secret out.

"Guess that doesn't matter anymore," he said to the workbench.

He could turn his head just enough to look at Hector's body in the pool room, "Why so blue, my friend? You aren't the one everybody hates, am I right?"

He toasted Hector again and turned back to the workroom, the alcohol beginning to give him the tingle on his skin that he was looking for. It wouldn't take much with the high proof he was pouring into himself.

"So, here I sit," Jack could feel a slur beginning to tickle his tongue. "Fuck thish... this is some good shit."

For a while, there were no sounds coming from upstairs. It had worried him before the few shots he had consumed. By the time there were sounds coming from above, he was well away from caring anymore.

"Good ol' Mark... what was that shong you sang? You know how it went."

After thinking for a while, the banker stumbled through it as best as his drunkenness would allow. As he was finished with the song, he went to prop his feet up in the tiny space available on the workbench and missed it with his swinging feet by a yard.

"Hey! I don' remember movin' that thin'."

He laughed to himself and scooted the chair closer and tried again, his feet hitting the right spot.

"Now, thish is fuckin' relaxin'," Jack raised his bottle in a toast. "To McQueen! May you have a nice place in hell to rot, your ash-hole highness. I'll be seeing you there soon, I'm sure! Sh-ave me a spot."

He swigged again, thoroughly enjoying the burn this time. McQueen wasn't a super bad guy to Jack. He was an asshole, alright, and deserved a good smack in the face or two, maybe even an ass paddling out behind a supermarket of his choice, but did he deserve to be murdered with a shovel? Absolutely not.

"Leshlie gave me that shovel."

So, who had killed McQueen?

The big question of the day. Jack knew he couldn't have done it unless he had picked up his childhood habit of sleepwalking again. All three of Cynthia and Milo Doll's children had a problem with sleepwalking until their early teens.

Jack automatically ruled out Hester and Leslie. Leslie simply wasn't strong enough and Hester just wasn't that type of gal. She probably could if she had to, though she wouldn't last long in a fight with the way her body was treating her, but, Jack knew, she would probably die defending someone she loved.

He could understand why Maria or Roger would suddenly snap and kill the fat man. Yet, they had both saved his life. Why would two people who are mentally programmed to save lives suddenly turn around and take one in the middle of the night outside in a vicious snowstorm?

That logically left Jeremy and Alicia. Both had the power to swing the shovel with deadly force. Jeremy had laid Jack out with a hell of a jab and Alicia seemed near the breaking point ever since they had climbed up to the bridge after the crash.

However, Jeremy had all but hovered over each person like a mother hen and Alicia seemed too concerned about getting to her friend's place in San Francisco.

On the other hand, both Roger and Jack couldn't peel Jeremy off McQueen when he had tackled him, and hadn't Jeremy mentioned that Alicia had gone off her rocker just after Jack had frightened her in the shed?

"Maybe *you* did. Maybe *you* didn't."

Jack raised the bottle again then stopped just before it touched his lips.

"Bonfire," he said, *fire* whistling slightly into the neck of the bottle.

Jack lowered the bottle and decided to have that shot after he used his last functioning brain cell on this thought of the bonfire.

The bonfire?

Why would someone be putting out the fire? Their only ray of hope in a lost, white wasteland. So much work had been put into creating it, so much so that one of them had died for the cause. Who would put it out or want to for that matter?

Another thought suddenly occurred that half sobered Jack.

What if "*it*" wasn't the correct word? What if the correct word was "*them*?"

Two fires being put out *two* times, not just the one that they had found McQueen half-buried in. What if the first one hadn't been buried by the storm, but someone had put that one out as well?

Jack shuddered and took two full swallows. It just didn't make sense.

"*Who in their right mind would want to remain in this hell hole?*"

"Bank robbers from the city not included, of coursh."

The thought of the money made Jack choke up a bit. Some fish was probably shitting on his cash for Mexico right now and there wasn't anything he could do about it.

The alcohol began taking him back again, away from the fires and the murder of McQueen, the accidental death of Hector and the robbery, and Jack embraced it.

"Somebody putting out fires, killing people, and everyone's a shuspect. Where'sh that novelist from Maine when you need her?" Jack laughed at his own joke.

He took another swig and became aware of the slightest of movement behind him. If Jack had cared to, he could have easily turned his head and seen who had crept up from the depths of the shadows behind him.

"I found your gun," was the whisper that entered Jack's ear.

It was the very same voice that had haunted Jack in his dreams.

"Get 'cherself back in my head where you belong, damn it. You're not gonna shcare me here," Jack commanded.

"That gun might just be a big help to us. You wouldn't believe where I found it. You really *don't* have the best luck, do you?"

"Well, I'm sho glad to be of service."

Jack tried to salute but fell out of the chair he had been sitting in, his drunken numbness saving him from any real pain as he crashed onto the dirty cement. He laughed to himself as his bladder let go.

"So, this is it? You're gonna shoot an unarmed man in the back?"

"No. You don't deserve a violent death. You have done some bad things, but you should still go in a peaceful way. We simply can't have someone like you here. It turns out you don't belong in this house with this family like I thought you did."

The light shadow on the wall in front of Jack shrank and grew darker as the voice got closer.

"Do you have any last requests or final words?"

Jack laughed, "Yeah, I do. I lived in the state of New York for almost twenty years and I have never seen Niagara Fallsh."

Jack laughed and brought the bottle to his lips for the last time. He drank one large swallow, belched, and put the bottle up on the edge of the workbench.

"Ish quarter to three..." Jack began to sing again.

Fingers were slowly encircling his throat like long spider legs, the fingertips gently touching his Adam's apple. They tightened after a moment, squelching off Jack's voice in the middle of a line of song.

"*With the way my luck seems to always go, it fucking figures,*" Jack Doll thought.

If the hands had loosened enough to let the dying banker's final sounds be audible, the noise that would have filled the room would have been laughter.

YOUR DESTINATION IS ON THE LEFT

"Dispatch." Pat said into her microphone.

"Mom, it's Sorenson."

"Get off my phone, I'm busy."

"Oh, yeah? What fingernail are you working on now?"

"Let's just say I'm getting ready for your next sign language class."

"Thanks for prepping me. Anyway, did you get a chance to call Buffalo?"

"Did that just before Misty left. They told me the bus had been instructed to make a detour to I-90 because of that overturned plow. I should have remembered that accident. I'm the one that took the call. I'm getting to be more like my mother every day."

"Where was the bus told to go?"

"I'd have been pissed if I were on that bus. They instructed the driver to backtrack all the way to Saratoga Springs and then cut down to Albany and then be on their way on I-90."

"I don't think they went that far."

"Why is that, Junior?"

"What colors are the TransCoach buses again?"

"Blue and red with some white in for good patriotic measure if I remember correctly."

"While I was waiting for the tow truck to show up at this accident here, I noticed that the sign to Crooked Street is bent with some blue paint transfer on it."

"You're shitting me."

"I shit you not, Mom. Could we get a plow out here to Crooked Street, please?"

"I'm already dialing. That road gets closed off a lot this time of year when there's too much snow. The driver had to be crazier than a shithouse rat to attempt going that way."

"Or just trying to save some time, as some crazy shithouse rats are known to do."

"There will be a plow out to you in less than twenty minutes if I can help it."

"You're my girl."

"Not and live, Junior."

*****

Jeremy pounded through the front door carrying four logs. Roger watched him as he placed them neatly on top of the stack by the fireplace.

"You out front choppin' trees down, man?"

Jeremy smirked, "No. I think these were the ones Alicia dropped earlier. Waste not, want not."

"What were you doing out there so long?"

Jeremy smiled and flushed. He walked over to the winged chair and sat down, "I know this may sound stupid, but I wanted to talk to Mark."

Roger raised his eyebrows.

"I know how it sounds but I wanted to apologize properly to him. Privately, I guess. Then I heard Jack singing and couldn't listen to that. So, I went out and reburied what was left of McQueen. That's when I found those and brought them inside."

Hester shuddered, "We heard him singing, too. Sounds like he still has alcohol hidden somewhere in the house."

Roger sat up, massaging his sore knee, "He tried to do an encore, but think he got sick before he really got going with it."

Hester shook her head in disappointment, "I will never understand the appeal of alcohol."

"Have you ever had a drink, Hester?" Leslie asked.

The old woman smiled, "Only once and it was just a sip. It was on Nate and I's first anniversary. My younger sister, Jan, had sent us some champagne. I should have known better than to have the drink I had. The fumes from a mimeograph machine used to make me giddy."

"What's a mimeo... mime... what's that?" Leslie asked.

Hester giggled and sighed, "Just me showing off my age

again. It was a machine we used to make copies before copiers were invented."

Roger felt like laughing at the guilt he suddenly had by wanting to ask Hester what color the dinosaurs were. Mother Watson leaped up inside his mind and slapped him upside the head to keep him from talking or laughing.

Alicia walked in from the kitchen carrying three logs. She looked at the growing stack of wood by the fireplace in confusion before she began placing them down, "I didn't think you brought that many in, Roger."

"I'm Superman, you know," Roger said, flexing a bicep, "Naw, Jeremy brought those in. The ones when you... from earlier..."

"Oh, right," Alicia said, shaking off the image and stink of McQueen, "Thank you, Jeremy. I could have brought those in myself in a little while."

"No trouble at all," Jeremy smiled.

As Alicia was sitting down on the floor, Jeremy asked, "Where's Maria?"

Alicia looked at Jeremy, "She was in the kitchen before, but I just saw her in the dining room. She's still eating."

Jeremy frowned, "I don't like her being in there by herself. So... so close to the basement."

"I agree," said Alicia as her nose twitched, "I went through there as fast as possible, myself."

"Could you go check on her, Jeremy?" Hester asked and then hastily added, "Please?"

Urgency built up in the pit of Jeremy's stomach as he walked quickly across the living room. On his way through the kitchen, everything seemed to go in slow motion as he pictured Maria downstairs with Jack.

Alone.

The nurse was standing in front of the basement door, her can of food forgotten on the dining table.

Relieved to see her upstairs, Jeremy grinned, "What are you doing there?"

Maria whirled around quickly, stumbling a little bit. She looked miffed.

"You scared me."

"Sorry, but with Jack and all... well, you know."

Maria turned back to the door, "I was debating whether or not to bolt this. It seems a little over-kill, but considering all that's happened... what do you think?"

Jeremy strode across the dining room and pushed home the bolt at the top of the door. He wiped a hand across his singed forehead, "There. Now we are truly safe, and no one could be mad at you. Let it be known that I am the one who locked the door."

Maria reached up and put her fingertips carefully on Jeremy's facial burns, absorbing a little of their heat, "You'll have to get these checked once we get out of here. Have you put any ice on these?"

Jeremy looked sheepish, "A little."

"You should do it more. It will help with the pains and healing. I know after it burns that itches are soon to follow."

He nodded.

"Cold water will help with that. Don't scratch those itches. It will just make the itching worse and you'll break some of those little blisters."

Jeremy put his hands on her shoulders and began lowering his lips to her mouth. A wall went up between them when Maria turned her head and said, "Jeremy, I can't."

She walked to the other side of the room, putting the table between them. Jeremy stepped closer with a look of concern spreading on his face, "I'm sorry, Maria. I didn't mean to upset you."

"It's not your fault at all. I just let things get out of hand the other day when I shouldn't have."

Jeremy looked pained, "Was it... bad?"

"No. You were fine. It's just that we shouldn't have done that."

In truth, the sex with Jeremy was one of the worst

experiences the nurse had ever lived through. He pinned her to the bed as he thrust into her. It made her feel claustrophobic and like nothing more than a sex toy to please his ballistic penis. Even after he came, it was some time before he pulled out and rolled off her body. His sex felt frantic, joyless, and desperate. There was no passion in what he was doing to her and any sexual turn on she had to begin with was quickly extinguished during the act. The thought of opening herself up like that again to him frightened Maria. She wasn't so sure that he would let her up again.

"It had been a while for me," Jeremy said. "A number of years in fact. My ex said that I was too needy for her. She said that she didn't think that I would be capable of surviving without her."

Maria understood where the ex would get this thought. What Maria allowed herself to say was, "My ex-husband felt like I didn't need him, that I was too ambitious. He wasn't crazy about me working as a nurse. I don't think he wanted me to have a job at all. Too macho to allow his girl to be working when he was supposed to be the provider, I guess."

Jeremy looked down, "I'm sorry about that."

"Me, too."

Sometimes, she missed the idea of being married. Her marriage to Daniel Watt had been a short one and she went back to her mother's maiden name, Crosser, faster than she had planned. They still talked once a week sometimes and had dinner at least once a month. They simply made better friends than partners. The few times that Dan had crossed her mind in the last few days, she knew that if he ever asked to be taken back by her, she would turn him down. Maria didn't want to lose the solid part of their relationship again.

"Could we still be friends?" Maria asked.

Jeremy flinched but said, "You must have been reading my mind."

Maria smiled, "What are friends for?"

*****

Hester shivered.

Alicia looked up at the old woman from her place on the floor, "Are you okay?"

Hester looked at the librarian and tried to smile but the strained muscles in her face failed to obey her commands.

The old teacher could only shake her head as an answer, trying to get the sudden fear out of her heart. She wasn't a big believer in the psychic world, but she was sure that some feelings just told the yet-to-be-spoken truth to a person's heart.

"Did you forget something again?" Leslie asked, taking one of Hester's hands as he sat next to her.

She looked down at the boy and decided to tell him the truth, no more secrets from anyone in this house anymore, "It's a bad feeling I have. It feels like something is coming and there's nothing I can do to stop it."

Leslie's eyes widened with fear, and he squeezed Hester's hand tighter.

"Leslie, I need a hug really bad right now-oh!"

The boy released her hand and hugged her as tight as his little arms would allow him to do so.

Her shaking grew in intensity. Roger leaped up and sat on the other side of Hester, his strong arms embracing her as well, as the old woman's trembling continued.

"You're scaring me, Hester. Should I get Maria?" Alicia asked, inching toward the swinging door.

Roger shushed Alicia, but Hester managed to stammer, "I'm so sorry... I... I'm trying to stop but I just can't seem to help it. I really don't mean to be... scaring you all. I'm really trying."

"We've got you, Hester. You're safe. Are you hurting?" Roger asked.

"No... I just seem to be having a moment, I guess."

Ever so slowly, like a ship righting itself in a hurricane, Hester's shaking slowly left her old bones and her brain settled back into position. The storm was blowing itself out.

"Could… could I have some water please?"

Alicia was off to the kitchen in a flash. She filled a plastic cup as quickly as she could from a jug of water, spilling a little with some shaking of her own.

Maria and Jeremy walked into the kitchen behind her, making Alicia nearly leap through her skin when Maria asked, "What's the matter?"

"I think Hester just had a little panic attack. Roger and Leslie are with her on the couch and she asked for some water."

"Is she okay?" Jeremy asked, rushing by the two women.

"Yes. I think so. She just needs some water."

Alicia and Maria followed Jeremy into the living room.

Jeremy walked quickly over to Hester, kneeled in front of her and took her gnarled hands in his, "Are you okay, Ma?"

Hester's shivers had totally stopped, and she blushed slightly, "I really didn't mean to scare everyone. I'm okay, really. I just got the shakes is all."

Jeremy breathed a sigh of relief, "It's okay to scare us. You are cared about here."

Relief seemed to be settling into the room, as if a jump scare in a film had passed and none of the horror was real.

Alicia was standing behind Jeremy and smiling warmly, "Hester, this is the best glass of water I ever made."

As she extend her hand with the cup, she froze.

"Alicia?" Jeremy looked at her.

She stayed half-bent in this position, hissing out, "Shhh… listen!"

A low rumbling sound could be heard in the distance.

Everyone in the room held their breath now and listened as the sound began to grow.

Alicia dropped the cup and sprinted to the front door, "Oh, please. *Please!*"

Maria, Jeremy, and Roger were right on her heels. Alicia slammed into the front door face first and fumbled with the doorknob. Hester and Leslie both stood and faced the party trying to run out of the front door.

"Can it be?" Hester asked in disbelief.

Alicia finally got the doorknob turned and pulled it open, backing into the three behind her without any other thoughts other than to get outside. She ran to the edge of the porch, scanning the distance, with the other survivors standing behind her in the doorway.

Alicia spotted it and pointed, "Look! LOOK! *IT'S RIGHT THERE!*"

Barely visible through the trees was the strobing, yellow light on the top of a huge snowplow. The light flashing just bright enough to make it through the dense naked, branches of the woods as it lumbered along Crooked Street.

Alicia was off the porch and into the snow, barefoot and not feeling any cold what so ever.

"Hey! HEY! *HELP US!!!*"

She waved her arms wildly and shouting for all she was worth.

Alicia's body filled with pure joy. She and Leslie *had* been correct since they woke up. The nightmare of the last few days would finally be coming to an end.

"We're here! Help us, plea-"

Alicia felt the overwhelming pain in her back before she heard the gunshot. Her brain filled with more surprise than anything else. She stopped running and turned back to face the house in utter disbelief, barely seeing the three figures behind a small cloud of blue smoke hanging in the air on the porch.

The next bullet struck her in the middle of her face. Alicia Brooms fell backwards in the snow, dying with the knowledge that she was completely right when she woke up that morning. She had, indeed, left that front door of the old house for the last time and she was never going back inside.

*****

The elderly driver of the plow glanced at his radio, wondering if those two static pops he was *sure* he had just heard meant that he was losing the signal for his music. Satisfied that he would be listening to his oldies without interruption after a moment, he put his full attention back on the twisting road, watching carefully as he approached a little bridge up ahead.

FAMILY

"What exactly did you find?" Pat asked in surprise over her headset.

"Half of the guardrail is missing on the northeast side of the bridge. I crawled down the slope a-ways and then saw the bus mostly buried in the snow on the other side of the river. I got up and over to the other side and- I - I found them."

It was only the second time in his career that the trooper's voice had ever cracked on the airwaves, "The bus has been split in half. It was the front half that I found in the snow, the rest must be in the river, although I can't figure out how in hell that happened. The half I could examine is mostly burned to a skeleton. I found five badly burned bodies in there and I'm going to guess now that there are no survivors."

Pat's heart panged with grief, but her professional exterior remained unruffled, "I'll get some units and a bus out there. Why don't you come back to the station after they arrive?"

"These folks have been missing for three days. I think it's a better idea if someone sat and waited with them for a while."

"*That's why you'll always be my friend,*" the dispatcher thought. "You got it, Junior. I'll let TransCoach know and have those units out to you as soon as possible."

Sorenson signed off and got out of his patrol car. He stood on the side of the road, looking down at the ruined bus, "I sure as hell hope nobody suffered."

*****

Roger's ears rang with pain as he brought his hands up to cover them. He saw Alicia's face explode before the librarian fell backwards into the snow. He bent over and backed himself up, hitting the doorframe. His breakfast rose in his throat as he turned to go back in the house when the end of a gun barrel filled his vision, making all feelings, thoughts, and movement freeze in their tracks.

"Don't you dare move," Jeremy Henderson said.

*****

Hester had been watching the others from the front windows when it happened. It was unbelievable how quickly Jeremy had pulled the gun from the back of his sweatpants and killed Alicia in cold blood. The teeth and gore Hester witnessed flying from Alicia's face would haunt her later, but she simply didn't have time to think about it.

She was watching Jeremy like a hawk. He had Maria by an arm and Roger at gun point. The last of the old teacher's school days were in the time of the Columbine Massacre, and Hester felt her classroom protection instincts flair.

"Leslie," she said in a commanding, hushed whisper, "I need you to go and get Jack right now."

The boy, wide-eyed and not exactly comprehending what had just happened, nodded and took off running through the room as fast as his little legs could carry him.

Hester's next move, as any good teacher would be for her students, was to put herself between the danger and the children. She limped as quickly as she could to the middle of the living room and turned her frail body to the front door, readying what was left of herself for the oncoming attack.

*****

Leslie dashed through the dining room and leaped at the basement door. He was worried about how much help Jack would be if he was drunk. Mama couldn't do anything after a night out, but he was sure Jack would at least try to help them.

He grabbed the cold brass and twisted. His fingers slipped off as he pulled, the door not moving. He pulled harder as he twisted and noticed on his third or fourth tug that the bolt at the top of the door was in place. He tried to jump and grab it, but his little legs couldn't boost him up high enough.

He looked around the room quickly and ran for the dining room chair that was closest to him. He pulled on its high back, dragging the heavy piece as fast as he could to the solid, unmoving basement door.

"*LESLIE!*"

Jeremy bellowed for him.

The boy climbed up on the chair and was able to finally reach the bolt's knob. He pulled it down, jumped off the chair and pushed it over onto its side. He threw open the basement door and took the steps two at a time.

"Jack?! Jack, we need help wicked bad. Jack?!"

Leslie saw Jack sprawled out on the floor asleep, the bottle he had been drinking from sitting on the workbench close by. The smell of potent alcohol burned Leslie's nose and stung his eyes as he bent over Jack's face.

"Wake up. Wake up! Jeremy has your gun! JACK, PLEASE?!"

The boy shook Jack as hard as he could, stopping when Jack's head rolled in a funny way.

Noticing that Jack's eyes were half open and glazed shook Leslie to his core.

"Jack?" he squeaked quietly.

"Get away from him, Leslie. Come here."

Jeremy was standing halfway up the stairs, pointing his gun at a frightened looking Maria and Roger standing together at the foot of the basement steps.

"Get upstairs, son."

Leslie took a few steps toward the staircase and hesitated, "Please don't hurt them, Jeremy."

"I said, *get upstairs*. Now, Leslie." Jeremy's voice was colder than the basement air.

The boy slowly walked to the bottom step, looking up at Maria and Roger before he began ascending.

Once the boy was behind him in the dining room, Jeremy started backing up the stairs, the gun pointed at the two frightened survivors.

"I'll let you up after I have a talk with Ma and the boy."

Roger's eyes were locked on Jeremy's, "I swear, if you hurt either of them, I'll-"

Jeremy fired the gun just above Roger's head, into a dusty box behind him.

Roger and Maria dropped to the ground, Maria covering Roger's head with her body. The explosion was still ringing in her ears when she looked up and saw Jeremy's silhouette at the top of the stairs.

"That was my last warning," Jeremy said, closing the door and bolting it.

Maria was up first, "Damn it, Jack, wake up. Jack! Come on."

She was kneeling over him with Roger right behind her.

"Shit, no."

She touched Jack's cold neck and felt nothing. Maria raised her fists into the air and brought them down on the dead banker's chest, "No. No. *No*!"

Roger knelt down and wrapped his arms around Maria. She was sobbing and trying to jerk her way out of his grip, but he held her fast.

"Why? Why is he doing this, Roger? We were almost out of here."

Roger looked down at what was left of Jack and felt a tear fall down a cheek, "I'm sorry, Jack," was all the lifeguard could think to say.

Maria inhaled and then exhaled deeply. She put a hand on Jack's bruised and burnt forehead tenderly and said, "We should have listened to you."

She looked up and around the room. The door to the pool room and Hector's body was open. She stood up to close it and then realized doing that would limit the precious light they had down there, so she just left it open.

Roger covered Jack's body with the blanket that was tangled around the banker's feet, "What are we going to do now?"

Maria inhaled, "I was just thinking that same thought."

They could hear faint cries coming from above.

"That sounds like Jeremy," Roger said flatly.

"I hope Hester's beating the shit out of him," Maria said, making herself smile despite the situation she and Roger were in.

She looked around at the storm windows, "Think we could open one of those and try to dig our way out?"

The windows were long and narrow, impossible for anyone but Leslie to try and squeeze through, but it was worth a try. She walked over the workbench and pushed some boxes to the gritty floor. She then crawled on top of the old but sturdy bench and looked at the window in front of her, her heart sinking as she looked around its edges.

"They don't open."

She looked at the grimy glass and bit her lower lip. The snow seemed to glow from the fading daylight outside of their prison. She was about to jump down when something caught her eye. She pressed her face to the cold glass, cupping her hands around her eyes and stared at a very faint profile just a few inches of snow away from her.

*****

Jeremy pushed through the swinging door to the living room. Hester and Leslie were standing together, holding onto one another, in the center of the room. Hester pulled little Leslie behind her scrawny legs, "Jeremy, what is going on?"

Jeremy walked over to the fireplace and pulled a cigarette from the black box on top of the mantle. He looked at the photograph of Mark and Almir and said, "Thanks for these."

He lit the clove with the same twig Mark had used before and shook the flame out and turned to Hester. Her eyes were glued to the gun swinging in his right hand. Jeremy noticed and then stuck it in his waist band, smiling, "Don't worry, Ma. I won't hurt you. I could never hurt my family."

Hester kept Leslie behind her and watched Jeremy carefully. He stood silently smoking, watching as a plume of smoke left his parted lips and spread out in the air. Hester's back and legs started to ache, but she wouldn't move. She stared at Jeremy and waited.

After another minute or two, Jeremy coughed and tossed the butt into the fire, "Go on and sit down. We need to relax in here."

Hester didn't move a muscle or break her concentrated gaze.

He put his hand on the gun butt sticking out from his waist and smiled, "Please?"

Hester backed up slowly with Leslie to the couch, never letting her eyes waver from Jeremy's.

A hushed rushing sound made Jeremy's head snap to the front windows. He could just make out two fire engines' flashing lights through the trees traveling down Crooked Street, heading for the bridge.

"I only did it for us," he said, bursting into tears.

Seeing the tears from Jeremy softened Hester's iron for a moment, "For us?"

"For the family," Jeremy sobbed and crossed to Hester, dropping to his knees, burying his face in the old woman's lap.

Hester brought her arms up in surprise as Jeremy placed his head on her. She watched carefully for a moment and then, fighting the nausea in her gut, Hester carefully lowered them to his back and began to rub gentle circles on the sobbing madman.

"We were destined to be together here," Jeremy said, "can't you see that's why we all survived the accident? We are here together for a reason."

Jeremy sobbed harder into Hester's tired legs. With childlike confidence, he said, "You're my mom now, Hester," his head snapping up and looking at Leslie wildly through his tears, "And you're my boy. Don't you see it? Can't you see it? Three generations under one roof. It makes me so happy, and they tried to ruin it all for us. They tried to take it all away."

He dropped the left side of his head back to Hester's lap, "McQueen tried to keep the fire going. Jack lied to us. Liars aren't a part of us, are they? They aren't like us at all. And then beautiful Alicia tried to run away from here with Maria and Roger trying to help her run away from us? They just don't belong to us like I thought they did. They don't want to be a part of this family. I love you all so much. This is the real family. The ones right here."

Hester asked carefully, "Where did you find the gun, honey?"

"It was under the snow on the porch just outside the window where Jack got sick and threw up. I found it that first morning when I was brushing the snow away," Jeremy smiled at Leslie, "Like father like son, right? Keeping little secrets. Now I know where you get it."

The tears had slowed, and Jeremy snuffled. Leslie looked up at Hester and then back to Jeremy. Hester felt a wave of admiration flood through her when the boy asked, "Can we let Roger and Maria up now, Daddy?"

Jeremy raised his head and looked at the boy, his eyes as dark as oil and his voice low with violence, "No, son, we can't. They aren't a part of us like I thought they were. They wanted to run away and leave us, too. I told you that already."

"Why do you say that, honey?" Hester asked.

"You saw. They were trying to run, too. We all saw what was happening. I thought Maria loved me, but she just wants to be friends. Friends! That's not love. That's not the mother Leslie needs to thrive here. And Roger threatened to kill me. *KILL ME!* He was going to kill your boy, Ma."

Jeremy's face grew red and a sickening smile twisted on his lips, "I won't let them separate us, though. That's not going to happen. I will protect you. You'll see. You'll be so proud of me."

More rushing noises could be heard from outside. Jeremy stood and ran out onto the edge of the porch. He could see another fire engine and other emergency vehicles going by through the thick trees. He pulled the gun from his waistband

and pointed the muzzle in the air, firing twice, "NO! You aren't welcome here. You stay away from us!"

Hester heard glass breaking down below. Leslie leaned in close and asked as quietly as possible, "Did you hear that?"

Hester nodded ever so slightly, "They must be trying to dig their way out. Please. Please, get out and get help. Please."

A thought occurred to Hester, and she said quickly in a whispered voice, "Leslie, hon, yell for Jeremy and be really loud."

The boy nodded, "Daddy!"

"Jeremy, honey, why don't you come back inside? It's terribly cold out there!"

Leslie looked at Hester and whispered, "Now, Roger and Maria will know we are okay up here, won't they? They don't have to worry about us."

Hester Maltby nodded once but wondered just how much longer she and the boy would be safe as Jeremy slammed the front door closed, chuffing like an angry bull.

LET IT BURN

"You realize that this could backfire and kill the both of us, right?"

Roger was pouring the last of the alcohol they found all over the boxes on top of the workbench. He looked again at the burned right arm that hung through the broken window and shuddered with grief.

Maria was holding Mark's Zippo. They were relieved to find it there, still clutched in his hand after digging in the snow to his body through the little storm window. No one had thought to take his lighter away before they had buried him next to the house.

Maria and Roger's hearts had almost given out when they heard two gunshots sound from above, picturing poor Hester and Leslie being executed by a crazed Jeremy was almost too much for either of them to bear. An entire year passed in their mind's eye before they heard Hester and Leslie call out and that inspired Maria and Roger to work faster on their plan of escape.

Maria tried the lighter, only producing tiny sparks that flew around the wheel until the sixth attempt when a little flame leaped up and waved happily at the nurse, "Even if this does kill us, hopefully Hester and Leslie will be able to get out."

Roger suddenly laughed, thinking that this may be the last chance in his life to flash the pearly whites his parents had spent so much money on, "You know, this means that McQueen was right the whole damn time?"

Maria looked at Roger, "How so?"

"If you remember, it was his ass that suggested to burn the whole damn house down that first day."

Maria allowed herself to laugh nervously, too, "So, I guess this is for McQueen."

Roger backed away from the boxes, determination in his voice, "And for Mark. And for Jack."

"And for Alicia," Maria said as she lowered the lighter to

the nearest alcohol-soaked cardboard flap.

*****

Jeremy reclined on the couch with his head on Hester's lap. Leslie sat in the winged chair, thinking of his real daddy, wishing he was with him now in Buffalo, watching television and eating ice cream.

"I have missed you so much, Ma." Jeremy said.

Hester was mechanically running her fingers over his oily hair, staring straight ahead.

"You should see the place where I work. I manage this stupid pizza joint, and nobody really likes me because they think I am too much of a pushover. I'm glad we can just stay here and be happy together. The family I always wanted to have and now we can have it. Are you happy, Mom?"

Jeremy looked up at the old woman. She managed to push the overwhelming sickness away from her throat long enough to say, "Why, of course, honey."

Jeremy smiled and Hester could briefly see a hurt little boy in his shark-like eyes. Jeremy looked over at Leslie, "Son. Are you happy?"

Leslie looked up at Hester, saw her brief nod, then looked at Jeremy, "Yes, Daddy."

A single tear left Jeremy's eyes and he looked back up to the ceiling again, smiling broadly, "I just knew you both would be. I've waited so long for a family like this. Such a long time. I love you."

Hester swallowed, "We love you, too."

Leslie looked at the fire and wrinkled his nose. He could smell smoke, but it was different than the fireplace smoke. Something wasn't right.

"Do you smell that?" the boy asked.

"What, son?"

Leslie stood and walked to the fireplace. The floor felt warmer on stocking feet.

"I smell smoke."

Jeremy smiled, "Of course you do, silly boy. You must get that from your mom. We have a toasty fire going."

"It's different, Jer-Daddy. I can smell it."

Jeremy sat up irritated, "Leslie, just let us enjoy this…"

Jeremy smelled it now, too. He ran to Leslie and picked him up, frantic banging and yelling could be heard from the other side of the house.

"What did they do?!"

Jeremy's voice had raised an octave and sounded panic filled. He ran with Leslie held tightly in his arms through the kitchen and into the dining room.

"Jeremy! Help! It's burning down here."

The smell of foul smoke was stronger in the dining room.

"*WHAT DID YOU DO*?!" Jeremy shrieked, hurting Leslie's ears.

He dropped Leslie, drew the gun, unbolted the door, and opened it. Roger and Maria fell into the room choking as thick, black smoke followed out close behind them. Jeremy looked downstairs through the smoke at the quickly growing wall of flames. He could feel the heat snaking its way up the basement stairs.

"I'll get you out, Leslie."

Jeremy picked up the boy roughly and charged across the room, both slamming into the backdoor. When he realized he didn't have a free hand to open it properly, he shoved Leslie hard into the glass, shattering it. Shards fell inwards as he threw the boy outside as far as he could, "I won't let these bastards hurt you. I love you!"

He turned, seething, to face the two destroyers of his home. The home he had waited so long to have. He raised the gun to Maria's face as he charged toward her, "This is for my family, you slutty bitch."

He pulled the trigger.

A cry of rage exploded out of Jeremy when nothing happened. He pulled the trigger repeatedly watching the revolver rotate indifferently in his hands. Roger lunged. Jeremy swung the gun upwards and caught Roger on the side of his head, sending the 17-year-old into the dining table. Jeremy's free hand laced its fingers into Maria's hair as she tried to dart around him. He brought the gun down on top of Maria's head, splitting open her scalp and breaking one of his own fingers with the butt of the gun. As Jeremy raised the weapon up higher for a heavier blow, he froze when he heard the gentle, sweet voice calling to him from the kitchen archway.

"Come here, my boy."

Jeremy brought his gaze up from Maria's battered head. Standing in the middle of the archway was Hester. She was smiling and had her arms opened wide. Her arthritic fingers beaconing to Jeremy, "Come on, now. Come to Mama."

Jeremy lowered his arm slowly, the fingers atop Maria's head loosened, his bottom lip began quivering, "They're ruining it. The family. The house. They want to take it from us, Ma. They want to kill us."

"Come here. Come to Mom. Mama needs you."

Hester's voice was calm and warm, heard clearly over the growing roar of the fire.

Roger was crouching on the floor just under the tabletop and he was holding a hand up gently to the broken skin over his shattered cheek bone. His eyes met Maria's. There was panic and fright in them, but determination. Neither of them moved.

"Come on over here, my little love. Give Mama a great big hug."

Jeremy let go of Maria and shuffled slowly over to the old woman, dropping the gun as he began to weep, "I'm sorry, Mom," he said, becoming more childlike with each step toward Hester's outstretched arms.

"There, there. Come to Mama."

He hugged Hester tightly, crying into her shoulder, "Why did they do it? Why, Mom? Why?"

"Shhh, now," Hester soothed, "Shhhhh. Mama's here now, and I love you so much."

Roger stood up shakily and took Maria's hand. Smoke and heat were quickly filling the room. They looked at Hester, watching her hold Jeremy, gently rocking him in a loving embrace, and letting him cry on her. That sly smile that tugged on the corners of Hester's mouth flashed and her blue eyes sparkled radiantly. She waved a hand at Maria and Roger over Jeremy's heaving shoulders.

"It's okay. Everything's alright now. Hush, my poor, little boy."

Roger and Maria started for the shattered glass doorway. They both stopped and looked over Jeremy to Hester, pleading with their eyes. Hester waved her hand again, the same hand that wore her and Nate's wedding rings.

Roger nodded to Hester and jumped through the opening, clearing the buried stairs, and into the deep snow.

Maria went to follow and then stopped. She did the only thing she could think of doing. She looked into Hester's eyes, kissed her fingers, and brought them to her heart. Hester winked at her...

"She's a fighter."

The old woman nodded and waved her hand again at the broken glass door.

*****

Maria leaped out of the house through the frame, nearly knocking Roger onto his face in the deep snow drift. He was holding Leslie tight against his body. The boy was clutching onto his right arm, a deep gash in a forearm was oozing blood freely between his little fingers.

"What about Hester?!" Leslie pleaded with tears in his eyes.

Maria swallowed hard, "She can't come but she... she sends her love. Let's get to the shed."

The three marched through the snow, making their way toward the tiny shelter. Maria stopped suddenly, "Roger! Get

Leslie inside and keep pressure on that wound. I'll be right back."

Maria was off, pushing her strong legs through the deep snow, churning her way around the side of the house and then out of view.

Roger held Leslie as tight as he could and made his way farther away from the house. The smell of soured smoke and pine filled the lifeguard's nostrils as the house behind him grew brighter.

*****

Hester continued rocking Jeremy gently as the heat intensified from all around. Flames were licking their way up from the basement stairway, ready to make a meal out of the dining table.

"It's okay. I've got you, my boy."

"I'm sorry, Mom. I love you so much. I really did it for the family. I promise."

"I know you did. I love you, too."

The smoke and heat stung the old teacher's eyes, choking her. The room quickly filled with flames. The roaring that had been building into a great cacophony of sound was slowly fading from Hester's ears and being replaced by another, gentler sound.

Hester could smell the salty sea breeze and could hear the hushed crashing of waves, the same sound the ocean makes as a cruise ship churns through the steady waters.

Hester Maltby smiled one last time with the thought of how happy Nate was going to be now that she had returned to her husband in the lifeboat he had put her in three days ago.

*****

"ROGER!"

The young man spun around and looked out of the shed's doorway. Maria was returning with a bundle of blankets, her hands looked burned.

Roger ran outside, picking up Maria with her bundle and stumbled back into the shed, "What the hell were you thinking?"

He put Maria down and took the blankets from the nurse. She turned and stuck a hand in her sweatpants pocket. She exhaled as she withdrew her injured hand, "I thought we would need these. The fire had come through the floor in the living room as I was leaving. I fell and burned myself. I am okay, though."

She tore a strip of fabric from a blanket and walked over to Leslie, "Let me see."

The boy showed the nurse the deep cut in his arm, the bleeding having slowed some. "See. I'm okay. It hurt wicked bad, but it's fine now."

Maria wrapped the strip around the wound and tied it tightly. She picked up some handfuls of snow from just outside the doorway for her burned hands and sat down on one side of Leslie, while Roger took the other. The lifeguard dutifully spread the blankets over their legs.

The three survivors then watched and waited.

The heat from the house could be felt in the shed, the light dancing wildly through the doorway to the dirt floor.

"Wow," Roger said, the shock from his broken cheek bone starting to wear off and allow pain to stab him, "If this shed had been any closer to the house, we would have been really screwed."

The house burned brightly in the early twilight. The three sat and listened to the crashing and small explosions as their former safe haven began collapsing in on itself.

"*How much longer?*" was the unspoken thought amongst the weary three.

"Damn it," Roger choked out and started to cry, the tears stabbing into his broken face.

Leslie joined in with his tears and soon Maria's flowed as well. The last three days and nights of their combined nightmare would soon be over, be it by salvation or by freezing to death together in this tiny shed.

Maria thought she heard a familiar sound over the ferocious fire. It was growing louder, closer. A crunching in the snow, "Do you hear that?"

"Hear what?"

"Shh!"

She strained to listen, fear bubbling up in her heart again. "Footsteps," she whispered.

The nurse, now sure she wasn't making up the sounds, leaped to her feet, grabbing Leslie's hand and leading him to the wall next to the doorway, keeping the boy hidden in the shadows behind her. Roger was instantly on the other side of the entrance, holding a narrow log like a crude baseball bat. Maria could see the house fire glisten in Roger's eyes and on the bloody wound on his cheek.

Roger and Maria looked at each other silently and nodded.

Roger brought his arms up slowly, building up power for the blow that was about to follow. Maria stuck a hand on Leslie's chest, flattening him against the wall of the shed, silencing him as she heard him whisper, "Please, be Hester."

A sinister shadow stopped moving for a moment near the open doorway before it continued to crunch its way closer to the shed.

When it seemed that the shadow's owner was within attacking distance, the lifeguard and the nurse nodded to each other again and leaped into the light.

Roger choked and checked his swing, dropping the log to the ground behind him.

Maria was staring up hatefully into the face of Jeremy Henderson, framed by the conflagration of the old house. She leaped like a ferocious tiger, clawing and screaming wildly through the doorway and into the darkening twilight.

EPILOUGE: ONE FOR MY BABY

December 30th, 2006

5:18 a.m.

"Ouch! Don't tear me up more, Mom!"

Sorenson sat in dispatch while Patricia Selleck swabbed some alcohol into the scratches on his face. "I wish I could be shown a man that can face both gun wielding maniacs and a little rubbing alcohol."

Sorenson hmphed, "You should have seen them. I'm not surprised that gal leaped at me. Those were people who were definitely at their wit's end. I tell you, as long as I live, I'll never completely believe it all, and I was right there."

Pat put two little butterfly stitches on the trooper's left temple, "You did a good job today. You always do."

"I can't believe that the two bank robbers from the city were there, too."

"What do you think they did with the cash?"

"The little kid said one of the robbers had it with him on the bus. It's either all burned up or it's sitting at the bottom of the river. All $600,000 of it."

Pat shook her head, "I'd swim naked down there to get that."

"I think the state has been through enough this week, don't you?" Terry Sorenson stood up and started for the door, "I've got to get some rest. I'll be going over to St. Paul's Hospital to get full statements from the three survivors tomorrow, well-later today."

Pat paused as she picked up her purse and her lunch bag, "They were transported all the way to Buffalo?"

"Yep. That's where they were heading and, well, I figured that, since all three were insistent on staying together, and we had that extra ambulance, well, why not? They earned it, didn't they?"

The dispatcher smiled and hugged Sorenson. She stepped back and said, "You're a good man."

Pat walked by the trooper and started off down the hallway.

"Nothing but the best," Terry Sorenson called out.

"Bite me, Junior," the dispatcher said, flipping him the bird over her shoulder.

*****

January 1ˢᵗ, 2007

10:23 a.m.

Almir Leon was lying in his hospital bed watching the news. His left side ached from where the air hose supporting his collapsed lung stuck out of his body.

His twin, Aram, had been with him earlier, having created more artwork on his leg cast and just shooting the shit. Almir sent his brother away when the 10 a.m. news began, saying he was tired and wanted to get some more rest.

The winter storms that had ripped through and devastated the Northeast in the last week were still dominating most of the news hour, however, a new story was slowly being released from Fulton County about the bizarre events surrounding the accident of a TransCoach bus. The tale of the three reported survivors was a harrowing one. The struggle to survive in a freezing, isolated house with a maniacal murderer. The local news had dubbed it: *The Crooked Street Disaster*, with one perky, ever-smiling reporter calling the handful of survivors: *The TransCoach Three*.

This was the story that Almir wanted to be alone to hear.

He hadn't told anyone except Aram that Mark was supposed to be on that bus. His boyfriend wouldn't have stopped calling him and simply not shown up here at Saint Paul's, even though Almir had told him that it wasn't necessary to worry that much.

Almir's liquid eyes watched the screen hoping to see his secret love's picture pop up and announce that he was one of the lucky few to make it out alive. After all, his Mark would be too stubborn not to be one of them.

The door wheezed open to room 511, and Almir expected to see his regular morning nurse come in to check his vitals and take away his half-eaten breakfast tray. He turned his head and was surprised to find a woman standing in the doorway that he had never seen before.

At first glance, she was a pretty Latina, dressed in a hospital gown and socks. One of her bandaged hands held a long, white envelope. Her face read exhaustion in a way he never wanted to understand. While she had horror written all over her face, Almir felt no fear in his heart when he looked into her glistening eyes.

She held up the envelope and walked to his bedside. Almir took it, wincing as his left lung protested this simple movement.

He turned the envelope over in his hands, the front of it had a scrawling message that read: *Promise Kept.*

Almir opened the envelope and pulled out what had been hiding inside.

It was spotted with water marks and streaked with creases, but, to Almir, it was the most wonderful sight he had seen in a while.

He was looking at two people in love, smiling and holding onto each other as one extended arm took their picture on a beautiful Boston afternoon.

Almir looked up from the photo for the woman, but she had vanished, the door to 511 gasping itself quietly closed.

Almir's gaze drifted back down to the photo in his hands.

"You're late, Miss West," he said, kissing the photo before

leaning it against his empty milk carton.

Almir Leon sighed as deeply as his broken body would let him and looked out of his hospital window to see the beginning of the first snowfall of the new year.

AFTERWORD

That's it. That's my story.

As a final word, *Nine Strangers* was created in a very bleak time in my life over the fall and winter of 2006 and into the first week of spring in 2007 while I was still living on 148th street and Broadway in New York City.

At the time, Mother, and my dear friend, Jaimie Howard (Noy), were the only two people who ever heard the tale in its entirety. All handwritten 388 pages of it they listened to over the phone. Mother made suggestions that worked their way into the story in a few places while Jaimie cheered me on chapter by chapter.

Once it was completed, as I had seen other authors do it, I signed and dated *Nine Strangers*, 03/27/2007 (Coincidentally, World Theatre Day. HOORAY!). I called the story *Detour* back then, which I never really cared for. I desperately wanted to call it *Lost*, but there was a popular television series on at the time that killed that idea.

Anyway, the manuscript was then sent to live in a drawer in my parent's house in Pahrump, Nevada, for the next 16 years.

I thought about the story a lot as I grew older, the plot points and the characters, the joy I had while writing it. I am not much of a typist, so I was content with the idea that I could say that I had written a book, even if it was nearly masturbatory in only myself really remembering that it ever existed.

When I found the two notebooks while visiting Mother and Dad in February of 2023, I decided to get off my 41-year-old ass and try to complete something my 24-year-old self had started.

The typing was slow going. I am still, unsurprisingly, not a great typist. I did, however, have some fun collaborating with the Matthew from 2006. As odd as it may sound, I found myself cheering on that 24-year-old dude, and it felt good. I wasn't very kind to him in the past, and it felt like I was making up for a piece of that. May we all have that opportunity to be more kind to the people that we are/were/going to be.

Why publish now after all of this time?

I suppose it's my extremely humble and stumbling love letter written in crayon to people like Stephen King, Agatha Christie, R.L. Stine, Mo Xiang Tong Xiu, A.E. Parker, Douglas Preston, Lincoln Child, and Hirotaka Adachi (Otsuichi). Hell, even Jessica Fletcher from *Murder, She Wrote* (I'll always miss and love you, Angela). The authors who have given me so much joy in life. It's my chance to give a little something back. Thank you for the work you have given the world. After all, one can never be bored when you carry a book.

However, since I am performer first (and a small town one at that), I am merely playing the part of a writer, and I thank you very much for allowing me to play that character to the best of my abilities as you read along.

I must thank Mother and Jaimie, the people who heard the whole story over the phone before anyone else and continued to encourage me, even when I got stuck for three weeks.

(A total side story, the moment in the chapter *Tensions* when Jack comes back inside through the backdoor into the dining room and Hester says to Jeremy, "He's frozen. He was gone so long that I forgot he was out there" ... that was all me. I forgot he had been out there for those three weeks when I couldn't think of what to do next in the plot. I am sorry, Jack.)

Dad, for buying the drawers that this story laid in comfortably for sixteen years. He's a very nice and patient man. Always has been.

To the residents of the real Crooked Street in Upstate New York both past and present. I know I took a lot of fictitious advantage of your geography, and I thank you so very much for letting me play with the surroundings. Remember, it was just me looking at real, hand-held maps back in 2006 and guessing where this story could feasibly take place. It's a wild kick to be able to look it all up on Google Maps now, and, without trying to boast too proudly, I did a pretty good job of picking a good spot off of paper with little, squiggly lines.

To my beautiful grandmother, Melba Pippin. She gave darling Hester Maltby her voice. I had originally envisioned a cantankerous battle-axe of a woman, one with a heart of gold and who swore like a sailor, but, the moment Hester opened her mouth going to the lavatory, there was our gentle and kind Melba. How I wish you all could have met her.

Almir Mestre Leon, who was the first person to read the story after it had been typed up (with typos *and* before any editing had been done) and then going on to create the perfect cover art you see before you ever read a word of this. His name also helped fill in a character that I fought over in my head anytime I read the part of Mark's tragically closeted boyfriend. The name fit and I was happy to include him in it. His friendship and encouragement have done more things to my present and future than he will ever truly understand. You can check out his art on Instagram under the handle: almir_lion_drawings. And, yes, he does do commissions.

Theresa Strong (Resa Pippin!) who had to sit through all of my frustrations of having to type this up and then patiently sitting through the edits.

To the Wenatchee Valley Museum and Cultural Center for letting me type this up in my office on my off hours, even if my sister from another mister, Luisa, was still trying to kill me.

Kristine Ringsrud, Vic Tapscott, Jamie Johnson, Ashley Peterson, T.J. Farrell, and Terry Sloan for their invaluable work of editing and helping this dyslexic actor get his act together in more ways than you can possibly imagine. If you see any errors, I claim all responsibility as they are entirely my mistakes, and I do solemnly swear that I will *never, ever* judge a misspelled word in a novel again.

To Becca Freimuth for taking one of the best headshots of me that I will probably use until I am 106.

To BTS for putting out the best music one could type to in 2023. Looking forward to seeing you all together again in 2025! ARMY!

My publisher, Wayne Drumheller, for making this happen and making the process easier than I thought it was going to be. He went above and beyond with his help, and I will forever be in his debt.

My kind husband, Phat Lam. He may not understand the drive for this book to be in print, but supports me before, during, and after for everything I do. (S'ok!)

To you, my darling reader, if you have made it this far. I really can't tell you how much it means to me that you took some of the precious time you have on this earth and used it to read *Nine Strangers*.

And finally, to Jeremy Henderson, Maria Crosser, Jack Doll, Leslie Pink, Mark Navarette, Alicia Brooms, Roger Watson, Harold McQueen, and Hester Maltby. How much I adore them and how I will always keep these beautiful characters close to my heart. I hope you enjoyed reading about them and their time in that abandoned farmhouse as much as I did putting them down on paper three presidencies ago. They sure have waited a long time to have their story told, and I am overjoyed that they aren't strangers anymore.

I bid you all a very heartfelt au revoir.

Matthew Pippin

Handwritten: 09/17/2006 - 03/27/2007
New York City, New York

Typed: 02/22/2023 - 03/06/2023
Wenatchee, Washington